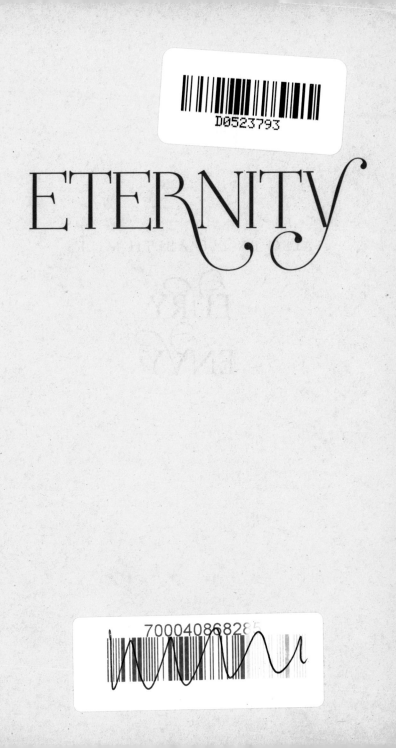

ETERNITY

ALSO BY ELIZABETH MILES

FURY

ENVY

ETERNITY

ELIZABETH MILES

SIMON AND SCHUSTER

First published in Great Britain in 2013 by Simon and Schuster UK Ltd
A CBS COMPANY

First published in the USA in 2013 by Simon Pulse, an imprint of Simon & Schuster
Children's Publishing Division.

1 3 5 7 9 10 8 6 4 2

Simon & Schuster UK Ltd
1st Floor, 222 Gray's Inn Road
London
WC1X 8HB

Simon & Schuster Australia, Sydney
Simon & Schuster India, New Delhi

A CIP catalogue record for this book
is available from the British Library.

ISBN 978-0-85707-209-2
eBook ISBN 978-0-85707-210-8

Printed and bound by CPI Group (UK) Ltd, Croydon, CR0 4YY

www.simonandschuster.co.uk
www.simonandschuster.com.au

PROLOGUE

Crow could feel the vision coming as he pulled out of Em's driveway. Maybe, if he drove fast enough, he could get home before it hit. He was getting used to the seeping sensation in his brain, the tingling, then the sharp, pricking pain as strange images took over. The visions had only been getting worse, more painful. Now he felt like his head was trapped in a vise. The road swam and blurred.

He wasn't going to make it.

He pulled over about a mile from Em's house. It was a moonless night, and the woods loomed like black walls outside the windows. Tightening his hands around the pickup's steering wheel, Crow breathed deeply. Pain exploded in his head. Starbursts. Colors.

It was coming. Soon, soon . . .

Drea was dead. He still couldn't believe it. She'd died in a fire Crow had somehow *known* was going to happen. Just like he'd known that something bad was going to happen to school pariah Sasha Bowlder . . . and that something even worse was bubbling beneath the surface here in Ascension.

Em was in trouble—he'd told her as much, just a few minutes ago, in her bedroom. Crow tried to push aside the memory of how shell-shocked Em had looked, how pale and thin, and how badly he'd wanted to reach out and hold her. Instead, he'd repeated what Drea had told him: *You're becoming one of them.*

Em had to know. Drea had been trying to save Emily Winters from turning into a Fury. Instead, she had burned to death in the Ascension High School gym.

The smell of ash seemed to be following him everywhere. Crow felt constricted, constrained suddenly, his lungs tight—he needed to be outside. He swung open the driver's-side door, its rusty whine echoing through the forest.

Gravel crunched below his boots as he stepped onto the road, and his headache redoubled, sending him stumbling backward until his hands were braced against the bed of the pickup. He closed his eyes and leaned back, succumbing to the dizziness.

Mirrors. There are mirrors in front of him, behind him, all around him. But it's not his own reflection he sees. It's Em. Beautiful, clear-eyed Em swirls in the glass. She is dancing with herself, but not herself.

Another girl—she has lithe limbs, brown-black hair, eyelashes like tiny feathers. But she's not Em. They are almost identical, but something is off.

Crow felt his knees contract, then turn to liquid and give way. He was on all fours, panting for breath as small, sharp pebbles dug into his palms. Smoke. He smelled smoke. He was choking on it.

The glass shatters with one high-pitched scream. Smoke is everywhere, choking him. Emerging from the shards are three blackbirds, their wings flapping noiselessly as they disappear into the night.

Crow gasped, the vision leaving him in a final flood of heat. As he stood shakily, brushing the gravel off his hands, one crystal thought emerged from the smoke and chaos in his head: *I must protect her.*

ACT ONE

SLEEPLESSNESS, OR THE SCARS

CHAPTER ONE

It happened so quickly. The socket sent out a small shower of sparks. JD jerked his hand away but not fast enough; pain surged in his fingers, and he could feel heat-induced goose bumps ripple down his arm. *Damn it*. He blew on his fingers, shaking them in front of his chest. *That's gonna leave a mark*.

JD stared down into the space between the hood and the headlight, noting the way he'd have to twist his hand in order to place the new bulb exactly right—without burning off his fingerprints, ideally. These lights were delicate; you didn't want to handle them too much before they went into their sockets, otherwise they'd flame out in a matter of days. It was hard for him to be careful lately—he felt like he would squeeze and crack anything he touched.

This morning was especially bad. He'd been leaning over the old Mustang for an hour, fiddling under the hood with this knob and that piece of wire . . . but in reality he'd just been enjoying the metallic silence. His arms were bare against the damp spring morning and his jeans were covered in black smears of oil and dirt. He'd have to go inside and change soon; he knew that. You couldn't show up to a funeral covered in grease. But he was putting it off as long as he could.

"JD? JD, honey, don't you think it's time to come in?" His mother's voice—gentle, tentative—floated out to the driveway. He looked down and realized that he'd had a death-grip on the screwdriver for who knows how long. He threw it forcefully into the metal toolbox, where it landed with a clang. As he flexed and unflexed his hand, he headed toward the house. Apparently he couldn't put it off any longer.

For the first time maybe ever, JD regretted his clothes: too many colors, too many patterns. Not one nice button-down, not one tie that didn't feature sunglasses or turtles or something funny. Did he really own *nothing* he could wear to Drea Feiffer's memorial service?

He'd have to swipe something from his dad's closet. His dad was a lot bigger, and JD would look like a kid playing dress-up, but he *already* felt like he was playing dress-up—trying on someone else's life, maybe. At least sometimes he wished he was. At any second he expected he might wake up and find that the

8

past week, since Spring Fling and the fire that had consumed Ascension High School's gym and Drea's death, had just been some awful hallucination.

One week. One week of floating, bad dreams, and sickening guilt. A week since he'd rescued Em from the smoke and flames—and in doing so, left Drea behind. A shudder of guilt ran along his spine. He flung open his dad's closet door and tried to focus on the silk ties, all variations of blacks, blues, browns, and grays.

School was closed for two days after the accident; even when it reopened, Em did not return. *She's going to take the week and see how she feels,* JD heard Em's mom, Susan Winters, say to his parents one night. Theories ran rampant at school: Em's lungs were permanently scarred due to smoke inhalation. She was horribly burned in the fire, doomed to be disfigured forever. The doctors had cut off all of Em's long, beautiful dark hair in order to address the blisters on her scalp and neck.

JD knew none of that was true. Em's trauma was mental—she'd been struck by the deaths, in quick succession, of Sasha Bowlder and Chase Singer late last year. And now . . . Drea and Em had only recently become close, but JD sensed that both girls had bonded quickly—that Drea had become really important to Em. Which, frankly, surprised JD. Just this past Christmas, Em was still cracking jokes about Drea's uniform when they went to the movies.

But something had obviously changed in Em since then. Something had changed in Ascension.

He hadn't spoken with Em in a week. He'd seen her only once, just out of his periphery: the wisp of a figure flitting past the window in her room, which directly faced his. She'd looked like a ghost; he might not have even noticed if it wasn't for her long brown hair. But he knew he'd probably see her at the church today, honoring their friend Drea: Drea of the half-shaved head and black nail polish and clove cigarette smell and dripping sarcasm.

His throat tightened up. Jesus. He was going to miss her.

He needed to talk to Em today, and know that she was okay. He couldn't bear to lose her, too.

JD selected a navy-blue tie to go with the gray suit he'd unearthed from the back of his dad's closet. It was vintage—pinstripe—but not over the top. Fumbling with the knot as he faced his parents' mirror, JD gave himself a once-over. He hardly recognized himself in his father's clothing. It might have been a stranger in the mirror: hair slicked back, fifties-style glasses, polished black shoes. Like one of those ad guys on *Mad Men*. JD wondered momentarily whether Em watched that show—whether she'd think he looked okay in a suit—and then hated himself for being so shallow.

He took a deep breath, then headed downstairs—going as slowly as possible, as if he could delay the inevitable.

"Poor Walt," JD's mom said as they piled into the family station wagon. "First his wife . . . now Drea . . ."

"He's going to fall apart," his dad said matter-of-factly as usual. "He's barely been holding it together these past few years." Mr. Fount and Mr. Feiffer knew each other from work—JD's dad bought fish for his restaurant from Walt Feiffer's seafood warehouse down on the waterfront in Portland. Over the years, Mr. Fount had made little comments here and there, about how Drea's dad smelled like booze early in the morning, or how he once saw him crying over a bucket of clams.

"It's a terrible coincidence. . . ." His mom trailed off, fiddling with her seat belt.

"What is?" Melissa piped up from the backseat.

"Well, it's just that . . . he caused an accident a few years ago. It was a fire—and Drea was almost hurt. He was drinking then, too. But now . . ."

"Let's just leave it at that, Mom," JD said.

In the backseat on the way to the memorial service, he watched the thawing landscape whirring past the car window. *Everything is changing.*

Truth was, any one of them could have died in the gym. It could have been *his* funeral today, and the only thing he'd have to show for his barely seventeen years on Earth would be a pile of stellar report cards, a few credits in school-play programs for lighting gigs, and years of romantic regrets. Well, just one regret, really.

Em. He'd known her his whole life and yet, weirdly, he seemed to understand her less and less. He was sure that he'd seen her making out with another guy that night at the Behemoth, the night of the bonfire, the night he heard her laughing at him. And not just any guy. This guy, Crow, was up for Asshole of the Year.

Em had gone from one jerk (Zach) to another (Crow), and just when JD had started to believe he might have a chance. It was infuriating and humiliating, and yet . . .

He had to get past all that, somehow. Because there was simply no way around it: JD loved Em. Always had. *Always*.

No matter what happened.

They'd grown up next door to each other; their parents had been close since their college days in Orono. From vacationing to carpooling to potlucking, the families did everything together, and JD and Emily had been inseparable as children. But not like brother and sister.

Maybe that was because he already *had* a sister.

He glanced over at thirteen-year-old Melissa, who sat next to him in the backseat, texting. Her face bore that signature expression of preternatural, blissed-out focus, the look that meant she was probably going to still be texting—or chatting or IMing or whatever—for the rest of the night. His younger sister had, without question, gotten 100 percent of the Fount sociability genes.

Mel didn't even know Drea, not really, except for running

into her the few times she'd come over to study. But JD had insisted that his whole family come to the funeral, and his parents agreed this was best. They had a way of sensing when someone needed them, and they'd always seemed to have that sense around Drea, probably because they felt bad for her—they knew her mother had died ages ago and her father was pretty much mentally MIA. The times Drea had been at the Fount household, his parents had gone out of their way to make her comfortable.

Or maybe that was because they'd assumed she and JD were dating.

Either way, here they all were, coming to the funeral, sharing in the agonizing discomfort of it. And JD was grateful for that.

He knew he was lucky to have them.

Still, the only person he really wanted to see right now was Em.

Em was family, and yet *not* family. More like a partner in crime. The cream-cheese frosting to his carrot cake. Without her, his life would have been blander, less sweet. As kids, she'd always been the one to get them into trouble, and he to get them out. She'd challenge him to race out to the half-rotten raft all the way in the middle of Galvin Pond; he'd remind her when it was time to return to shore, and carry her, piggyback, when she got tired of walking home. She'd convince him that pranking the baby-sitter by hiding her cell phone in the middle of a Jell-O mold was funny; he'd talk them out of a grounding when their parents came home. Without Em, JD would have been just another geeky tall kid who did really well at science fairs. With her, he felt brighter. Happier. Less like a loser.

With Em, he was like a knight in shining . . . vintage polyester.

Somewhere deep inside him, JD could admit that his bizarre self-confidence had its roots in his friendship with Em. In middle school, when popularity started to matter, Em and the impossibly cheerful Gabby Dove had effortlessly assumed spots at the top of the hierarchy. While his shyness and complete lack of interest in competitive sports did JD no favors among the guys, Em never blew him off. She still wanted to come over for movie marathons; she still giggled when he made up fake fortunes for their fortune cookies. And he had his own friends—Ned, whom he'd known since Boy Scouts, and Keith, another member of the Young Engineers Club. Recently, he'd hung out a bit with this guy Aaron who was in Ascension's vocational program, studying to be a car mechanic. Aaron had given him some great pointers on his mission to fix up the Mustang. And Drea, of course, whom he had bonded with over history trivia and an appreciation of cop dramas on TV.

At some point, JD had realized that there were no "requirements" he had to fulfill in order to keep Em in his life. She didn't judge him or expect him to measure up to some standard. And because of that he had started to . . . be himself. He liked old clothes—old stuff in general, actually, vintage watches and junky record players and shit that never got sold anymore. So he wore vintage T-shirts. He liked lights, especially theatrical lighting, so he signed up to design the lights for school plays. He did his thing, and Em did hers, and they always came together to check into each other's worlds.

But that girl was lost to him now . . . had been since winter break.

"What did you do to your hand?" Melissa's voice broke him out of his reverie, and he looked down at the red blisters that were blooming on his left hand.

"Just a little burn," he said as he tugged down his sleeve. "You might want to disengage from that thing before we go inside," he added, glancing at her phone as they pulled into the church parking lot. She rolled her eyes, but placed her cell on the seat between them.

The lot was, surprisingly, full of cars. JD felt a flicker of anger. Hardly anyone had been nice to Drea when she was alive. She was a weirdo, at least by typical high school standards. Did Ascensionites think they'd get extra credit if they showed up for the memorial service? He hated how people only cared after the fact. It was like that after Sasha Bowlder committed suicide, too.

Or maybe it was the guilt. The kids in his school had laughed at Drea and Sasha when they were alive. They'd accused them of being witches and performing midnight rites in the Haunted

15

Woods; they'd whispered about them getting naked and painting themselves with blood. Maybe all the recent shock was forcing his classmates to get their heads out of their own asses.

"There's that girl who had that terrible accident a few weeks ago," his mom whispered to his dad, who nodded with solemn recognition. It was Skylar McVoy, who was limping into the building—wearing an oversize black dress that made her look tiny and frail. She was on the arm of an older woman. JD shuddered. He'd barely known Skylar before the Gazebo's glass ceiling had collapsed on her; now that section of the cafeteria had been cordoned off and she was a minor celebrity, having escaped with horrible, but not life-threatening, injuries.

His family filed into the church and sat in a pew toward the back, with JD scooting the farthest into the row and Mel immediately following. He shoved his hands deep into his pockets, trying desperately not to stare at the open casket at the front of the room. Melissa nudged him with her elbow and cocked her head, giving him a look that asked without actually asking: *Are you okay?* He gave her a thumbs-up and did his best to approximate a smile.

But he was definitely not okay.

Dust motes revolved lazily in the light streaming through the stained-glass windows. It was warm in the church, too bright. The smell of musky incense mixed with sympathy bouquets was unfamiliar—his family never went to church. He couldn't get comfortable; the bench was too hard and he felt like he was overheating. In the process of wrestling off his coat, he nearly elbowed the girl on the other side of him in the face. "Sorry," he whispered.

She was small, with wavy, honey-blond hair and an elfin face. She was wearing all black, except for a bright red ribbon tied tightly around her neck. He'd never seen her before—maybe she was part of Drea's "non-Ascension" crowd. Drea had hung around at punk clubs and attended dub-step shows religiously— she'd made friends from all over.

"That's okay," she said. She didn't look like one of Drea's music friends, though. She looked like a plastic model of a person, almost too perfect. Her face seemed oddly frozen into an expression of neutrality, like one of the dolls Mel used to play with. "I'm Meg."

"JD," JD muttered absently. He wasn't in the mood to make small talk. Wrong place, wrong time. He scanned the room, looking for Em. His heart skipped. There. Em and her parents were sitting close to the front with Gabby and the Doves. Her head was down and he could see her shoulders moving ever so slightly. She looked broken. Beautiful, but broken.

Everything is changing, JD thought again. Life was short and he couldn't waste any more time. He had to forgive Em, and then tell her how he felt: that he loved her. He had realized he loved her years ago, and remembered the moment exactly.

They'd been on the couch in his den, watching a documentary about the death penalty for their freshman year civics class. It was just some boring assignment; he was getting ready to turn the movie off and pop in another movie so he could hear her laugh. But when he turned to Em, he saw tears streaming down her face.

And his first, overwhelming instinct was to reach over and comfort her somehow—but he realized he, too, needed her comfort. He wanted to smell her hair, to scoop her up, kiss her, and tell her it would all be okay. Instead, he'd shoved a box of tissues at her and turned back to the movie, heart pounding, earth-shattered.

That was the day JD admitted to himself that he was in love with his best friend.

The service began with a brief sermon, and it wasn't long before a heavy pressure started to build in JD's chest. He felt heat pricking at the backs of his eyes and the bridge of his nose, and he forced himself to look around the room to distract himself. His eyes drifted from Em's back to the dark, wooden, satin-lined casket to the heaps of flowers toward the front of the room. Sent by grieving—or guilty—classmates, probably. One of the arrangements in particular stood out: an enormous bouquet of red orchids. They looked strange and garish next to the other flowers, in muted shades of cream and white, and reminded him unpleasantly of blood. His stomach twisted.

"... and now, we welcome to the podium Drea's good friend Colin Roberts, who will perform a song he wrote for today." JD snapped back to attention and watched Crow walk to the microphone, holding his guitar in one hand and brushing his black hair out of his eyes with the other.

There he was: Asshole of the Year. What did Em see in this guy? What had Drea seen in him? Crow hadn't even finished high school. Rumor was, he dropped out—before he could be kicked out. JD had hung out with Crow only once, at a party at Drea's house. They'd barely spoken, so JD knew only two things about Crow: He played in a band and he used to be really good with computers. Oh, and he smoked a lot of pot.

There was no question in JD's mind that he and Crow were after the same girl. It was Crow who Em went to meet that night at the old mall. Which meant it was Crow who was to blame for what happened to JD there; he'd been hit in the head with a falling industrial pipe, an accident that nearly got him smothered in concrete and left to die. Luckily, Em had managed to get him out of there with just a scar above his eyebrow to show for it, but it was her fault that he'd been hurt in the first place.

Which meant it was Crow's fault.

Crow cleared his throat and spoke into the microphone. "Many of you barely knew Drea," he said, not even trying to conceal his disdain for the crowd in front of him. But then his voice broke as he went on. "Maybe ... maybe it's not too late for you to pick up a thing or two from her anyway. She was always open-minded. Obsessed with everything unique and different. So if you want to honor her, try to be a little bit more like her from now on. Be like how she would want you all to be if she were still around to see it. Break away from the fold." With that, he brought up his guitar. "Drea, this one's for you." And he began to pluck out a song, slowly at first.

Then he found the melody and his music washed over the room, at once sad and defiant.

Just like Drea.

JD was more than a little annoyed that the song was so good. Crow could really sing, too, in that raw, rough way that girls were always into—belting his voice into the air and tapping his foot to the beat. JD imagined Em staring up at him in the front row, listening to that voice, finding comfort in it. God, it made him feel sick how girls loved musicians. He lowered his head, consumed again by feelings of confusion and resentment.

He felt an elbow in his side.

"Here," Red Ribbon Girl, Meg, murmured, offering a tissue. He was about to tell her he was okay, he wasn't going to cry, but she pressed the tissue into his hand before he could resist. She must have mistook his annoyed expression for anguish. She turned her petite face at an angle and stared at him with that same doll-like expression: "Ya know, I've always thought death was really just the beginning of something else. Something we can't understand." Her voice was light and girly, and yet it felt like ice sliding down his back.

JD nodded and turned back to the altar, hoping that the girl would leave him alone. She was clearly trying to be nice, but her whole attitude was so clinical it just came off creepy.

Crow was playing the final notes of his tribute. When he finished he turned and walked offstage without even acknowledging the quiet and respectful round of applause. Everyone clapped. Everyone except JD.

You may have won over this crowd, he thought. *But Em will see through your bullshit eventually.*

At the end of the service, JD squeezed his mom's shoulder.

"Do you think I should go up there?" he asked, motioning toward the casket, where some mourners were lining up to pay their final respects.

"Only if you want to, JD," his mother replied.

Of course he didn't want to. He didn't want to see Drea's face, frozen in an eternal expression of death. He didn't want to see what they'd done to her, how they'd "fixed her up" with makeup she'd never have worn. What if it was a cookie-cutter version of Drea Feiffer up there—made to look fake and plastic and everything she'd railed against her entire life? Plus, he thought open caskets were creepy. Who wanted to see their dead loved ones like that? But he owed her this. One last good-bye.

"All right, I'm going to do it," he said.

As he pushed his way against the tide of the shuffling crowd, JD spotted Drea's dad, Walt Feiffer, struggling with the same bouquet of giant orchids JD had noticed earlier. It was on the verge of tipping over, and Walt was attempting to right it. He was alone.

JD sighed and looked around. If no one else would help Drea's dad, he would. He made his way over to the altar. Just as he was about to offer a hand, Walt let the flowers drop to his side—though it looked more like a shove—and JD wondered if Walt hadn't been wrestling it to the ground this whole time.

"Can I help, sir?" JD barely recognized his own voice; it sounded strained.

Walt turned around. His eyes were red, and he smelled like alcohol. He was crying, too, letting tears stream down his face. JD was embarrassed for him, and felt guilty for being embarrassed. Walt had lost his daughter. He had the right to cry. And drink.

"First my Edie, now my Drea," Mr. Feiffer said, slurring slightly. "What do I have left?" Another sob escaped the man's throat.

"I'm so sorry, Mr. Feiffer," JD said. "Drea was a friend of mine." The words of condolence stuck in JD's throat. His mind flashed back to the scene in the gym: the hysteria, the heat, the smoke. Could he have saved Drea?

It was too late now.

Until this moment, he hadn't understood or fully processed

the true horror of it: Drea was gone, and she was never coming back—ever.

He couldn't do anything about it.

No one could.

He turned to the casket. He could see the top of Drea's head, except it wasn't her head—or rather, it wasn't her hair; the undertaker must have put a wig on her. Was that because her burns were so bad, or because they wanted her to look more like a 1950s housewife than a rebellious teenage girl? JD swallowed hard and took another step closer.

Drea didn't look like herself. Her navy-blue dress was plain and demure, and the wig—a straight brown bob—was jarring. Her features were placid, like she was in the middle of a deep sleep. Her hands were folded across her ribs, and there was a single flower tucked between them. It was bright red and intricate, like the orchids Drea's dad had been wrestling with.

Good-bye, Drea. I'll miss you.

"Did you put that there?" Walt Feiffer had come up behind JD and was pointing shakily at the flower. "Get it out of there. Get that away from my daughter." He was in a frenzied panic, reaching over JD with such force that he practically tackled him. JD stumbled forward, closer to the casket than he would've liked, watching in horror as Walt tore the flower out of Drea's hands and crushed it under his boot on the floor. JD fixed his eyes to the spot on the ground; the flower's petals were smeared and broken but the center remained more or less intact. He was reminded of the occasional dead bird he'd come across when he rode his bike as a kid.

JD looked up and noticed how those nearby looked quietly away, as if nothing out of the ordinary had happened.

The reaction was intense, but JD remembered that if anyone was entitled to it, it was Walt. He needed to cut the guy some slack. After all, Mr. Feiffer had already lost his wife, many years ago, when Drea was still a little girl. JD couldn't remember the details—Drea never talked about it—but he did recall that Edie Feiffer had died in an equally terrible accident. Locked in a freezer or something? And now Walt had lost his daughter, his only child, too.

Meanwhile, Mr. Feiffer had started fumbling with a cigarette and a silver Zippo. His hands were shaking violently. He was drunk, definitely. JD didn't have the heart to remind him that they were still indoors—in a church. He did the only thing he could think of: He motioned for the lighter, took it, and lit the flame so Walt could take a long drag.

"She was a wonderful person, Mr. Feiffer," JD said, hearing the lameness of the words even as he said them.

Mr. Feiffer didn't even respond. His eyes were fixed on something invisible. Like he was gazing at nothingness. JD turned to go.

By that time, the crowd had thinned out significantly, and

Em was nowhere in sight. He trudged out of the church feeling more unsettled than ever.

Back at home, JD's mom pulled out a homemade casserole from the freezer. "JD, honey, will you bring this over to Sue and Dave's for me? They have a lot going on right now and I have a feeling they could use a good home-cooked meal."

JD tried to recall the last time he'd gone over to the Winters' house—certainly not since he'd gotten hurt at the Behemoth. With the exception of their almost make-up at the dance, before the fire, he and Em had barely exchanged ten friendly words in the last two months. He knew a lot of that was his fault. He'd been pissed at her for choosing Crow. He'd blamed her, too, for the accident that had nearly killed him. She'd tried to apologize a dozen times and he'd blown her off. But he was tired of being angry, and hurt, and not doing anything about it.

He was tired of missing her.

"Let me change," he said, feeling in his pockets for his phone, which had just started buzzing. It was Ned.

"Hey, dude, I need you in the booth tomorrow," Ned said, sounding his usual combination of frazzled and pumped. "One of the soundboards is on the fritz and I'm running rehearsal, so there's no one else to check it out."

Ned was directing this spring's student play, some Greek

drama, and JD had promised to help out. He'd done lights and sound on a few previous shows—the engineering part of it came naturally to him. Plus he loved the calm, remote darkness of the booth, high above the stage, where you could see everything and everybody, but no one could see you.

"Yeah, that's fine," JD responded. Couldn't hurt to have some distractions lined up. "I'll see you tomorrow." He ran upstairs, replaced his gray suit with a more comfortable pair of jeans and his favorite yellow-and-black woolen flannel, then came back to retrieve the food from the kitchen.

It took about one minute to walk from his back door to the Winters' front stoop; it was just enough to remind him of the last time he'd set foot in Em's house: the day he left her flowers and a bar of chocolate. And a note. *Always, JD.* He could still picture the way Mrs. Winters had looked at him—like she had known that the gift was more than just an apology. That it was a confession, too, and a pledge.

He still didn't know exactly what Em's reaction had been to the gift.

"JD! What a nice surprise," Em's mom said when she appeared at the door.

"My mom thought you might want some casserole," he said, holding up the dish.

"Oh, how sweet of her," Sue said. "Let me take this into the kitchen." Then, with only a second of hesitation, she added:

"Em is resting upstairs. I'm sure she'd love to see you, hon."
She turned and walked down the hallway toward the kitchen.

JD took a deep breath as he started up the stairs. This was it.
His chance to come clean, to start over, to start *something*.

Em's door was partly open; he knocked softly and, hearing
no response, entered. Em was lying on her bed, still wearing her
clothes from the memorial service, having fallen asleep while
reading. Her dark hair was splayed across a mountain of white
pillows, and her eyelashes fluttered ever so lightly from dreams
JD hoped were good.

He felt a pang of disappointment and also relief. And, deeper
than that: love. Plain and simple. She was so beautiful. He moved
quietly across the room to turn off the lamp. As he did, he caught
the title of the book she'd been reading: *Conjuring the Furies*. The
book was old and worn, and JD could see that it was heavily
flagged with Post-its.

Curious, he picked it up and flipped through the dusty pages.
Mostly Greek and Roman mythology, probably for the indepen-
dent English project that all of Mr. Landon's students were working on in his absence. The former Ascension English teacher had
been found dead last month, and the long-term sub had assigned
semester-length research papers. Or maybe Em was planning to
get involved in the school play?

JD stopped short at page thirty-eight: a detailed drawing of
a bleeding snake. The caption read: *Eye for an eye, tooth for a tooth.*

Only blood will bring them back. He felt a sudden surge of nausea. He remembered the night he'd found Em in the graveyard, covered in mud, holding a dead snake. He'd been scared, worried, and disgusted all at once. She was grieving—going crazy because of all the deaths. That's what he'd told himself at the time.

It was warm in the Winters' house, but he shivered involuntarily. Creepy stuff. He'd bet money that this book wasn't grief-counselor-approved. Should he mention it to her parents?

He turned the page to a new chapter: "Justice versus Revenge." He adjusted his glasses and began to read.

> *Once summoned, the goddesses of vengeance don't know when to stop—nor do they want to. They can't distinguish between appropriate punishment and malevolent retaliation. The desire for revenge is subsumed by its evil underpinnings, leaving tortured victims in its wake.*

JD felt like throwing the book across the room, or burying it. He didn't go for energy and juju stuff but he could swear he felt bad vibes seeping from its pages, like toxins. Before he could close the book, Em stirred sleepily and opened her eyes. He could tell she'd been crying, but she managed a small, tentative smile. He smiled back, closing the book quietly and placing it down on her bedside table.

"Hi," she said. Her voice sounded small.

"Hi," he said. He felt awkward standing above her; he kneeled down next to the bed so their eyes were level. "My mom sent over some food, a casserole and—" He cut himself off before he could start to ramble. "Listen, Em, I know you're having a hard time right now. And I wanted to tell you . . . I wanted to make sure you know . . . that I forgive you. I'm not mad at you anymore. I'm here for you. Always."

She was half-asleep again, and he couldn't force out the last bit of his speech. The most important part. The part about being in love with her. So instead, he kind of half-stroked her shoulder, pulled up the afghan that was folded at the bottom of her bed, tucked it around her, and left.

As he trekked back across his lawn, he replayed the last few minutes in his head. Em's sleepy smile. The way his palms had tingled when he'd kneeled next to her. At least he'd said some of what he needed to say. There was some satisfaction in that.

But a sense of dread cut into any contentment he might have felt, and he blamed it on Em's ancient book. He couldn't shake the memory of the words *Only blood will bring them back*. What the hell did that mean? Hadn't they all seen enough blood by now?

CHAPTER TWO

Through sleep-fogged eyes, Em peered at her alarm clock. Seven o'clock. Gabby would be there soon.

After the memorial service yesterday, and especially after Crow's speech and song to the crowd, Em had decided that her self-imposed break was over. A week of avoiding the everyday pressures of Ascension had apparently done nothing but heighten her anxiety. She could only watch so many movies—and spending her days alone allowed her mind to circle back, always, to what Crow said the night of the fire. Her mood had alternated between fierce rage (like *hell* she was "becoming one of them") to a deep concern something within her was changing undeniably.

Either way, it was time to face reality—nothing would be

gained by lying in bed, scared and angry. And reclaiming her life is what Drea would have wanted and what she would have done. It was funny how much she had learned from Drea about true strength: about sticking up for the people who mattered; about loyalty; about ignoring what other people thought or said about you; about pushing through your own fears.

Em had made Gabby promise to pick her up on Monday morning, normal time, no questions asked. Gabby had sounded skeptical over the phone, but she'd agreed.

There was a knocking on the door and Em jumped.

"What?" she called, too sharply.

"You awake, sweetie? Gabby will be here in about half an hour. . . ." Her mom's voice floated tentatively through the door.

"I'm up, Mom," she called back, trying to make her voice sound as groggy-normal as possible. Em moved over to her nightstand and forced the motions of her morning routine— after only a week, it felt unfamiliar, like trying to squeeze into someone else's jeans. She began to run a comb through her long layers. "I'll be down in a few."

She moved robotically, washing her face and brushing her teeth, trying to think of normal things. Math class. Spring break. Digging through her dresser drawer, she found a blue henley, one of her favorites—worn thumbholes, soft as flannel. She was pulling it over her head when she began to gag, a wrenching, sudden feeling of sickness that burst from her stomach into her throat.

31

ELIZABETH MILES

The smell. It wasn't her.

Someone else had worn this shirt.

She tugged frantically, trying to get it off her body, finding her head stuck in the collar, like hands around her jaws. *Get off me. Get it off.* The feeling wasn't too far from what she imagined it would be like to be thrust into a barrel of snakes.

Finally she was free of the fabric; she threw the shirt as far as she could muster. That smell. Like flowers drooping—just slightly dead, emanating their last bit of sad sweetness. Disgusting. If her mom was using new detergent, she'd have to throw it away.

With a shudder, she plucked a plain white T-shirt from the drawer.

Gabby was already honking outside; Em looked out the window and could see her car idling in the driveway. She hurriedly finished dressing, pulling a black hoodie over her head and kicking through the pile of clothes on her floor. She needed a pair of jeans—any pair—that didn't look like it had been balled in a corner for seven days. Finally she found a pair of dark denim that wasn't too wrinkled and slipped them on, nearly tripping over herself as she rushed out of her bedroom. She flew downstairs before stopping short; if her mom was in the kitchen there would be an awkward pep talk. Confirming the coast was clear, Em shoved a pile of books into her bag and grabbed a yogurt from the counter.

"Thanks, Mom!" she shouted as she slammed out the front door.

As soon as she settled into the passenger seat, she felt instantly relieved. Gabby handed her a steaming cup of hot chocolate and gave her a quick once-over.

"You look good," Gabby said, raising her perfectly groomed eyebrows in approval.

"Really?" Em responded, pulling down the sun visor to look at herself in the mirror.

"Really," Gabby said. "More beautiful than ever. Welcome back."

She smiled back. "That's what best friends are for, right?" She reached over and squeezed her hand, then winced. "Circulation, much? Your hands are freezing."

Emily wrapped her hands around her cup of cocoa as Gabby reversed out of Em's driveway, barely missing the mailbox, as usual. Em felt her spirits lift a little. Normal. A normal beginning to a regular day. It was amazing how much she had come to crave the everyday, regular-routine stuff of life, and to appreciate it. Just like she had a new appreciation for the people she loved. Gabby had been inconceivably generous with her forgiveness during the past few months. First there was the fiasco with Zach over the holidays, when Em had betrayed Gabby in the worst possible way—by hooking up with her best friend's sleazebag boyfriend. Then Gabby had to adjust to Em's blooming friendship with Drea—a girl they used to make fun of together. And Em had waited some time before telling

Gabby, her oldest and best friend, that she was in love. In love with her next-door neighbor JD Fount.

Honestly, Em had started to wonder if she even deserved a best friend like Gabby—who, even now, bounced her head back and forth in perfect time to the radio. Em took a sip of her hot chocolate, wishing it tasted as good as she remembered. But all this thinking about how she'd betrayed Gabby made her want to puke. And all for him. Zach.

He loomed like a specter over their friendship. Zach McCord, Gabby's slimeball ex. He'd played both of them, cheating on Gabby and making Em feel superspecial, when really she was just another trophy for his collection. She had to admit that she was grateful he'd left school. There was a rumor that Zach had fallen prey to a mysterious illness or accident that left him unable to play sports, but really, Em was fine knowing as little as possible about Zach's new life—she was just happy he was no longer part of theirs.

Em was still amazed at how she'd deluded herself into think-ing she and Zach were meant to be. She'd been longing for love, but she'd been looking in the wrong place. And she'd ruined everything by being so stupid, so wrong.

How could it have taken her so long to see that *JD* was the one for her? The boy who'd challenged her to epic snowball fights when she was a kid, who'd sat and watched movies with her one summer when she had broken her ankle and couldn't play outside, who'd made her laugh and knew all the words to her favorite cheesy musical, *Guys and Dolls*.

For the millionth time, she wished she could go back and do it all differently.

Gabby would be well within her rights to ditch Em completely—to advertise for a new co–queen bee. A new best friend. But Em was determined not to let that happen. She'd screwed up so much recently. Her chances with JD were almost certainly over; he believed she'd bailed on the pep-rally bonfire (and him) to meet some other guy at the Behemoth. He thought she was a selfish liar. And she had no way to prove that it wasn't true. She couldn't tell him what had really happened—she'd made a promise to the Furies, and she already knew all too well what could happen if she broke it.

And then there was her overwhelming guilt about Drea; it was impossible not to believe that her own safety from the fire had come at the price of Drea's life, no matter what the counselor said. It was her fault. And Drea had been trying to save her, to exorcise her of whatever demons she believed were consuming Em.

She couldn't—wouldn't—let anyone else down. From now on, she would be the one to play heroine. She would save her friendship with Gabby. She would save Ascension from the wrath of the Furies, before any more deaths occurred. She would save herself.

It was up to her now.

"When did Skylar come back to school?" Em asked Gabby when they reconvened in the library during lunchtime and plopped down at the research table by the windows. With the Gazebo section of the cafeteria under repairs after the glass roof collapsed onto Skylar's face, there was overflow during fifth-period lunch. Gabby, Fiona, Lauren, and a few others had taken to eating in the library, where they were often shushed but rarely bothered. That was another thing that had changed since the slew of tragedies had hit: Back in the day, the girls would never have missed the opportunity to be right in the center of the action. But now it didn't seem so important.

"Today's her first day back too," Gabby said. She bit her lip, looking worried. Before her accident, Skylar had developed a *major* girl-crush on Gabby. "I called her a few days ago, just to see how she was doing. It was superweird; she kept saying all this sad stuff like how she didn't deserve my friendship."

Em had spotted Skylar by her locker before third period. Skylar had avoided her eyes. She had a new haircut that had to be a wig. When she'd seen Skylar in the hospital last week, part of her head had been shaved and a row of stitches had stretched from her forehead past her hairline. Em was sure this cut and style was chosen to conceal her scars: long bangs, layers around her cheeks. Still, it was impossible to miss the feather-colored scars crisscrossing Skylar's nose and cheeks.

36

At least she was healing. Em involuntary shuddered as she pictured Skylar just before the Spring Fling—lying in the hospital bed and practically incoherent, her face slashed and bandaged.

While the school board blamed the accident on structural deficiencies in the Gazebo glass, Em knew that there was another culprit. Or rather, three of them, who went by the names of Ty, Meg, and Ali. Em was certain the Furies had marked Skylar, but she didn't fully understand why. There were glaring clues: the orchid Em had spotted pinned to Skylar's dress at the bonfire in the Haunted Woods, the fact that Skylar, too, had met the mysterious trio.

"I saw her waiting for the bus on my way to school today," Lauren piped in. "She looked like she wished she could melt into the ground."

"Talk about tragic," Fiona said, stirring a thermos cup of soup in front of her. "I heard from Amy Martin that she's planning on trying out for the school play. Apparently the guidance counselors want her to get more involved and stuff . . . to help her cope."

"Ned's play?" Em had a fuzzy, pre-Furies recollection of JD's nerdy friend Ned carrying on about the play he planned to direct in the spring: A version of the Greek story of Cassandra, whose prophecies were perceived as madness. Ironic that Skylar might play a role in a Greek tragedy onstage while embroiled in one offstage, as well.

Fiona shrugged. "I guess so. God, do you *remember* what she looked like at the Fling? She certainly knows how to put on a show."

The night of the Fling, drugged-up and bandaged, Skylar had looked almost as if she were possessed. Her entrance at the dance had been anything but subtle. She'd stumbled in, hopped up on painkillers, wearing a too-small dress and a crazy-lady veil that half-concealed her gauze-covered wounds.

The dance. Though she tried to quell the thoughts before they overtook her, Em began to flash back to the moments following Skylar's disastrous appearance. The gym had gone black. Hysteria set in when students realized the doors were stuck. Drea had gone into a corner to prepare what she believed to be a ritual that would banish the Furies. And then Ty had appeared.

The girls got quiet, a show of respect for Em. They'd noticed how close she and Drea had gotten.

"So, how's your first day back?" Gabby asked.

"It's not that bad, actually," Em said. And it wasn't, thank god. She'd felt relatively . . . normal today, which was a good sign. "I'm never going to be able to leave the house again, though—too much homework."

"I can help you with all the math stuff," Fiona said. "It would actually be good practice for the PSAT."

"And I've got all the French homework," Lauren added.

"I can tell you every single couple that's fought and made up in the past seven days," Gabby deadpanned. The girls laughed as the bell rang, jolting Em from the few moments of true freedom she'd felt in weeks.

It was time for gym. They all said good-bye, and Em hoofed it across campus.

In the antiseptic locker room, she distractedly made small talk with Jenna, who had just "totally failed" a math test, and Portia Stewart, the starting forward on the girls' varsity soccer team and Em's go-to girl during yearbook season for write-ups in the sports section.

"I can't believe we have to go outside in this weather," Jenna whined, finger combing her hair into a high ponytail. "It's—it's inhumane is what it is."

"Jenna, it's like fifty degrees outside," Portia reasoned. It was one of those cusp-of-spring days marked by damp air and gray skies. It was almost guaranteed they'd do a whole lot of laps around the track—not to mention Ms. Hadley's version of handball, which involved students hitting small rubber balls against the dark green walls that lined the tennis courts. To be honest, Em didn't mind it that much. She hadn't exercised at all recently—though you wouldn't be able to tell, the way she was losing weight—and she appreciated the every-other-day chance to focus only on her heaving breaths and burning calf muscles. To shut off her mind for a bit.

"Yeah, but the point is, we wouldn't even be out there if the stupid gym hadn't—" Jenna cut herself off, her eyes wide with embarrassment.

"Burned to the ground?" Em asked, struggling to keep her voice neutral.

"Em, I'm so sorry. . . . I wasn't even thinking."

Em shook her head and managed a weak smile, hoping they could both just drop it. But the mention of the fire, so sudden and unexpected, made it hard to breathe. She couldn't even be mad at Jenna, though; what she'd said was true. Since the fire had damaged the interior of the Ascension gym, all phys ed classes were being held outdoors until further notice.

"Well, at least Hadley keeps us on the track and the courts," Portia said to defuse any awkwardness. "We had to do sprints on the grass at practice yesterday and Sarah Stokes totally wiped out on the mud." She giggled. "It looked like she'd crapped her pants."

"She probably did," Casey Cornell snickered, coming up from behind them. "Remember when she peed her pants at the ski mountain in sixth grade?" Em had never liked Casey—she'd always seemed just a little too fake, a little too plastic. Her clothes were generally more suited for Ft. Lauderdale than Maine, and Gabby always said she looked like a Bachelorette waiting to happen.

Ms. Hadley stuck her permanently scowling face into the locker room. "Girls! Hurry it up! I want you outside in three minutes!"

Em slipped on her gym shorts and a loose-fitting T-shirt and headed outside; as she did, Jenna jogged up alongside her. "Em. I really am so sorry about what I said earlier. . . ."

"Jenna, seriously—don't worry about it."

"Okay, well . . ." she started. "It's just good to have you back, is all. But aren't you going to be freezing?"

Em looked around, noticing all the other girls were pulling on sweatshirts or yoga pants to brave the misty afternoon. But she knew she'd be perfectly comfortable. It was as if her internal temperature had increased over the past month or two. Like her anger at the Furies was a fire burning constantly inside her.

"I'll be fine," she responded. "I'm going to go warm up."

Out by the track, Hadley was already barking at the students: "I don't want to hear any griping about the weather. Start moving and you'll work up a sweat."

She was already burning up. As she folded herself in half, hands dangling by her toes, Em tried to quiet her mind, which was suddenly full of the Furies and everything else. Just the mention of the fire made her feel crazy, made the stories flare up in her brain. The gym, sure, but also that house in the woods . . . the one Drea had told her about.

Drea's research had unearthed the tale of three sisters hounded to death by Ascension townspeople more than a century ago. Accused of being witches or gypsies or husband-stealers. The fire was set in an effort to drive them out. And while the sisters' charred remains were never found, the towns-people *did* find the body of a male, a boy, in that house in the Haunted Woods. They'd assumed he was a servant. That odd detail had stuck out.

She closed her eyes, feeling the pull in her hamstrings, trying to block out everything but the sensations in her body. Then she swooped her torso and arms upward, reaching for the sky, leaning to the left and the right.

"Okay, now start jogging," Mrs. Hadley instructed the group. "We're going to run for fifteen minutes. If you can't run any-more, start walking. But I don't want to see you strolling. This is work, people."

Em had never been much of a runner; while Gabby enjoyed sweating it out on the treadmill, Em had always been a Response Runner—that is, her running routines were generally a response to jeans that felt tighter than usual. But today it came naturally. She was barely panting.

"Nice work, Winters," she heard Hadley shout as she marked her first lap. "You been taking steroids?"

Lap two. *Pound, pound, pound.* She was an asteroid hurtling toward an unavoidable fate.

She ran past Casey a second time, and felt resentful eyes bor-ing into her. Didn't care.

Lap three. *Go. Go. Go.* Her skin soaked in the dampness around her. She was pulling energy in like a magnet. The running came easily—she whipped along, enjoying the wind against her face and the steady pounding of her feet against the asphalt. It was more comfortable sprinting than standing still. She felt like she could keep going forever. Part of her wanted to. As if she could outrun every thing and everyone that reminded her of the fire, of Drea's death, of the Furies.

But then, just as she was starting to relax, to feel a whiteness in her whole body, a cleanness, like she was floating, something happened: a terrible sound, like high-pitched wind chimes keeping an off-kilter beat, went tearing through her mind. The trees lining the track blurred together in fast-forward. The speckled asphalt below her feet created fractals—patterns that repeated themselves over and over. It was like everything was folding in on itself. Soon, she could hear nothing else but the unmistakable timbre of Ty's laughter reverberating in her mind. She ran faster and faster, trying to drown it out with the air whooshing into her ears and her increasingly strained breath. When fifteen minutes were up, she stood on the sidelines with her hands on her hips and an expression of what she hoped looked like nonchalance on her face. *Oh, hey, no big deal that I just lapped every one of you.* Inside, her heart was pounding.

Then they were moving on to handball—dividing themselves into teams and "serving" the ball by bouncing it against the ground and slapping it against the wall. The goal was to hit it in such a way that one's opponent couldn't return the shot. Bo-ring.

Em teamed up with Jenna against Casey and Portia. She waited for the first serve, shaking her head in an attempt to quiet the lingering echo of Ty's laugh. Any peace she'd found while running had disappeared completely.

When the ball came whizzing toward her, she held her palm flat, enjoying the sting as her skin made contact with the rubber surface. It was a nice kind of pain. She swung, propelling the ball forward. Her arm was simply part of a machine. The ball shot away from her hand like a cannonball, hurtling toward the wall. She could practically hear it whistling through the air. It hit the wall with an explosive thud, sending several chips of green paint onto the asphalt below. Em watched it go. She felt calm. Like she'd done it before.

"Shit," she heard Portia mutter with a mixture of fear and respect.

The ball came shooting back in their direction with amazing force. Suddenly, it was as though time was moving in slow motion. The blue ball was the size of a nectarine or a plum; it probably weighed a pound or two and it seemed to be hurtling forever in the air. *Zoom*. There was no way to stop it.

She saw where it was going. The bullet of a ball smashed directly into Casey Cornell's face.

There was a sickening crack and a moment of stunned silence before Casey collapsed to the ground, wailing, covering her cheek.

Em felt twenty sets of eyes on her—fearful, wondering, accusatory. A sick feeling opened up in her stomach. People were looking at her as though she were a criminal.

Her fault.

I'm worried you're going to hurt someone, Crow had said.

Ms. Hadley began barking out orders, instructing a terrified-looking Jenna to go retrieve the ice pack from the office and telling Casey to tip back her head; her face had begun to bleed. Spots of blood spilled—one, two, three—sharp red on the pavement.

"Why would you *DO* that?" Casey blubbered, practically hysterical.

And now everyone was watching Em, inching away from her as though she were contaminated, contagious.

She couldn't keep Crow's warning from thundering back into her mind.

You're becoming one of them.

Without thinking, she turned and ran—away from the crowd, away from what she had done and the violent power that had overtaken her. She cut across the wet grass and felt the cold seep into the tips of her sneakers. If she could have run away from herself, she would have. . . .

Was this the darkness taking over? Was it inside her already, burning her up?

CHAPTER THREE

"Destruction! They call me crazy, like a fortune-teller. A poor, starved beggar-woman . . . and now the prophet undoing his prophetess has brought me to this final darkness. . . ."

Even in rehearsal, Skylar had nailed her monologue. It was only a reading; she and the other actors sat in a circle in the middle of the stage—but still, it gave JD chills.

This Cassandra play was actually going to be pretty cool, JD reflected as he left the techie meeting on Monday afternoon. Cassandra was a classic tragic figure, with the ability to predict a future that nobody believed. Her prophecies were a curse: ultimate power paired with ultimate hopelessness.

Ned had some good ideas for the production, which would kick off AHS's Spring Week—a student play, a music assembly, an art show, and a lacrosse game. They were going to use muffled sound cues and displaced voices to contribute to the sense of insanity in the theater. And Ned had decided to cast Skylar McVoy in the leading role just from hearing her read a passage in class. While JD was somewhat skeptical about working with a girl who had more than one screw loose, he trusted Ned's directorial instinct.

Rehearsal ended late. Driving home, JD passed by the Dungeon, Drea's favorite coffee shop. It was the first time he'd been by the place in more than a week, and just seeing it opened the floodgates in JD's mind—everything he'd been trying to tamp down for days. He thought of how Drea had survived on Red Bull and ramen noodles, and how she'd been able to name every Best Actress winner back to 1976. How she'd flicked at her fingernails when she was thinking hard. How her eyes were so dark they looked almost purple—like her hair, or at least the half of it that wasn't buzzed.

Admittedly, JD had been avoiding the Dungeon. He had his subconscious to thank for that. Pain was supposed to ease in time—but it seemed that with every passing day her death became more difficult to process. His throat tightened and his chest felt heavy. He was shocked and devastated by one crippling thought: that he'd never see Drea again.

In the months before she died, JD had become increasingly suspicious that Drea was developing a crush on him. There were the late-night study sessions, and the flirty anonymous texts that he suspected were her weird, secretive way of confessing her feelings. She'd once hinted as much. His cheeks got hot remembering how close they'd come to kissing the night before their AP Physics midterm . . . She'd been leaning over his leg, pointing to a diagram in his textbook, wearing his yellow buffalo-plaid flannel because it was cold. It was big on her, and falling slightly off her shoulder. He'd bent closer to grab his highlighter and she'd looked into his eyes, questioning him, daring him. But then, just when he decided to go for it—JD Fount was going to kiss Drea Feiffer—she'd put her hand on his chest and said a single word: "Em."

And he figured it out then that Drea might like him, but somehow knew he was in love with Em, that she would only be a substitute. His chest swelled like someone was inflating a balloon in there—thinking of Drea, how smart she was, and how sweet, under all that metal and that big, fierce mouth that got her into so much trouble.

He missed her. Maybe he should have kissed her that night. Because she was funny and brilliant and because of his own dumb luck, a girl like her had liked him.

Stopped at a red light near the shopping plaza, he spotted a familiar flop of dark hair . . . it was Crow, with his guitar case slung across his back, standing in the parking lot, deep in conversation with the same girl whom JD had sat next to at Drea's funeral service—the one with the honey-blond hair and the ribbon around her neck (it was still there, he noticed). Meg. That was her name. If she was one of Drea's friends from another nearby town, it would make sense that Crow knew her too. And he definitely seemed to *know* her. They were talking so intensely that their faces were just inches apart. JD watched as Crow grabbed her arm with one hand and gesticulated madly with his other one. They appeared to be . . . close. Boyfriend-girlfriend close.

He felt a flash of anger, wondering whether Em knew about this girl. Why did she always fall for these two-faced guys? First Zach McCord, who gave "shithead" a new definition; and now Crow, who was more consumed with his image and his stupid guitar than with Em's happiness. And now, apparently, he'd found a distraction with this other, ribbon-wearing chick . . .

JD couldn't understand what seemed to be willful blindness on Em's part, at least where her heart was concerned. She deserved better. She deserved someone who understood her, who knew how to care for her and what flavor ice cream she liked best (rum raisin), what her favorite movie was (*Dirty Dancing*), and how to make her laugh until she spit soda from her nose (tickle her ankles). JD knew that he was jumping to a whole lot of conclusions—and being slightly judgmental, which was Em's long-standing criticism of him, but he couldn't help it.

His phone beeped, and he reached over to grab it from the

passenger seat. The text was from Jenny, one of Melissa's best friends.

Melissa got hurt. Someone's taking her home.

"Terrific," he muttered. "Now what?"

As the light changed from red to green, JD glanced in the rearview mirror just in time to see Crow getting into his red-and-silver pickup truck. Red Ribbon Girl was nowhere to be seen—it was like she'd disappeared completely in the few seconds JD wasn't looking. Strange. The *click-clack* of his turn signal seemed louder than usual.

He stepped on the gas, only to see a flash of white just in front of his tires, directly in his path. JD sucked in his breath and swerved to the right, slamming on the brakes right in the middle of the intersection. Cars going the other way honked and moved around him. As the car skidded to a stop, JD's heart still pounding, he made momentary eye contact with a thin white cat, mangy and mean, standing right in the middle of all the traffic, just staring back at him. It appeared to have something hanging from its mouth. Something red. For a second, he was almost sure it was the red ribbon he'd seen the girl wearing just minutes before. Christ. Was he hallucinating now? The cat's eyes shone black in the quickening dusk.

Cats had always unsettled him; they gave the impression that they knew so much more than they let on—and this one was no exception. JD beeped his horn and the cat paused for another second before turning and moving off languidly into the shrubs on the side of the road.

He drove the rest of the way home with his hands white-knuckled around the steering wheel, then burst in the front door calling his sister's name.

"Mel? Melly? What's up? Where——" He stopped short when he saw her sprawled on the living room couch, her right ankle wrapped in sports tape and propped up on a million pillows. She looked at JD with the wide-eyed excitement of someone who has just discovered a new toy—or in her case, social-networking platform.

"I hurt my ankle, JD, practicing for the spring cheer-squad tryouts," she said. "I thought it was broken!"

"Why didn't you call me?" JD said. "I got a text from Jenny."

Mel shrugged. "My phone was dead again." She was always killing her phone battery from all the use it got. It was getting to be a miracle for that phone to make it past two p.m. without a recharge.

For the first time, he noticed a soda and a bag of popcorn sitting next to her on the coffee table. She looked like she was having the time of her life. His heartbeat started to slow.

He came to sit down next to her. "Are you okay now?"

"I'm fine," Melissa said. "Ali says it's just bruised."

"Ali . . . ? Who's——"

"I'm Ali," a voice said from the doorway.

JD turned to see a girl with practically white-blond hair leaning easily in the door frame. She was holding a bag of ice.

And she was gorgeous. Like, magazine-cover-supermodel gorgeous.

"Um, hell-hi," he stammered. His brain seemed to be trying to work through sludge. "And . . . who are you?"

"Ali saved me," Melissa piped in. "Me and Jenny were practicing near her house—you know where she lives, right, kind of near the Behemoth? And I slipped 'cause it's so freaking muddy! And Ali was just right there—"

"I just happened to be driving by at the right time," Ali said, handing Melissa the ice pack. Her movements were easy and practiced. Maybe she really was a model; he could picture her on a runway. "And I offered to take her home. I hope that's okay."

"I guess . . . I mean, thank you," JD said, still mystified over the appearance of this girl in his living room. "Mel, did you call Mom and Dad?"

"Not yet," Melissa said. "I haven't even plugged my phone in yet. It all happened so fast, you know?"

"You've been away from your phone for more than five minutes? Wow, you must really be hurt," JD said. He reached over and mussed Mel's hair, and she shrieked and ducked away from him. He sniffed. "Is something burning?"

"Nothing burns unless I want it to," Ali said with a smirk before she headed back in the direction of the Founts' kitchen.

She walked like she owned the place. Like she'd been here before.

"Ali's making me Pop-Tarts," Melissa said. "She said she wanted to stick around until someone got home."

JD looked at Melissa's ankle, which was encased in a mound of white medical gauze. "And you're *sure* you're okay? How do you—how does *she*—know it's not broken?"

"Ali's studying to be a nurse," Melissa informed him. "And yes, I can stand on it. It just hurts. I'll be fine, JD. It's not bad at all. Don't tell Mom and Dad, though. I want to milk this. I have a stupid English test tomorrow and I haven't even studied." She shook out a handful of popcorn into her palm and ate the whole thing in one go. He couldn't help but laugh. There was the Melly he knew.

Still, he couldn't quite relax. Something was off. He didn't know if it was the adrenaline from his drive home, or the presence of the new girl, or what, but the energy in the room was electric.

All of a sudden, without having made a sound, Ali was next to them, putting a plate of pink-frosted Pop-Tarts on the coffee table and sitting down on the love seat across from them.

"Thanks, Ali," Melissa said, scooping one up and biting into it greedily. "Delish."

JD grinned. "I think you may have a new president of your fan club," he said in a stage-whisper to Ali, who laughed. She had kind of a low voice but her laugh was high and tinkling, like falling glass. Melissa reached around to punch him and JD fake-winced, pretending it hurt. "So, Mel tells me you're studying to be a nurse—do you live around here?"

Ali shifted in her seat, rolling her shoulders back. JD caught himself staring at her chest and immediately looked away. *Christ.* He was sweating. She was straight out of a Victoria's Secret catalog.

"I'm taking classes up at UNE," she said. "I was just visiting some relatives today."

JD nodded. The University of New England was known for its nursing program—Em's parents were always talking about it. "Well, thanks. You know, for doing your job—even in the field."

Ali smiled. "I love it. Some people are freaked out by blood, you know? But I never was." Her smooth voice provided a sharp contrast to the words coming from her mouth. "It's almost like I get a rush from it."

JD felt his stomach clench up. He didn't like blood. There'd been too much spilled this winter in Ascension. "Plus you're good at being in the right place at the right time," he said to change the subject. "I'm not sure Melissa and Jenny would have really known what to do on their own."

"Um, I'm not an *idiot*," Melissa said. "We would have just called *you*. And if you weren't too busy moping somewhere, you would have come to get me."

"Moping?" Ali asked. Her eyes, icy blue, seemed to bore into him.

"JD is, like, mope-city these days. Not that you don't have a reason to be," his sister added quickly as JD shot her his look of death. "But admit it: You've been basically a zombie."

He looked over at Ali with an expression of both apology and embarrassment. "I'm sorry," he said. He pushed his glasses up his nose and cleared his throat. "It's nothing. I just . . . I lost a friend recently, and I've been dealing with that."

"Oh, that's awful," Ali said, bringing a hand briefly to her mouth. Her nails were red. Blood colored. Suddenly he wasn't finding her so pretty anymore. There was a pause. Then she looked at him with eyes full of sorrow. "I know about tragedy," she said quietly. Her voice seemed to drop octaves as she spoke her next sentences: "I know how you feel. Sometimes it seems like the wrong people get hurt, doesn't it?"

JD felt a ripple of discomfort shimmy along his spine; something about this girl was . . . different. He was about to ask her what she meant when Ali leaped up from her perch.

"Well, I've intruded long enough," she said, and JD noticed that all of a sudden she was back to cheerleader mode. "I better get going. I'm so glad you're okay, Melissa. I hope I see you again—oh!" She cut herself off, pointing at a picture on the mantel. "You know my cousin Ty?"

JD squinted at the photo, confused. "That's our neighbor Emily," he said. "Emily Winters. She lives next door."

Ali frowned for a second. But then she smiled, and her face

was once again transformed: radiant, gorgeous. "So weird . . . they could be twins!" In a quieter voice she said, "Very pretty."

"JD has a total crush on Em," Melissa blurted out.

JD stared at her. "I give up with you, Melissa. You're worse than *Gossip Girl*."

"Sorry," she said, not sounding very sorry at all. "But it's true, isn't it?"

Fortunately, Ali only laughed. "Well, if you like Em, you'll have to meet my cousin Ty," Ali said as she walked toward the Founts' front door.

"Ali, wait," Melissa called out. "When are you going to show Jenny and me those drills, the ones for high kicks?"

JD rolled his eyes. "You wanna talk about crushes? I think you have one on Ali." He ducked to dodge the pillow that Melissa lobbed in his direction.

"Oh, don't worry, you can't get rid of me that easy," Ali said musically as she sailed out the door. "You'll see me really soon— that's a promise. And I *never* break my promises."

The house felt eerily quiet with Ali gone. JD stood there for a moment, thinking of what to do next. It was weird—Ali was clearly very sweet, but she'd left him somehow feeling sour.

"Is that Ali's glove?" Melissa asked, pointing at a bright red leather glove on the floor.

JD picked it up and ran outside, strangely grateful for the excuse to get some fresh air. To thank Ali again, too, and try to shake off the bad feeling he had. But outside, he found that Ali had already disappeared.

Had Ali brought a car here? He didn't remember seeing one when he pulled up, but then he'd been stressed out and worried about Mel, so maybe he just hadn't noticed.

He looked at the glove still in his hand—it was kind of old-fashioned. Who wore driving gloves anymore? He stood on the porch another moment, inhaling the wet smell of new growth. The sky was navy, and spring peepers were chirping somewhere in the woods. New life. That was what Ascension needed.

He turned to go back inside, and as he did, he instinctively looked up to Em's window to see if she was home. Her lights were out. Her windows were dark. No one was home.

CHAPTER FOUR

Crow's obsession with music extended to an active online presence—where he shared his favorite music and tirelessly promoted his band, The Slump. Plastered all over his Facebook, Twitter, and Tumblr was news about everything band related, from the latest numbers hitting iTunes to tour info and recordings of gigs. He even had his own YouTube channel with an extensive following, where he posted videos of covers and his own songs.

What was supposed to take two minutes took half an hour. Em's one goal was to find out where Crow would be on Monday night; she needed to talk to him about what had happened in the gym earlier. Yet she felt compelled to watch video after video of him. His voice was fantastic and he played just about every instrument there was: piano, ukulele, mandolin. The list went on.

Em had watched a series of posts made over the last month, but she'd noticed a trend that disturbed her. Crow's earlier videos had been engaging, funny, and even a little bit flirtatious—but in recent posts he seemed careless and sometimes incoherent. His voice seemed to have gotten grittier and lower. More tortured. But it was still beautiful. It still got her every time she heard it.

"I'm trying something new," he said into the camera in this latest video, smiling breezily as he held up a harmonica. "Because I'm drunk and tired and pissed off . . . and when you play a harmonica in a minor key? It can sound like all those things. . . ."

He took a swig out of a pint glass. "And don't worry, moms and dads—this is apple juice." He smiled, big and plastic, then went on to hum a melody and stomp out a beat. Despite the grainy recording, it moved her. When Crow blew into the metal harmonica, the notes seemed to bend and expand. It was bluesy and haunting—but just thirty seconds into the video, the music stopped abruptly.

"This is shit!" Crow yelled suddenly—then threw his harmonica at the camera, which fell to the floor and ended the video. The whole thing was bizarre. Others could write it off as the outburst of a moody rock star, but Em felt it was something else entirely. Knew it, in fact, because she felt the same way—the hopeless frustration, the feeling of being deeply misunderstood . . .

She signed off, realizing that she was borderline stalking him.

Plus she'd found out what she needed already: His next gig was tonight at the Armory, a newish, all-ages club in Biddeford, about twenty minutes up the highway from Ascension.

Which is how Em decided where *she'd* be that night. Who knows if she'd get ahold of him otherwise? He had this irritating pattern of never having his phone on when she called. She remembered he always used to answer for Drea, and wondered if he did this on purpose to torture Em. Maybe after climbing in her window last week and telling her she was becoming a Fury, he'd had second thoughts about wanting to hang out with her. It would be just like him to offer help one minute and then avoid her the next.

Or maybe he regretted their kiss that day in his truck.

Or maybe he just spent a lot of time rehearsing with his band.

But he was one of the only ones who knew anything about the Furies, and she needed to tell him that she was starting to fear that Drea was right. Em was turning, slowly. She was still trying to explain away Drea's wild ideas. Drea had been obsessed with the Furies, blaming them for the death of her mom and the subsequent collapse of her family—her dad was a drinker, and their house stayed upright only because she was there to make sure it didn't fall down on top of them. It was very possible that her need to destroy the Furies had just gone a little too far. Em totally got that. Thinking about the Furies for too long would drive anyone insane. You might start to think they were following you. Like predators stalking their prey . . .

But then again, the signs were there, and they were becoming impossible to ignore.

The heat. Her unnatural speed and strength.

Those seeds.

If only she hadn't swallowed those five seeds, binding her to the Furies forever . . .

But of course, if she hadn't swallowed the seeds, then JD would still be in danger. Or worse, dead.

She didn't know who, or what, to believe.

Her first day back at school had been harder—much harder—than she'd anticipated. Now she was feeling ragged and raw, like any little thing could set her off into screaming. She felt like she might snap in two. She was still on somewhat restricted driving rules, and anyway, she wasn't sure she was up for getting behind the wheel just yet. So she would have to ask her mother for a ride to Crow's concert.

As she padded down the carpeted stairs, she reminded herself that Crow had always seemed decent and honest—sometimes too honest—from the first days she'd spent with him.

Either way, based on what she'd promised the Furies, there was practically no one she could talk to about this. He was one of her only potential allies. And he *seemed* to know more than he let on. Meeting him on his own territory? It had to be worth a try.

Thankfully, her mother was thrilled that Em actually wanted to leave the house after so many days of hiding in her bed, and eagerly agreed to drive her out that night, making Em promise a million times to call if she couldn't get a ride back home. "I'll come get you, no matter how late it is, okay, honey?"

Em hugged her mom, assuring her she'd be fine, and got out of the car.

"Em?" Her mom called her back.

She turned and ducked into the open passenger-side window. "Yeah, Mom?"

"Are you sure you're all right?" Her mother looked older then, grasping the steering wheel with thin hands. "I feel like I'm losing you."

"I'm not going anywhere," Em said firmly. "And being here tonight? It's what I need."

Her mom offered a tight smile. "I'm trusting you, Em. Call if you need to."

As she watched her mom's car disappear around a bend, Em readied herself to talk to Crow. She wasn't going to let him pull his sleepy-eyed caginess on her, not tonight. She wanted *answers*. How much did he know? If he'd been lying to her before, she was going to find out the truth now. If this was all head games, it needed to end.

And if it was something more, well . . . she'd find a way to make it stop. Somehow.

The chilly spring air felt great against Em's always-burning skin and it fueled her forward as she pushed open the heavy wooden door and walked into the Armory. She was on a mission.

The club's crazy architecture fit right into her mood—dark, gothic, dramatic—and the music from The Slump, who were already midset when she arrived, wrapped around her like a warm cloak. The place was really an old church that had been repurposed into a music venue; pews still served as seating around the downstairs stage (what used to be the altar), and a long mahogany bar ran the length of one entire side wall, lit by ornate iron sconces. A spiral staircase led from the foyer to a velvet-draped balcony level, where dark corners and metal poles clashed with the piety depicted on the stained-glass windows. There were so many places where people could hide. Do things and not be seen.

Em felt a sudden tightness in her throat. How many people had confessed their sins here? How many people had asked, and been granted, forgiveness?

And would Em ever get that chance?

She was surprised to feel tears burning the back of her eyes, and she blinked quickly. She was dying to talk to Crow, but he had just begun a set, so she leaned against the back wall, fiddling with her UNDER 21 wristband and listening to Crow strum the opening notes of a new song. False start. He leaned his lanky body over the strings to tune them. When he did, a piece of his long black hair fell into his eyes. She felt a bizarre itch in her fingers—like she wanted to reach up there and brush the hair out of his face herself.

He started up again. This time the notes were good, strong, powerful. Crow's voice was powerful too: liquid and dark, like something you wanted to drink. Crow owned the stage. Once he got going, it was impossible for Em to take her eyes off of him. All thoughts of the Furies were temporarily defused, as though they were floating up to the Armory rafters along with the ringing notes of Crow's chords.

The last song was one he'd just written, he announced before he started playing—it was called "Vision." He took a swig from his beer. "I think it's going to be part of a series," he said cryptically before playing the first chord. He grimaced; it hadn't come out just right. For a second he looked up with a mad glint in his eye and Em flinched, reminded of his YouTube breakdown that had gotten more than two hundred views. He didn't even feel a need to hide it. . . .

But then he leaned over and tried again. Once he started singing, his lyrics were poetic and somewhat mournful; Em found herself leaning forward to catch every word.

"*Haunted by my dreams*
Like startled birds so fast
With visions of the future
And memories of the past."

In the church chamber, the wailing of the guitars soared

overhead, while the pounding of the drums coursed through the floor. The highest notes, like those of a choir, seemed to linger long after the next chord was strummed. And Crow's voice cut through it all—forceful and passionate, like a preacher giving a sermon.

She'd been spending time with Crow for a month or so, and she'd always known he was a good musician—his videos only proved that over and over again. But here, in the old church, Em was blown away by his talent. She grew warm thinking of the afternoon she'd gotten into his car to escape a harsh winter rain storm . . . the song he'd played for her . . . the way he'd slipped off his shirt for her to wear . . . the way his lips had brushed against her jaw . . .

It was crazy—she almost felt like Crow was singing right to her, stirring up emotions that she'd tried to ignore. And his words, they were so real. Like he could somehow see inside her head, like he knew her secrets. Like he knew what she'd come here to tell him. Like this was her confessional, her moment to ask for forgiveness.

Somehow, Crow's song made her feel less alone. She wasn't the only one caught up in this mess. She had the uncanny sense that Crow was part of it too.

With a burst of feedback from the monitors, The Slump's set came to a close. There was loud applause, and as the crowd broke apart, with most people making a rush for the bar, Em watched as

Crow jumped easily down from the stage and walked straight in her direction. So. He *had* seen her in the crowd. She'd wondered. There had been a moment when their eyes had met, and it was as though an electric current had run straight through her. . . .

She shook out her shoulders, slung on her black blazer, and reminded herself why she'd come here: for answers.

Then he was standing next to her—very close. She resumed her pose against the wall, feeling her shoulder blades against the brick behind her.

"You know this isn't a real church, right, angel?" He put his hand on the wall above her head and looked down into Em's eyes. There was a sheen of sweat along his hairline and he smelled like fire.

She felt her knees buckle ever so slightly but managed to swoop sideways and out from under his arm. "I had to leave my halo at the door," she said. "Beautiful set."

For a second, she saw a real flash of pleasure in his face, lighting up his greenish eyes, turning them temporarily golden. Then he shrugged. "Just a few things we're playing around with," he said nonchalantly. There was whiskey on his breath.

"Well, it was good," Em said firmly. Crow smirked and she added, "But I didn't just come to hear you play. We need to talk." She looked around at all the people still milling around the club, waiting for the next band. There it was again—the feeling of being watched.

"I'm gonna need another drink if we're going to get all serious," he said, turning and striding toward the bar without waiting
for her to respond.

She trailed after him, watching girls lower their eyelids flirta-
tiously as he passed by. He was oblivious.

"I'll have a another," Crow said just a little too loudly when
he got to the bar. "And a PBR chaser. And whatever she's having." He tossed a thumb over his shoulder in Em's direction.

"Just a seltzer, please," she said. "Are you using one of your
fake IDs?" she added under her breath.

"Like I need it," Crow shrugged. "I'm a regular." When his
drink arrived, two inches of brown liquid with one lonely ice
cube, he slammed half of it in one sip and followed that with a
swig of beer. So much for asking him for a ride home. He stared
at her, daring her to pass judgment.

"Can we find somewhere to talk?" she asked, looking around
the bar to avoid his gaze. His eyes were so intense—as though he
could see directly into her.

And maybe he could. She *trusted* him. She really did, despite
what everyone said. She realized she knew virtually nothing
about him except that he'd dropped out of high school . . . or
been kicked out, depending on who you asked. But when she
heard his music there was an understanding there, an honesty that
just felt right. Plus he just couldn't have made up what Drea said
out of spite or sketchiness. She couldn't make herself believe that.

"How about over there," he said, pointing to a small wooden love seat in a corner dimly lit by a glowing tea light.

Once they sat down and Em had arranged it so her knees weren't touching his, she forced herself to ask the question that had been burning inside of her all day. "Do you think it's true? What Drea said?" Was it her, or did every candle in the place flicker at the exact same time, like a gust of wind was passing through?

There was silence as Crow studied his beer can. Em could feel the *ba-boom, ba-boom, ba-boom* of bass drums through her feet.

"Honestly? I have no idea," Crow said, shaking his head.

That makes two of us, she thought. The condensation from her glass made her hands cold and wet.

"Something happened today," she said finally. "In gym class. It was like . . . it was like I had turned into someone else."

He didn't say anything. She couldn't even tell if he was really listening to her, the way he was looking off into the distance. He took another deep draw from his drink.

"I . . . hurt someone," she said.

"What do you mean?" he asked.

She bent her head, embarrassed. "I became, like, Super-woman for a few minutes. I threw a ball and it—it hit someone . . ." Then, at the exact same time, they finished the sentence: "Right in the face."

She whipped toward him. "How did you know?"

He laughed humorlessly. "Listen, angel, you're not the only one stuck in this shit show. I have a feeling I'm tangled up in it too." The words "upinit" smashed together like a traffic jam.

"You mean, because Drea told you about the Furies?" She still wasn't sure how much Crow knew.

Fortified by another sip of beer, Crow leaned forward and spoke to the floor. "Worse than that," he said. "See, I knew you were going to do that, what you did today in gym. I saw the whole thing—I saw you running like a track star on speed. I saw you break that girl's cheekbone. I'd already seen it all."

It was like a valve had opened within Crow; the words were spilling out of him.

"Where?" she asked. "What do you mean, you saw it?"

"What do I mean . . . ? Just what I said. I've been having these . . . visions, I guess you'd call them," he said. His knee was jangling up and down to its own rhythm. "I've been seeing things—like movies in my mind. Not memories, exactly. But things that have happened. Or will happen. Or . . . I don't know." When he looked at her again, his eyes were reddish. Tired.

She nodded, but couldn't speak. Was this Crow's drunken idea of a practical joke? Or was he just drunker than she'd even realized?

"I know what you're thinking," he said defiantly, "but I'm not just wasted. I mean, not *that* wasted. I saw you, Em . . . in my mind. There was so much blackness around you. Spilling out from inside of you. I knew you were going to hurt someone. And I don't think it's over. I think you're going to keep hurting people. The damage isn't done." The last words came out in a slurred rush. He drained what was left in the beer can.

No. I don't want to hurt anyone. His words tapped into her worst fears. "I didn't mean to hurt Casey," she said weakly. "I'm not . . . like them." Not yet, at least.

He barely heard her. "But here's the really bad thing," Crow continued. "That darkness that I saw in you, in my vision? It follows me around. I'll have another vision. Guarantee it," he said, holding up his empty glass. "Refill?"

She glanced at the key chain dangling from his belt loop. "I'm worried about you driving home."

"Don't you worry about me, babe," he said, leaning in close. "I can take care of myself. It's you we should be worried about." And with that he made his way back to the bar.

As she waited for him to return, her eyes were drawn to the church balcony. To the high stained-glass window that depicted a scraggly tree being split in two by a bolt of lightning. She stared at the oddly shaped cuts of glass, pieced together to form a whole image. An image of destruction. The window swam, a kaleidoscope of colors. Then there was a flash of white-blond hair.

She did a double take. There was someone up there.

Ali.

Ali was here. Spying.

She *was* being watched. Her stomach seized up and she considered running. Leaving this place, leaving Crow.

But when she narrowed her eyes and kept them trained to the spot where she'd seen movement, there was nothing. Nothing but dark corners and fleeting shadows.

"So here's what I know," Crow said, breaking her concentration. He'd come back with another glass of whiskey in his hand. "You and Drea were playing 'Buffy the Vampire Slayer,' except not vampires but Furies. The goddesses of revenge. Evil." His voice was rising; his tone was suddenly performative. It was as if he were trying to make a scene.

"Shhhhh," she hissed. "They'll hear you."

"Who will?" He was mocking her, but she thought she saw a spark of fear in his eyes.

"Crow, how much do you know? What else have you seen in your . . . visions?"

"I know too much," he said, sitting down heavily. "I knew about—I knew about Drea."

Em felt the familiar wave of panic and hopelessness rush through her. "You knew that she was trying to get rid of them?"

"More than that," he said dully. "I knew what was going to happen to her."

"You knew about . . . the fire?" She shook her head. "But that's impossible."

"It's not *impossible*," he said. His jarring tone made several nearby patrons turn their heads. "It's not impossible just because you don't understand it."

"This is serious, Crow." She tried to pull him back into their conversation, but his focus had shifted. He was looking at her through narrowed eyes, as if he were examining a specimen under a microscope.

"Sure, sure. Let's be serious." He scooted his chair toward her and leaned forward.

"Crow . . . don't."

"Don't what, princess? I gotta ask a question, and I gotta get close to ask it." He grabbed the underside of her chair and pulled it toward him, so close their faces were just inches apart. "If it's impossible, why the hell do you think I showed up that night when I did?"

Em opened her mouth to speak, then realized she didn't know how to answer that. Why *was* he there? The timing seemed suspicious. . . .

And then, all of a sudden, he was leaning in to kiss her. A piece of her wanted this—badly—but she couldn't have everything. Em pulled away and felt the armrest jam awkwardly against her back.

"No," she said shakily, placing her palm against his chest. "We—this isn't right, Crow. You know that. We're—we're friends."

He swayed backward a little. But not that far. His lips were still so close. . . . She could feel the heat from his body. "What's the matter, angel?" he said. "I'm not good enough for you?"

"You know that's not it," she said quickly, softly—almost like she was pleading with him. "It's just . . ." She couldn't finish. *JD*, she wanted to say. But she felt like an idiot speaking his name out loud, when he had barely even spoken to her in a month.

"You're drunk, Crow. And I don't want to mess up our friendship. . . ." The bench dug into her shoulder blade.

"I don't believe that's all you want from me," he said. His eyes were still on her. Burning. Sending a leap of warmth through her stomach, a spinning, dizzying heat through her head.

What *did* she want from him? Reassurance? Protection? Help? She didn't know anymore.

He reached up and traced her face lightly with two fingers. Everywhere he touched was like fire. "Tell me," he said in that low voice, like a song. "Tell me what you really want."

What did she want? She wanted information. She wanted his secrets. To see his visions. To learn from them. To know the *truth*.

She wanted everything to be different.

Em tilted her face to his, trying to read his eyes, trying to understand what was happening—what his role in it was. And that one small gesture was all Crow needed. He reached out and grabbed the back of her head, pulling her slowly toward him. Their lips were so close that she could taste him—that smoke, that sweetness.

The booze.

"No," she said, suddenly realizing how wrong it was. "Really."

"Everything okay over here?" Suddenly a bouncer, big and thick-necked, was behind them, pulling Crow back by the collar of his plaid shirt. "I don't think you're wanted here, buddy."

Every ounce of gentleness Crow had had just moments before was gone in an instant. "Get your hands off me." He stood up, shrugging off the bouncer's arm roughly.

Em put her hand on his arm. "Let's just go, Crow." Em needed to get him out of there in one piece.

"You hear that?" He ignored her, getting in the bouncer's face. "She's fine. Everything's fine. So I suggest you stop acting like I'm some kind of criminal." He punctuated the word with a nice, hard shove.

The bouncer was thrown off for less than a second, which was all the reason he needed. "You're out of here!" he yelled, clipping Crow's shoulder and herding him forcefully toward the door.

"What are you doing, man?" Crow argued. "It's early. I'm not even that drunk."

"You can't kick him out," Em said, chasing after them. "He's in no shape to drive."

"You're right, he isn't," came the bouncer's surly reply, "but he sure as hell can't stay here."

"Asshole," Crow muttered. The doors burst open and Em was relieved by the crisp air.

"What the hell are you doing?" she asked.

"He started it," Crow said pointing in the direction of the Armory. He got out a final round of expletives, then repeated: "I'm not even that drunk."

"You *are* that drunk."

They stood in silence. Crow looked up at the sky. He interlaced his fingers behind his head so his arms splayed out like wings. It was cool enough that Em could just barely make out his breath in the air. "Fine, I am drunk."

"Good. We're in agreement. Now give me your keys," she said, holding out her hand.

"You know how to drive stick?" he asked aggressively. "I don't want you bottoming out on the Ridge."

She didn't. Dammit. Why hadn't she taken JD up on those lessons this summer? "Crow . . . I . . ."

"You don't," he said smugly. He grabbed the keys out of her hand.

She still wasn't going to let him drive, manual transmission or no. "Well, then, I guess you'll have to call someone to pick you up." Em went for the keys, which he held up high and just out of her reach. "I'm not letting you get behind the wheel like this," she said jumping for them.

His eyes narrowed. "You can't tell me what to do," he said. "You can't tell me you don't want me and then tell me how to act."

75

Em stopped jumping. The words stung. They were standing so close she thought he might try to kiss her again. But instead he turned and started stalking across the parking lot in the other direction. "Crow!" she called after him. "Stop! You can't drive!"

"I feel like they're poisoning me." Crow wheeled around and his voice broke into the quiet. He threw the keys at her feet and winced, like he had a sudden headache. "The visions . . . I want them to stop. It's like blackness inside me."

A car came around the bend and waited for them to get out of the way. Illuminated by the bright white glow of the headlights, Crow looked almost otherworldly. "I want to help you, Em," he said, "but I think I'm going to get hurt if I do." Then he ran off into the night, leaving Em with his keys on the ground in front of her.

CHAPTER FIVE

"Yup, you're totally becoming one," Melissa said, standing in the doorway to JD's room and pulling her strawberry-blond hair back with a headband.

"Huh?" he asked. He'd been in another world, thinking about Em, and specifically of that book on her nightstand and wondering if he should ask her about it. He didn't even know how long Melissa had been standing there.

"See? Case in point," Melissa said, putting her arms out straight in front of her and staggering theatrically around his room. "I said, you're totally becoming a zombie. You need a life."

"A liiiiiife," he said, sounding the word out for effect. "How does one procure such a thing? Teach me, oh social one. Does it involve faking injuries to make friends?"

"I was not faking it," Melissa said. "I really twisted my ankle and you know it. It was pure serendipity that Ali and I met. Speaking of which, I need a ride to Pete's. Ali invited me for pizza."

"Didn't she leave, like, two hours ago?" JD said. "You're a little too young for an exclusive relationship."

She chucked a pillow at his head. "I texted to *thank* her again. And she invited me."

He swiveled back toward his computer. "Tempting, but no. First of all, I have homework to do. Second, I'm not—*not*—a chauffeur." Even saying the word—Gabby and Em's old nickname for him—made anger spark inside of him. He pushed it aside. "And last, there's pasta on the stove. Why are you going for pizza?"

"Let's start with the last one first," she said. "I'm going for pizza because I'd love to get out of the house. Even zombies need to socialize, you know." She plucked a hat off his bed and chucked it at him.

He didn't want to admit that she was right.

"And I *know* you're not a chauffeur," she added. "You were invited." She smiled brightly at him.

JD tried to keep his voice neutral, but he knew he'd already given in. "By whom?" he asked.

"By Ali, silly," Melissa said. "She said she wants you to meet her cousin later or something. So let's go already."

When they arrived at Pete's Pizza, Ali was already waiting for them in a red vinyl booth. Her skin shone flawlessly under the reddish lights of the restaurant. She had on a low-cut turquoise tank top, despite the fact that it wasn't exactly beach weather. Her hair was pulled back in a high ponytail and again he had no trouble picturing her rolling around in a bikini on the beach with cameras flashing. Everything about her was perky and oddly— almost eerily—perfect.

"Hey guys," she said, smiling.

"Thanks for the invite," he said as he scooted into the booth, trying not to stare too long into Ali's ice-blue eyes. He tugged off his peacoat and adjusted the collar of his cable-knit fisherman's sweater, hoping he looked at least semi–put together.

"I ordered a large pepperoni with mozzarella sticks on the side," she said once they'd settled in. "Hope that's okay."

"Perfect, I was actually praying for a heart attack tonight," JD said, grinning but making a mental note: *Someone likes to be in charge.*

"Well, luckily you have a nurse nearby if it happens," Ali responded. "Speaking of which, Mel, how's your ankle?"

"A little better than it was," she said. "I've been icing it like you said to."

"And making me run back and forth getting things for her," JD interjected.

Mel glared at him while Ali laughed. "I bet I'll have to sit out of practice for a while, though. . . ."

JD tuned out while his sister chatted, letting his gaze fall unfocused on the windows and the parking lot outside. He bent his head to one shoulder and then to the other, listening for the snapping cracks at the base of his neck. He did that sometimes when he was stressed, despite the fact that Mr. and Mrs. Winters both told him it was bad for his posture or something.

Em. He thought of how much she loved Pete's Pizza, especially her favorite combo of pepperoni and pineapple. He was halfway through his second set of cracks when he took in a sharp breath: As though he'd conjured her, Em Winters was coming through the door of the restaurant.

"Oh, good," Ali said just as JD was about to call Em's name. "Ty's here!" She waved to the newcomer and patted the bench next to where she was sitting.

As the girl came closer, JD could see it wasn't Em after all. Her cheekbones were wider and her eyes were green and catlike, nothing like Em's, which were big and brown and varied in darkness according to her mood. (They got lighter, weirdly, when she was angry; dark and chocolate brown when she was relaxed.) This girl didn't have the single freckle above her left eye.

But otherwise, Ali was right: Ty and Em were total doppelgängers.

"This is the cousin I was talking about earlier," Ali said, introducing JD to Ty, who stuck out her hand for him to shake, which made him feel awkward. Maybe she was older? He was surprised at the firmness of her grip.

"Nice to meet you," he said.

"The famous JD," she responded, as though she'd been hearing about him for ages, which didn't really make sense since he'd only met Ali today. She spoke with a casual drawl, as if she was from the South or someplace where time moved more slowly. "Meg is going to be jealous!"

"Oh yeah, meeting me. That's on everyone's bucket list," he said drily. "Who's Meg?"

"Meg's the third one of our little trio. We've been wanting to meet you for a long time," she repeated. Again, it was an odd thing to say, but JD still felt kind of flattered.

Once introductions were made, Ty joined the group, chiming in seamlessly as Ali and Melissa discussed the intricacies of some dance-tumble move for the cheerleading squad. JD sat back, unable to take his eyes off of Ty. Of course, as soon as he studied her more closely, the differences between her and Em became sharper: her voice was deeper, her mannerisms more extravagant, her laugh louder and throatier. She wore a bright red flower in her hair, and it reminded him of something, though he couldn't remember what.

He was simultaneously attracted to her, immediately and

instinctively, and put off at the same time. Like he was looking at a mirage, a mist that might vanish if he tried to touch it.

"So, what do you do around here?" Ty asked JD as they waited for the food to arrive. "Other than school, I mean."

Nothing, he nearly said, but he could see Melissa looking at him, silently praying for him not to be a geek. So he said: "Well, I like messing around with old cars . . . and right now I'm helping my friend do the lighting for a school play."

"Oh, cool," Ty said, flashing him a smile that showed off her perfectly white teeth. "I've always been interested in theater. Lighting, especially. Isn't it funny how one thing can look completely different depending on what light you shine on it?"

The pizza arrived, steaming and greasy, and as soon as Ty took a bite, her eyes practically rolled back in pleasure. "Ummm, *thisissogood,*" she said, her mouth full, eyes wide.

JD nodded and finished chewing. "Pete's never lets you down."

She wolfed down the rest of her slice and grabbed another one. "No, really, this is de-lish," she said. Meanwhile, JD noticed that Ali had barely touched her own pizza.

"I guess I'm less hungry than I thought," she said offhandedly when she saw him eyeing her plate. "Mel, want to come get refills on the soda? Then I'll play you at Big Buck Hunter," she added, pointing toward the handful of arcade game consoles in the corner.

"She literally has no idea what she's missing," Ty said when Ali and Melissa had gone off toward the counter. "I'm totally going to have a third piece!"

"Eat up," JD said. He liked girls who could eat. That was one thing he'd always loved about Em: her crazy sweet tooth and obsession with all things chocolate. "I think I'm done. A little too grease-heavy for me."

She looked at him seriously for a moment. When he stared back into her eyes, it was almost like looking into the center of a fire, where embers smoldered black-red. It sent shivers down his spine. "You have no idea how long it's been since I've had pizza," she said, going in for another bite. "You must think I'm such a freak, huh?"

"I think you're hungry," JD said.

Ty threw her head back and laughed, but it was different from before. Now the sound was surprisingly hoarse—like the laughter of a much older woman. Like she had dust in the back of her throat. The happy, hazy feeling surrounding JD dissipated momentarily.

"So, how long have you and your family been in town?" he asked. "Ascension's a little screwed up right now. . . ."

"Oh, you mean because of all the murders?" She dabbed at her mouth with a paper napkin, leaving a smear of red lipstick behind.

"Well, they weren't *murders*, technically. There were two

suicides and two accidents and . . ." He trailed off. "This is a kind of morbid conversation topic, huh?"

"When bad things happen, you can't just pretend they didn't," she said.

He nodded, reaching for the stack of napkins. "That's true," he said. "Although lots of people seem to be good at doing that."

"Oops, don't take this one," she said, whisking her lipstick-marked napkin away from him. "You don't want to end up like Chase Singer did. . . ."

JD's jaw dropped. "Excuse me?"

She smiled, looking temporarily embarrassed. "Sorry, that really *was* morbid. I was just thinking of that lipstick mark they found on Chase's cheek."

"Oh . . . I didn't . . ." JD trailed off, wondering if he'd heard that specific detail before. It seemed like something he would remember, but he didn't. "You—you knew Chase?"

"Just by sight," she said casually.

And just then, it hit him where he recognized Ty's flower from: Drea's service. Bright crimson, like the one that had ended up in Drea's casket.

He was hit with a wave of nausea. "Where did you get that?" he asked, pointing to her hair. It occurred to him that perhaps she had sent all those orchids. He remembered how strange they had looked against the other bouquets: just like droplets of blood.

Ty removed the flower from where it was tucked into her hair and twirled it in her fingers.

"Isn't it pretty?" she said.

"Were you at Drea Feiffer's memorial service?"

"For a little bit. I kind of hung back. Were you close with Drea?"

"We were friends," JD said, feeling his throat constrict. "It's been a hard week. It just doesn't seem right. Doesn't seem fair." He looked down at his lap. Jesus. This is why he didn't go out—he'd just met this girl and so far they'd talked about nothing but death. "How did you know Drea?"

"Old family friends," Ty said vaguely. She held her hand out as if to give him the flower, but when he reached for it she withdrew her hand quickly. Ty spoke again, but softly this time, as though through a sheet of silk. "You mention fairness . . . and I was always a big believer in justice. An eye for an eye, and all that. But these days, I'm seeing things differently. Some things just aren't fair—you can't *make* them fair. You know? Some things just happen. . . . And all we can do is let them."

As she finished speaking, she placed the flower back in her hair.

JD nodded slowly. Her speech had left him feeling a little overwhelmed, like he'd been hit by a wave, or put under a spell. A good one. And she was right. Some things just weren't fair, and he had to accept that and move on—whether it was Drea's death or the fact that something was going on between Em and Crow.

"Don't you two look serious," Ali said teasingly as she and Melissa came back toward the table.

"You know me," Ty said with a surprising edge. "Always—" She was interrupted by a low wolf whistle from across the restaurant.

JD swiveled around. Some frat boy in a baseball cap with a puffy beer face and squinty eyes was leering in their direction. Melissa was fidgeting uncomfortably. JD felt the impulsive desire to leap up and cover her.

"Hey, man, keep your eyes on your food, okay?" He made his tone good-natured yet firm, praying the guy would turn back to his pizza.

Ty put her hand on his arm. Her fingers were cold and smooth, like river rocks. "Just ignore him," she whispered with a flirty smile. "Though I appreciate the chivalry."

"Guys like that always get what's coming to them," Ali said, sliding into the booth. Melissa slid next to JD, and he put his arm around her.

"They sure do," Ty said, but she suddenly seemed distracted. JD watched her eyes squint just a little, like she was trying hard to remember something.

And that's when the hacking started, first loud and punctuated, then lower, gurgling. JD turned around. The frat boy, the one who had whistled, was leaning out of the booth, struggling to breathe. He had his hands around his throat. JD couldn't even see his face, just the visor of his cap. Everyone in the restaurant was watching.

"He's choking," someone shouted.

"Does anyone know CPR?" That was the waitress's voice, high, hysterical.

JD almost missed Ali's muttered comment: "See?" He was already getting out of the booth.

He was by the guy within seconds. He hoisted him to his feet, then spun him around to perform the Heimlich maneuver. Channeling his memories of sophomore-year health class, he wrapped his arms around Frat Boy's stomach, made a fist, and thrust upward. Once, and again. On the third try, something was dislodged, and the guy gasped.

"Oh my . . . Oh my god." He coughed. "Thank you. Thanks, man."

A little old lady sitting at a wooden table with her husband started clapping. "You saved him," she said. A round of applause swept through Pete's; JD felt his cheeks flush as red as the back of the booths around him.

"No problem," he said, backing toward the doorway. He couldn't stay inside any longer. He was dizzy, pumped from a combination of adrenaline and fear. "Look—smaller bites, okay? Come on, Melissa." With that, he swept out into the parking lot, relishing the way the fresh air cooled his face. He paced the asphalt, waiting for the girls to follow him outside.

"You're a hero!" Melissa said, bursting out the door after him with Ty and Ali close on her heels. "That was amazing. How did you know how to do that?"

"Even zombies can save lives," he said lightly. "Ready to go?"

"Let me just say good-bye," she said, turning to give Ali a hug.

Ty took the opportunity to take a step closer to JD. "It would be awesome to get a phone call from a hero," she said with a wink.

He felt the heat rising back up his neck. "I, ah—I don't have your, ah—," JD stammered.

"My number? Don't worry, I have yours. I did my recon," she said, clicking away. A second later, JD felt his phone buzz in his pocket.

The number was blocked.

Another chill washed over him. He couldn't tell if it was one of excitement or apprehension or both. He unlocked his phone and read the text: *Guess who?*

ACT TWO

PROPHETIC, OR ALL THE PRETTY FLOWERS

CHAPTER SIX

Surrounded by the chalky-strong smell of gym clothes and disinfectant, Em sat in the girls' locker room during fourth period on Tuesday. She was cutting class, but this was more important. She was worried about Crow, and his confession about seeing visions had reminded her of the book—the one she'd stolen from Sasha's locker last month: *Conjuring the Furies*. She carried it with her everywhere and had practically memorized most of it, although there was one section, the one she was reading now, that she'd previously just skimmed over: "The Role of the Prophet." She remembered it talked about visions. She had to figure out whether there was something she'd missed, some key clue that she'd ignored.

According to the book, prophets were reborn over and over

again through the centuries, living lives tortured by incomprehensible visions, as vulnerable to forces of evil as to sources of good.

No one knows if they descended from above or arose from the underworld. Some prophets are responsible for calling the dark essence of the Furies out from their dark lairs and into the real one. Others, gifted with an ability to identify the Furies' snowballing thirst for vengeance, are able to combat the influence of those and other dark spirits. Prophets are usually, but not always, male.

As much as one percent of the population may be unrecognized prophets—many of them artistic types who try to channel their visions into their work; others are driven crazy, or persecuted by the mainstream into believing they are crazy.

Some become entangled with the Furies unknowingly, Em read, *drawn unconsciously to do the Furies' bidding. They may, however, recognize that they are part of something heinous; if they trust their visions, they may be able to battle the Furies.*

The passage went on. *Do not confuse the prophet with the patient. Many victims of head injury or trauma display symptoms of prophecy. They may hear the Furies, but it is temporary.*

So, "prophets" were different from "patients." Patients were people who had brain defects and who shared some of the same symptoms as prophets. They were missing the part of the brain that apparently stores and processes trauma. The part of the brain that keeps most of us sane and normal, that protects us from succumbing completely to exposure to evil and chaos. If that part of the brain is damaged or missing, it's like the floodgates to evil open up. And that's how the Furies can get in.

Crow didn't seem to have anything wrong with his mind.

No, Crow was a prophet, not a patient. She was almost certain of it. The disturbing visions. The desire to escape from them, or turn them into art . . . It all sounded just like him.

But how deep was his connection to the Furies? Could he help her? Or would he hurt her more?

She packed up her books and started walking back up the hill from the gym to the library, where she had plans to meet Gabby for lunch. Halfway up the hill, her cell rang. It was a blocked number.

She picked up anxiously. "Hello?"

"Emily, it's Crow." He sounded distant.

"What happened to you last night?" she asked. "Where did you go?"

"To jail," he said. There were loud voices in the background.

She stopped walking and covered her other ear to hear him better. She stood in the middle of the walkway and students streamed around her. "To *where*?"

"I was arrested last night," he answered sharply. "Don't ask. I need money. For bail."

"Wait, Crow, hold on," Em said. She suddenly felt itchy all over, like she'd stood in a hot shower for too long. "What are you talking about? What can I—"

"Go to my house," he said. "Get my guitar—the acoustic, the Fender, from my room. Then, please, can you go down to the pawn shop on Route One? And get some money? To bail me out? Two hundred should be enough. I'm sorry, Em."

His guitar? The one thing he loved? His one source of happiness?

"No way," she said.

He misunderstood. "Em, there's no one else—"

She couldn't bear to let him think she would just leave him there. "No, of course I'll bail you out," she said hurriedly. "But I'm not going to sell your guitar. Just don't . . . I'll be there as soon as I can."

"Did you see the article about Landon?" Em heard Portia say later as they waited for their French teacher to arrive. The hair on Em's arms prickled. The very last place she wanted to be was here when Crow was sitting in a jail cell, and the very last thing she wanted to talk about was a dead teacher.

The school paper had just run a short obituary of their former English teacher, published on the anniversary of the *Spring Awakening* humanities quiz show he'd started at Ascension a few years back as part of Spring Week. School administrators were promising to bring back the *Jeopardy!*-style event later this season, before SAT and final-exam pressures started to build. Em had placed well last year but she hadn't decided if she would participate this time around. Not likely.

"Shitty luck," said Andy Barton, the football player and former friend of Zach and Chase. "That ice is dangerous." He didn't really sound too beat up about it.

Henry Landon had been found, drowned, in a small pond near the Haunted Woods, where people ice-fished in the winter. The reports said there was no appearance of foul play; the ice had simply cracked below him.

"I know this is, like, so bad to say, but . . ." After a suitable dramatic pause, Portia went on. "I always felt like he was a little bit perverted."

"Like how?" Leaning back in his chair, Andy leaped at the chance to delve into the topic of perversion. Meanwhile, Em tried to ignore the irritation billowing in her chest. It was impossible not to listen.

"I think he . . . paid more attention to me . . . in class on the days I wore . . . low-cut shirts," Portia said. "I bet I would have gotten an even better grade if I let him give me extra help, if you know what I mean. I think he was into that sort of thing."

"Well, I hope you'd let me videotape it." Andy smiled slyly. "That dude didn't deserve such a hot piece of ass."

Portia shifted uncomfortably. Oblivious, Andy continued, tilting his chair so it balanced on his two back legs. "Anyway, if he was really a creep then he probably had it coming."

"'Had it coming'?" Em interjected. "So he deserved to die?" She couldn't help herself.

"No, obviously *not*," Andy said as he rolled his eyes. He looked to Portia for sympathy, but she hung her head low and pretended to be fascinated with her French worksheet. "What's with you, anyways, Winters? You and Landon close or something?"

God, she hated people like that, who managed to turn everything upside down and make their own shitty comments seem totally natural. As if *she* were the one who was out of line. Her body tensed—including every muscle in her hand, which clutched at the pen so firmly that it shook.

"Maybe I hit a nerve?" he asked, tipping back and forth on his chair. He then went on to say something about always being misunderstood. Em wasn't listening anymore. She could sense her temper starting to boil, and all she wanted was for Andy to *stop* talking. She wished something would happen to just make him *shut up*.

"Oh, shit!" Andy cried in a stupidly strangled voice as his chair wobbled out from underneath him. As he came down on the tile, there was a clang of metal against the floor and a loud thud as his head flew backward against the desk behind him.

"Oh my God," Portia said, kneeling down on the floor and reaching for his head. "Andy, are you okay?"

"It's nothing," he said quickly. He propped himself up on an elbow and reached behind his head, but flinched immediately after touching it. When he drew his head back, there was a spot of blood.

"But you're bleeding . . ." Portia continued.

"What's going on?" Ms. Oullette said as she came into the classroom. By now a handful of students had gotten out of their seats and formed a semicircle around Andy.

"I'm *fine*, guys. Really." And aside from a tiny cut, he was mostly—except for the fact he was red with mortification.

"Well, fine or not, you'll need to check in with the nurse," Ms. Oullette said. Andy nodded and accepted Pete Nash's hand, using it to pull himself off the floor.

"Ms. Oullette," Pete called over his shoulder, "Andy probably needs someone to accompany him to the nurse's office—like me, maybe. Who knows if he's concussed or not?"

"Nice try, Mr. Nash," she responded drily, "but you wouldn't want to miss the pop quiz I was just about to administer."

There were a bunch of exaggerated groans as Andy slunk out of the classroom. He looked at Em as he passed, and she stared back with wide, unblinking eyes. *I did that,* she thought, terrified. *I hurt him. Just because I was angry.*

Em could barely focus during the quiz; she wouldn't be surprised if she'd completely failed it—but she didn't even care. After turning it in she excused herself to go to the bathroom, slung her bag on her shoulder, and never came back.

• • •

When you combined all the money from last year's summer gig at the YMCA day camp, plus her savings from occasional baby-sitting jobs here and there, Em had about three hundred dollars. She'd been hoping to put it toward a new laptop, but getting Crow out of jail was slightly more important. After raiding the Mason jar at the back of her closet (her "savings account"), Em sped to the police station with two hundred dollars in twenties, tens, fives, and singles.

"Thank you," Crow mouthed as soon as she'd signed the paperwork and they brought him through the heavy sliding doors.

"Thank you, officers," she said, praying that no one she knew would see her coming out of the Ascension Police Department with Crow at her side. "What is this?" she hissed as soon as they were back in her car. "What were you thinking? What happened?"

He reached over and put his hand on her arm. She'd never seen him so serious.

"I'm sorry, Em," he said, and she could tell that he meant it. He was sober. Tired. And his eyes were full of gratitude. "I don't want you to . . . I went back. After you left, after your mom picked you up. I kept messing with that guy—the bouncer. I was so pissed off, Em. They called the cops on me, and I got arrested for disorderly conduct."

Em shook her head slowly. "But that doesn't make sense. Wouldn't they have just let you out this morning?" She remembered the same had happened to Gabby's brother, Sam, the night he turned twenty-one and started stripping drunk in a gas station parking lot. They'd taken him overnight and let him out the next morning; he reported back that he'd been thrown in a big cell with a bunch of other drunk people and a whole lot of vomit on the floor. Nothing too traumatic, though definitely impressionable enough to never do it again. But either way, there was no bail involved.

"Yeah, I just . . . I might have told an officer to fuck himself. . . ."

"What?!"

"And then smiled at a judge the wrong way . . ."

"You had to see a judge this morning?!" This felt way out of her league.

"Listen, Em, it wasn't that big of a deal. It's just that I pissed off some cop and so he pulled up my record—and now that I'm eighteen they don't cut me such a break. . . ."

"Crow, stop." She took in a deep breath, trying to form a coherent thought in her head. "It doesn't matter how it happened, not really. I'm just . . . I'm really worried about you. You're going off the rails. Drinking too much, getting into fights, getting arrested, telling off cops? All of this could've been avoided. Why couldn't you just talk to me? Why the hell did you run off like that last night?"

"I don't know," he admitted. "It's the darkness . . . these visions. They're driving me crazy." He rubbed his palms on the front of his jeans, his large hands shaking. It was torture—for both of them. As he did his best to deal with these visions, he only spiraled deeper—further and further away from her. She couldn't withhold any information from Crow. Not anymore, not at this point.

"Can we go somewhere to talk?" she asked, looking around.

"Aren't we talking now, princess?"

"I'm serious. Somewhere private."

"My house?" he said quietly. "Let's go get my car and meet back at my house."

She looked at him skeptically. He tilted his head but she couldn't read his expression. "No funny business," she reminded him. It took a moment to realize what she'd committed to: She was going to Crow's house. Alone.

At his split-level ranch, not far from Em's street, Crow brought her up to his bedroom, a large space over the garage. "Sorry," he said before opening the door. "It's kind of a mess."

And it was: an explosion of notebooks and guitars and guitar picks, jeans and empty cigarette cartons and black clothing and Dr Pepper cans. The rich and musty smell of candles and incense hung in the air. *Nothing like JD's room,* she found herself thinking, before pushing the comparison from her mind.

"A seat?" he said, gesturing to the bed, which was covered in rumpled navy-blue flannel sheets. She scooted so her back was against the wall and he joined her, careful to leave a few inches of space between them.

"So, you first, or me?" Crow asked.

"I'll go," she said, reaching down to grab the book from her bag, where it always was. "There's something I have to show you." She flipped through the pages like they were on fire. "Look at this. I think . . . I think this is you." She pointed to the chapter about prophets and passed the book to him, waiting breathlessly as he read.

"A prophet." The words came out of his mouth like bricks, like he was using them to build a wall. "Tortured by visions."

Em nodded. He looked back down at the book, frowning as though he couldn't decipher the words on the page. Then he took in a deep breath. "This . . . this is crazy."

"Crazy," she said softly, "but real."

"So that's what's going on? The Furies have a direct line into my brain? No thank you." He ran a hand through his hair, making it stand up.

"I'm still not sure exactly how it works, but I know you're involved," she said. "I just don't know whose side you're on."

"I think you wondered that about me before you even read this book," Crow said, a weak attempt at lightening the mood.

It was true. She had never completely trusted Crow. But now, she allowed herself to feel a moment's pity for him. Crow was cursed, just like she was. Except one glaring difference: Crow hadn't chosen his fate. But by betraying Gabby, she had.

"I've been trying to figure out a way to stop them," Crow said, fingering the pages. "They've been getting more intense. More frequent."

Almost like he was becoming more possessed by the evil.

"I don't think you *can* stop them—unless the Furies go away," she said, hoping to enlist his help for that very purpose.

Crow groaned. "You sound like them," he said. He reached into his pocket for a stick of gum. "I'm trying to quit smoking," he said, indicating the wrapper in his hand.

"I sound like who?" Em persisted, her heart in her throat.

"Meg, and Ty . . ." he said.

"How would you know?"

"I know who they are, Em. When they came to town . . . that's when the visions started again. I've met them. I know they're part of this. I know *they're* the bad guys you and Drea were up against."

"What do you mean? When did you meet them? You've spoken to them? What did they say?" She asked the questions in rapid-fire succession. Em felt overwhelmed, heat reaching up and through her skin like she might combust.

"We don't *talk* about anything, Em. They just harass me, show up to fuck with me. They don't answer my questions. They don't tell me what the visions mean. They're like puppeteers with an unwilling puppet."

"How do I know that, Crow? How do I know I can trust you?"

"Can you trust anyone?" Crow answered.

"I want to trust you," Em said. If Crow had an inside line to the Furies' hearts of darkness, maybe they simply had to learn to harness his abilities for good rather than for evil. "Did you have any visions last night, or today?"

"I did, actually." He cleared his throat and looked at her. She nodded at him to continue. "You were looking for something. Frantically. Running all around like crazy. Digging in the mud."

"Mud?" she repeated.

"You were in a field. . . . There were lots of flowers," he said. "And then they started overpowering you. Overpowering me. I felt like I was suffocating right there in the jail cell."

She waited for more, but none seemed to be coming. "Well . . . ? And?"

He stared at her. "It's not a fairy tale, darling. That's it."

"What do you mean, *that's it*?" she asked, throwing her head back. It thudded against the wall and she ignored the pain. "What does it *mean*?"

Crow frowned and shook his head. "I don't know," he admitted. "Sometimes I can't really figure that part out."

Em forced herself to take a deep breath.

One thing was obvious: Crow didn't understand his visions. He hadn't even known what he was until tonight. She tried to read his expression but couldn't. "I should tell you something else," she said instead.

"Oh, there's more good news?"

She grimaced. "Something else happened to me today. Another one of those . . . episodes. I got angry. . . . This kid in class was talking about Mr. Landon—our old English teacher— and then saying all this stuff to make a girl uncomfortable, and I was just like, *Please shut up,* and then his chair just . . . fell back. He hit his head and started bleeding. It was terrible. It was like I willed it to happen." She shuddered.

Crow snapped his fingers in front of him, trying to call up some buried information. "Landon, is he the teacher that chick found in the woods? Drea was freaked about that."

"Skylar?" *Skylar.* Yes. Of course. Skylar was hunted by the Furies. All of this was connected. "Yes," she said. "Yes, he was." There was a heavy silence. She looked at the big red numbers on the alarm clock next to Crow's bed. It was already after midnight and suddenly she felt so weary.

"I should go. . . ."

"No, don't," he said grabbing her hand. He let go of it just as quickly, realizing he'd somehow overstepped a boundary. "I need to ask you what you think . . . about what Drea said about you. Is she right?" He sounded as scared as she was.

Exhaustion was building in her chest and her head. "I'm not sure," she said—though every instinct inside her screamed the opposite. How could she possibly make him understand? That her time could be running out. That she could feel it looming closer: the darkness that wanted to inhabit her, to swallow her forever.

"You want to try to get some sleep here?" he asked. "I'll stay on the floor."

"No. I should get going soon. . . ." She began to make a mental list of all the pieces she'd collected today. About Crow being a prophet, about Henry Landon possibly being a victim of the Furies, about Skylar. Em had always suspected that Skylar's aunt knew more about them than she was saying. Em had to find a way to discover what Skylar—and her family—knew. Why hadn't she thought of that before? Em had so many questions. . . .

But she was fighting to keep her eyes open. Crow's inched closer to her, and he moved his hand up her scalp; he massaged it with his fingers and it felt like lapping waves on the back of her skull, lulling her toward sleep.

"I'm going to try to understand them, Emily," he was saying. "The visions must be telling us something. I promise to help you, Em, even if it means giving in. Giving in to the darkness."

She started thinking of a million different responses. Ways to explain that she could see the blackness was already seeping through his blood—that if he went down even deeper, he might never come out. That she was turning bad. Hurting people, just as he'd predicted.

But her thoughts came in abstract wisps. The gears in her brain were revolving slower and slower. . . . She couldn't fight the exhaustion any longer. She let go, into sleep, like a bottomless well. Her sleep was thick and dreamless. Like falling down into absolutely nothing.

CHAPTER SEVEN

Over the next two days, JD found that he couldn't stop thinking about Ty: her uncanny similarity to Em, the throatiness of
her voice, and especially, what she had told him about Chase
Singer. The intimate detail—the fact that Chase's face had been
marked with lipstick when he died, which meant (had to mean)
that he had been *kissed* by someone wearing lipstick before he
died—stuck in JD's mind like a celery string between his teeth:
annoying and uncomfortable.

JD didn't hang out with any of Chase's friends, discount-
ing Em, but he had woodshop with Aaron Johnson, who played
football, and they sometimes sat together at lunch talking about
old cars and machinery.

During fifth-period lunch on Tuesday, JD blurted out to

Aaron: "Hey, weird question: Have you ever heard that Chase Singer had lipstick on him when he died? Like, on his cheek?"

It was strange, given the local media's blanket coverage of Chase's death, that JD didn't remember that striking, if small, description. When he Googled the news reports from a few months ago, there was no mention of any lipstick mark. The only distinguishing marking was the red flower he'd had in his mouth, and even that detail hadn't come out at first, but had finally been admitted by the police after rumors had spread about it. JD wondered what other secrets had been covered up. And he wondered, too, about that red flower that kept showing up in all the wrong places.

"Nope, never heard that one," Aaron said.

Tina, Aaron's girlfriend, was sitting on his other side with a plate of French fries. "He had some trashy girlfriend," she piped in. "They'd probably been . . . you know."

"Just before he jumped?" JD shook his head. It didn't make sense. Would Chase have gotten it on with his girlfriend right before he planned to off himself? "Who was the girl?" This was the type of gossip that a year ago Em would have chided him for not knowing. *You can't ignore their existence and hope they'll go away,* she used to say about her popular group of friends.

"You sound like Tina," Aaron said, fake-sneering as he finished a bite of his sandwich. "Are you starting a gossip blog or some shit like that?"

"Shut up, babe," Tina shot back. Then, to JD: "He was with Lindsey for a while. Lindsey Cutler? From Trinity? But he blew her off for some mystery college chick."

"No one ever hung out with her, as far as I know," Aaron pointed out. "So they just *assume* she was trashy."

"She had a laugh like a ninety-year-old smoker," Tina said. "That's what I heard. And she dressed like a Real Housewife. *And* she was a bitch. She stood Chase up when he tried to take her to Lumiere de la Mer. Becky and Jamie saw him waiting there for, like, an hour once. It was totally depressing and weird, they said."

"Becky and Jamie's little dates at that French place are what's depressing, if you ask me," Aaron said, ripping open a bag of potato chips.

"It's their tradition! Anyway the food is supposed to be really good," Tina said. "Not that I would know, since *someone* never takes *me* out for dinner." She playfully punched Aaron's arm.

JD felt himself drifting from the conversation, and began to pack up his stuff. The bell was going to ring soon anyway, and he was perturbed without knowing why. Something Tina had said had caused alarm bells to go off on his head, very faintly . . . but when he tried to focus, to figure out what was upsetting him, he lost it. He was relieved when the bell rang and it was time for rehearsal. "Just curious," he said. "Freaky shit. See you later, guys. I'm off to class."

• • •

The staircase that led into the rafters above Ascension's theater was narrow and dark. After school, JD ascended the steep ladder and pulled himself up on the catwalk. It was second nature to be up there now, balancing on the creaky boards in the dark. He ducked under the heavy metal lights and was careful to avoid the snaking wires zigzagging at his feet. Heights never scared JD, and despite the fact that only a few inches of wood stood between him and the giant open space of the auditorium, he loved being up there.

He was there now investigating what he had to work with in terms of lights for Ned's show; meanwhile, Ned held rehearsal on the stage. As JD wove his way along the platform, making notes and checking various cables, he could see and hear perfectly what was going on below him. He'd always liked the perspective from up above—the bird's-eye view.

Skylar was front and center, delivering one of Cassandra's monologues.

"Oh, misery, misery!" Skylar's voice punched the air around her, powerful and confident, a complete contrast to her physical presence. "Again comes on me the terrible labor of true prophecy, dizzying prelude." Her tone was frenzied and she waved her hands in front of her as if to ward off the looming prophecy.

JD found himself rooted to the spot, poised over a hanging light, waiting for her to continue. *Wow,* he thought. *Ned was right. This girl is good.*

"For this I declare," she was saying. "Someone is plotting vengeance."

JD's wrench slid from the nut he was tightening. There was the clang of metal on metal.

"Hey, keep it down up there," Ned yelled up from his seat in the audience. "I thought you knew what you were doing."

"Yeah, that's why I'm getting paid big bucks," JD shot back, and gave a few over-the-top, obnoxious clangs for good measure.

"I meant to tell you, Fount—I think I'm going to have to pay you in pizza. . . ."

JD smirked and turned his headlight toward the next fixture. This one had frayed wires; it needed to be taken downstairs and looked at in the workshop. He got to work, cranking his arm to loosen the bolts and unclamp the light from the pipe it hung from. When it came free, he hoisted it down, his muscles flexing to control the movement. Stage lights were funny beasts: heavy enough to warrant strength, but fragile enough to require delicacy.

Just as he set the light on the board next to him, he felt his phone buzz in his back pocket. He reached around and pulled it out to see a text from Anonymous. It had to be Ty.

Care to be lured away? I'm in the parking lot.

He felt his neck get warm. Technically, he should stay. There was still inventory to finish and all the cleanup backstage. But there was always tomorrow . . . and he needed to bring this light downstairs anyway. He began to make his way carefully back along the ledge, hesitant to admit the truth even to himself: He was drawn to see Ty again. Not because he had a crush on her. It was more like some sort of magnetic curiosity. As if he were playing a video game and needed to see what the next level would hold.

And he wanted to find out how she knew that stuff about Chase. Had she been lying to JD when she'd acted all oblivious about it? He had no idea why she would lie, but he also felt instinctively curious about her, like she held secrets he needed to know more about.

Onstage, Ned was telling the actors to take five. It was the perfect chance to tell Ned he'd be back tomorrow, ready to talk light plot and sound design. JD had almost reached the stairway when he heard Skylar's voice again. She was in the wings now, backstage, and her tone was hushed and urgent. JD froze—he was probably not supposed to overhear what she was saying. But given the urgent tone of her voice, he couldn't help but listen.

"No," she said shrilly. "That's impossible. They can't just . . . let her *go*. Let them all loose. Isn't that, like, against the law?"

JD held his breath, wondering who she was talking to. Through the grate by his feet, he could see her blond hair, her frantic pacing.

"No. Please," Skylar said. "Isn't there another place we can send her? She *cannot* come stay with us. I can't . . . You don't understand. . . ."

Creeeeaaaak. The floorboard below JD gave a groan, and he winced. Skylar whipped her head from side to side, then looked straight up. Right through the grate. Busted.

She snapped the phone away from her ear as though it were on fire. He quickly made his way to the stairs and intercepted her just as she was about to run back onstage.

"I'm sorry," he said. "I just didn't want to interrupt."

She looked at him like an animal in a cage, her arms crossed tightly over her chest. Said nothing. Just stood there, quivering.

"Are you okay?" he asked warily. He knew he was butting in to the private affairs of a girl he barely knew, but she just looked so . . . scared.

"Just mind your own business," Skylar snapped, brushing by him and throwing her shoulders back as she did.

Fair enough. JD shook his head, grabbed his backpack from the light booth, and headed out to meet Ty. He pushed through the double doors and squinted as the afternoon sun flooded his eyes, which had gotten used to the dim theater lighting. Through half-lowered lids, he saw the silhouette of a girl leaning against the hood of a car—tall, graceful, her hair haloed with light. He was close enough to touch her by the time he could make out Ty's features.

"I've been waiting forever," she groaned playfully, hopping around to the driver's-side door. "I'm glad you decided to meet up. Come on, let's go. I have a surprise for you."

The car smelled heavy and sweet, like a perfume he couldn't identify. "Where are we going?" he asked as they passed Ascension's forests, fields, and buildings in Ty's maroon Lincoln. The sun was getting lower in the sky; soon the horizon would be a muddy wash of pink and orange and purple. Ty looked like she was dressed for a nightclub, in tight black jeans, a flowing red top, and earrings that dangled as far as her collarbone. He wondered if he'd made a mistake.

"I told you, it's a surprise," Ty said in her singsong voice. "But I hope you're hungry. I packed us a picnic."

Now that she mentioned it, JD realized he hadn't eaten anything since lunch. "I could go for something to eat," he said. But he worried: Was this a date? He wasn't an idiot—he knew most guys would kill to be him right now. Ty was ridiculously gorgeous and, from what he could tell, perfectly nice—but there was something . . . off about her. He had a gut feeling there was more to Ty than met the eye, and it wasn't necessarily beautiful.

And then there was Emily Winters. There was always Emily Winters, and would always be.

Ty turned down the industrial road on the edge of town, near the old train yard. He'd passed this place a million times on his way to the highway, but he'd never had any reason to explore further. "What's down here?" he asked.

"A blast from the past," Ty said as they rounded the corner and a decrepit brick warehouse came into view. Broken-down train cars lined tracks that were overgrown with husks of dead grass. The entire landscape was brown—rusty metal, muddy ground, dirty bricks. "Ta-da! Isn't it beautiful? Sometimes I feel like I can still hear the whistle of the trains in the distance."

JD knew enough local history to know that the freight line hadn't come through this part of town in decades. He sat for a moment, squinting his eyes, looking at the abandoned building, its broken windows, and graffiti. "It's, ah, very retro. . . ." he said. It wasn't exactly what he'd been expecting, but then again, he couldn't have imagined Ty pulling him out of theater early or packing him a picnic. He cleared his throat. "Looks like a spot that serial killers would take their victims, actually," he said. "Should I be worried you're trying to kill me?"

Ty laughed. "I thought it would be the perfect place," she said as they got out of the car. What she thought it would be perfect *for*, he wasn't sure. "It's different, you know?"

She took his hand in one of hers—naturally, easily, as though they'd been holding hands forever. JD began to sweat. This was definitely a date. Which meant at one point, she might expect him to kiss her. Which meant he should start being nervous approximately now.

She led him toward a low broken window on the side wall of the warehouse. Faded stalks of grass, old cigarette butts, and shards of broken glass formed the carpet below their feet.

"Careful," JD said, noticing Ty's strappy sandals. "You're not exactly dressed for urban adventuring." He reached over to grab the picnic basket—an ornate wicker thing with a bright red ribbon wrapped around the handle.

"And you are?" She smiled huge, revealing paper-white teeth.

"These pants were probably made when this warehouse was still functional," JD said in defense of his gray corduroys. "And suspenders are very practical."

"Whatever you say." She giggled as she put one leg through the window and then the other, snaking her body carefully to avoid snagging her clothing on any jagged edge. He followed her lead much less gracefully, managing to snap off a piece of the window ledge with his workboot as he jammed his foot through.

Once inside, she motioned for him to follow her down a hallway. Their footsteps echoed in the dark. The place was vast, cavernous, full of large, empty rooms, presumably places where old machines used to sit. It smelled like damp and bird shit and mice. Dusty shafts of sun filtered weakly through the broken windows and pitted roof, but did little to penetrate the dark. JD fought to ignore a buzzing anxiety, a fear that spiders might drop on him from above or rats would suddenly swarm them from the darkness.

It was, without a doubt, the worst picnic place he could imagine.

He cleared his throat. "So, how'd you find this place?"

"I like old things," Ty said. "Always have. My cousins and I like to explore. See who can dig up the best stuff. Ascension is crazy old. There's a lot of cool places around here. Stories like you wouldn't believe ... haunted places. Places where they staked witches, or burned them alive. Well, women who they *thought* were witches, anyway." For a second, her voice rang out, steely, harsh. Then she turned to him, and her teeth flashed in the half-dark. "Do you believe in ghosts?"

"Well, it seems like this would be the place to find them," JD said, trying to joke. But he was uncomfortable. There *was* something about this place that freaked him out, made him feel as though he were being watched.

"Let's find out. . . ." Ty said, trailing off as they came to a tight, rickety stairway not unlike the one that led to the catwalk at the theater. "This way."

She grabbed the basket from his hands and led the way, climbing so quickly it was almost as if she floated above the rung-like steps. He followed much less surely, planting his feet nervously and gripping the railings on either side.

The top of the stairs opened up into a bright, window-lined room. The walls were brick and the floors were thick slabs of wood. Iron pillars stood around the otherwise empty space. It was dusty and in disrepair. No one had been here in a long time.

The sun was just starting to set, and the glass burned orange-red. Ty walked over to the window and looked out. JD wanted to join her, but the moment seemed loaded. He didn't want it to seem like he was making a move or something. He wasn't even sure he *should* make a move—whether she wanted him to, whether he wanted to.

"Come look at this," she breathed, shielding her eyes against the glare.

He hesitated for just a second, and then moved closer. The scene outside the window was a perfectly composed juxtaposition of industry and nature—the rusty, unused train tracks, overgrown with weeds, butting up against the forest, dark with evergreen branches. A scene of unrestrained wildness. For a moment, he felt like he was inside a museum exhibit, encased in glass.

"Wow," he said. "Looks like a photograph." Their arms were touching. He took a deep breath.

"Feels nice to get away from it all, doesn't it?" Ty said before turning back to her basket and starting to assemble the "picnic"— a baguette, some Brie, a bunch of grapes, an apple, and a bottle of red wine. Classy. He wondered how old Ty was—it hadn't occurred to him to ask.

"Great spread," JD said. "Did you bring a knife?"

"Of course," Ty said, reaching deep into the seemingly bottomless basket and pulling out what looked like a hunting knife. It was silver, and there was a snake engraved in its hilt. Not exactly your typical kitchen utensil.

JD drew back in mock fear. "Whoa. I didn't know you were packing heat."

"What can I say?" Ty shrugged and batted her lashes. "I always come prepared."

"Good to know," JD said. "I'll call you next time I need help gutting a deer."

"I'm good at that," Ty answered evenly. JD wondered if she was kidding or not. The she laughed—that low, hoarse laugh that made her sound kind of like a woman from a black–and–white movie. It was sort of sinister, actually. *She had a laugh like a ninety-year-old smoker,* Tina had said. He didn't know why the thought popped into his head just then, but it made him totally uncomfortable.

It wasn't possible. . . . It wasn't at all possible that *Ty* had been the older girl Tina was talking about, the one who had dated Chase briefly and driven him almost to madness. The one who had led him on.

But then again, Ty had mentioned that Chase died with a lipstick mark on his face. Why would she have known that? Again, the detail haunted him. He wanted to bring it up again, but how?

Trying to shake off the eerie feeling in his gut, he set to work slicing the apple, and they settled onto the floor, munching on bits of fruit and cheese. Everything felt slick and heavy in his mouth, and even as he started to feel full, he felt like he couldn't stop eating. She poured the wine into clear plastic cups and he sipped his freely, enjoying the way it loosened his tongue and calmed him down a little.

"So, do you see Ali often?" he asked. He figured he'd start by finding out how much time Ty even spent in Ascension, and go from there.

"Oh, we spend a lot of time together. The three of us travel everywhere." She reached into her bag and dug out a strip of photo-booth snapshots. The picture was black-and-white, timeless. "That's us," she said. "Me, Ali, and Meg."

JD was startled to see that the third girl in the picture was the same Meg he'd met at Drea's memorial service, the one with the red ribbon around her neck. She was wearing it in the photograph.

And he'd seen her with Crow, too.

"We're inseparable," Ty said. "Or at least we used to be. I actually think we're growing apart. We want different things." Her eyes drifted back to the window, where the sunset had turned dusky, pinkish, like a faded rose.

"Really? That's too bad." JD took another sip of wine. He didn't usually drink, but he was starting to feel warm and more relaxed. It had just really hit him that he was on a date with a girl who could have passed for a supermodel. He still couldn't quite believe it.

"It happens." Ty shrugged and fiddled with the hem of her shirt. For a minute, she was quiet. Then she blurted: "It's been happening for a while. I want . . . I want to live my own life, I guess. To *have* a life. And she and Meg don't really understand that. So I'm taking matters into my own hands." She looked vulnerable then, more like Em than ever. The impression was so strong he almost reached out and kissed her. He almost couldn't stop herself. But then she smiled again and the resemblance faded. "People change, you know? And I'm changing. I know I am." The thought seemed to please her.

Ty's words made something stick inside of him. *Change.* Would he, JD Fount, ever change? Had he ever taken matters into his own hands, or fought to have a life? Even his younger sister thought he was lame. When was the last time he'd really been proactive about anything, anything that mattered? He kept letting himself get jerked around . . . but maybe he deserved better.

"Hey, are you all right?" Ty reached out and touched JD's arm. He hadn't realized it, but he'd been balling his fists.

"Oh, yeah . . ." he said sheepishly, stretching his fingers. "You just got me thinking. I've been growing apart from someone too."

Ty raised her eyebrows. "Wanna talk about it?"

Maybe it was the wine, or the way that Ty was looking at him so sympathetically. Or maybe it was the weirdness of the place, the space high up in an abandoned building with the sun smoldering pink outside their window, but JD suddenly felt compelled to share everything. "This girl I've known . . . forever. My friend Em."

Ty looked at him, wide-eyed. "Not Em Winters?"

He immediately regretting being so open. Ty now probably thought he was pathetic too. "Do you know her?"

"Kind of. Just a little. We have a mutual friend. She came up in conversation the other day." She shook her head. "Life is so weird like that."

"Who's the mutual friend?" JD asked.

"Oh, I'm not sure if you know him—he doesn't go to Ascension," Ty said, plucking a grape from its stem and popping it into her mouth. "His name is Colin. He's a musician—"

"I know who Crow—who *Colin* is," JD said, feeling the familiar burn of resentment in his chest whenever he thought of Crow. "What was he saying about Em?"

Ty cocked her head to one side and gave him a smile that indicated she knew more than she was letting on. "He just mentioned he knows her, that they've been hanging out, that's all. . . ."

JD tightened his hands into fists again. He desperately wanted to pump Ty for information, but he refused to embarrass himself so blatantly.

"Are you and Em, like, a *thing*?" Ty asked.

"We're—no," he said after a moment's hesitation. "She lives next door to me. I've known her forever."

"And you love her," Ty said matter-of-factly, as though daring him to correct her.

JD looked away. Was it that obvious? Heat crept into his

neck. There was no point in denying it. So he just said: "I've just . . . I've seen her get hurt. She has terrible taste in guys."

"She must, if she's not into *you*," Ty said playfully, but the compliment only made him feel worse. Because Em *wasn't* into him, and that was the point.

He could feel Ty watching him closely. "Last year, Em fell for the world's biggest d-bag. He cheated on Em's best friend—with Em. I warned her about him, but she ignored me."

"Sounds like she made a pretty bad mistake," Ty said, popping a grape's skin with her teeth. "Did she pay for it?"

"Did she . . . what?" JD looked confused. "What do you mean?"

Ty shrugged. "I just mean, did she learn from her mistake?"

JD shook his head. "I don't know. I think so." Had she? He didn't know. "What about you?" he asked pointedly. If Ty was going to put him on the spot, he should be allowed to do the same to her.

"What about me what?" she asked.

"Any unrequited love of your own?" What he wanted to ask was, *Who are you really? What are your secrets? Did you know Chase Singer more than you're letting on? Did you date him?*

Ty shrugged, pulling a strand of hair around in front of her shoulder and tugging at it as she talked. "Not really," she said. "I've never really been able to date someone seriously. Every time I try, it ends badly." Her voice was less musical than usual.

ELIZABETH MILES

Suddenly JD felt terrible. Here he was, suspecting this girl—who was basically a stranger to him—of lying, of knowing Chase, of maybe even having seduced Chase on the night of his death. It was absurd, and now he'd gone and made her feel sad. He really had a way with the chicks.

The light was quickly waning, and the magic of the evening felt drained. "I think we should start heading back," he said. He placed his cup back in the basket, along with the remaining food items.

"And miss the rest of the sunset?" Ty pouted. "Some urban explorer you are. . . ."

"I've got homework," he said, unable to come up with a clever response. When he stood, JD felt dazed, unsettled with the turn this conversation had taken.

She led the way back down to the main level, but as JD was descending the narrow staircase, one of the boards broke loose under his foot, and he felt himself falling forward.

Ty reached out and he grabbed her hand, steadying himself.

"Sorry about that," he said. "The ground just completely came out from under me."

"I saved you," Ty responded, laughing in that same husky way that she had at the pizza parlor. "Looks like you owe me one."

CHAPTER EIGHT

"W . . . T . . . F," Gabby said as she slid into the red vinyl diner booth. She drew out every letter. "You better tell me more about this Crow sitch. *Especially* if I'm going to be expected to cover for you. Thank god your mom fell for the I-was-having-a-boy-crisis-and-needed-Em-please-don't-ask-any-more-questions bit."

Em cringed, imagining what could have happened if Gabby hadn't thought so quickly on her feet. "You saved my ass, Gabs," she said. "I'm definitely buying your meal."

The past forty-eight hours had been hell. Though she'd slept well in Crow's bed, she'd basically been awake ever since. She'd lain wide awake in her bed the last couple of nights, staring at the ceiling and getting up periodically to peer out from behind her curtains. The feeling of being stalked was constant. And she'd woken up with a hot, black anger flowing inside of her, like a physical force.

It was undeniable now. Ever since that night with Crow, she'd gained a horrible clarity—that the transformation was definitely happening, and quickly. She had no idea how to reverse it.

She would lose her life, her family. Her soul.

Which was why she was desperate to talk to Skylar McVoy in private. But all day at school, Em had been unable to corner her; the one time their eyes met across the hall, Skylar pivoted and scurried away, almost as if she were deliberately avoiding a confrontation.

Now it was nearly six o'clock, and Skylar's rehearsal would be ending soon. But first, Em had to deal with someone she'd been desperately putting off: Gabby.

She had never intended to fall asleep in Crow's bed two nights earlier, and was mortified—and panicked—when she woke up with her face mashed into his pillow, a little spot of drool next to her mouth, her shoes discarded on top of his sheets. She must have kicked them off in her sleep. The truth was, she hadn't slept so well, so soundly, in forever.

But while she was dreaming in Crow's bed, her parents had called Gabby early that morning.

"Em left us a note that she was going to your place, but it wasn't clear that she was sleeping over," Susan Winters had said suspiciously. "It seemed strange for a Tuesday night. We tried her cell, but it's off."

Gabby had told them Em was in the shower—she wasn't an idiot—but after hanging up with Mrs. Winters, she'd called Em in a frenzy. *Are you okay? Are you even alive? Where are you? You better get home.* All that stuff. Em had promised to explain everything later. But for two days, she'd been promising Gabby an explanation more detailed than the one she had given—which happened to be the truth. "I was with Crow," Em had said. "He's helping me with something."

Obviously that hadn't satisfied Gabby—in fact, she'd let out such a prolonged screech in the library yesterday that she'd nearly gotten them kicked out—and she'd finally guilted Em into an early dinner and a gossip session at the diner tonight, claiming she was craving a tuna melt. Em wasn't thrilled about meeting at a diner with notoriously slow service; she looked at her watch, counting down the minutes until Skylar's rehearsal got out— then scolded herself. *Gabby,* she thought. *You're spending time with your best friend, Gabby.*

"Bribes don't work, Winters," Gabby said once they'd ordered (a tuna melt for Gabs, just a strawberry milk shake for Em), leaning forward. "Spill it—everything. How long has this been going on? How far have you gotten? What about JD? I thought you had a big thing for him?"

Em couldn't help but be slightly amused by the rapid-fire

questions. "It's not what you think," she said. "I didn't *mean* to sleep over. It was an accident." He'd been perfectly respectful, as he promised; Em had woken up to find him curled in a blanket on his floor next to the bed. It was weird to see how peaceful Crow looked in sleep—boyish, even. His mouth open ever so slightly, his scowl gone, his eyes fluttering lightly. She'd realized she was staring, and coughed loudly to wake him up.

"So," Gabby said, not skipping a beat. "My best friend is sleeping with the Grim Creeper, a pot-smoking high school dropout. Should I call an intervention now, or wait until you become the new Teen Mom?"

Em dropped her head into her hands. "Nonononononono," she mumbled, half-laughing. "Gabby. Calm down. First of all, quit it with the nicknames—they've gotten me into enough trouble. And second, I am *hanging out* with Crow, and it is very unromantic." She thought of his hand running through her hair and blushed; Gabby slapped her arm and gave her *a look*. "Okay, okay. We've kissed, like, once. But really, I *do not* like him like that. Like you said yourself, I'm still head over heels for JD. Crow is just . . . a distraction."

"You, Emily Winters, are completely out of your mind," Gabby said, shaking her head and sounding a lot like Em's mom had earlier this morning. "I can't believe I lied for you so that you could hang out—no, I'm sorry, *make* out—with Crow." She took a huffy bite of the sandwich that had been placed before her.

Em looked down, disappointed that her shake looked so thick. "We're just . . . it's because of Drea," Em said, the excuse coming to her all at once. "You know he was friends with her too. He's kind of . . . broken up about the whole thing. We just wanted to talk about her. So I went over, thinking I'd just be there for a little while, and I ended up falling asleep."

The explanation seemed to placate Gabby slightly; it was like a tacit agreement between them that Drea and Em's unlikely friendship was off-limits. Em felt bad lying to Gabby, but in this case a lie really was better (not to mention more believable) than the truth. She was scared to get Gabby mixed up in this mess.

"Are you in trouble?" Gabby asked. "Did your 'rents buy it?"

"They seemed to go for the fell-asleep-at-your-place thing," Em said, knocking on the non-wood tabletop. "I mean, they made a big deal about being clearer next time . . . but I was already late for school, so they didn't go on for too long. They haven't mentioned it since."

"It almost seems like you *knew* you were going to sleep there," Gabby teased, raising a perfectly plucked eyebrow. Em could tell she wasn't going to just let this one go.

"I promise, Gabs. Nothing is going on between me and Crow. Nothing." More than anything, Em wanted that to be the truth.

"Whoa, that's crazy," Gabby said, suddenly transfixed by Em's hands.

Em looked down and sprung her hands away from the glass.

129

There was steam rising between them, condensation from the heat of her hands against the cold milk-shake glass. Like she'd been sizzling on a stove.

She looked all around her and, with the strangest feeling of déjà vu, she tried to change the subject. "So what have you been up to?"

"I met with Ned about makeup on Monday night and then—"

Em put up her hand. "You met with *who*?"

"Ned—JD's friend? The director? I'm going to do hair and makeup for the play!" Gabby smiled proudly.

"Now who's keeping secrets?" Em asked playfully. "That's awesome, Gabs. I had no idea."

"I just decided on Friday," Gabby said. "I figure it's something good to put on the old college application, plus I'm good at it. And it won't take up too much time. I mean, the play is coming up so soon. It basically just means I have to be there on Tuesday night."

"Very practical," Em agreed. "So you'll be spending time with JD, huh?" She tried to sound casual, but Gabby knew her too well.

"Already thought of it," Gabby said breezily. "I'll take copious notes on what he does and say good things about you whenever I can. Plus, there is *no* reason for you to worry about those theater girls. They are cray-cray."

"What would I do without you?" Em smiled. Here was an unforeseen benefit of telling Gabby about Crow: Out of nowhere, Gabby was rooting for JD.

Em felt a sudden rush of love for her best friend—her loyal Gabby.

Would she lose this, too?

Em was getting good—too good, maybe?—at following people, at tracking them down. If she couldn't corner Skylar on their mutual territory, she'd have to go one step further.

After dinner, Em drove straight to Skylar's house. It had started to rain, and the constant squeak of the windshield wipers was oddly comforting in the otherwise silent car. She'd decided against calling—there was less chance, this way, that Skylar could avoid her.

She was desperate and could think of no better options. Crow had said he'd help her, but what had he done? Nothing yet, other than write a few songs.

Em knew Skylar probably couldn't do anything either. She was just another victim. One who'd somehow managed to escape the Furies' long-lasting curse. But then there was Skylar's aunt Nora.

Nora was knowledgeable about local lore and history. She knew Ascension's secrets. She knew its ghost stories. Last time Em showed up at Skylar's house, Nora had acted as though Em had leprosy. For the first time, it hit her that maybe Skylar's aunt had some intimate knowledge of the Furies—had, in fact, *recognized* the darkness in Em.

Even though the woman seemed to despise her, Em had to find out what Aunt Nora knew.

The old Victorian house was close to downtown Ascension, and as she drove up Em saw several lights were on. That was a good sign. She parked her car and made a run for it, ducking her head as drops pelted down on her. Once she got onto the covered porch, she wiped the rain off her face and knocked loudly on the door, hoping both that Nora would answer and that she wouldn't.

But it was Skylar who came to the door. Her wig was askew and it took everything Em had not to reach out and adjust it. Em wondered about the scars on her scalp and shuddered.

Skylar flipped on the outside light, bathing Em in an orange-yellow spotlight. "What are you doing here?" she said.

Em held out a hand, as though to prevent Skylar from closing the door in her face.

"I'm sorry," she blurted out. "I know we haven't really . . . spoken since your—your accident. But we really, really need to talk."

"I don't—" Skylar began to speak, but Em cut her off.

"You know as well as I do that what happened to you wasn't just random. It was retribution." There was no time for mincing words—Em had to make sure that Skylar was paying attention.

She was. Skylar's eyes grew wide and sad. "I was being punished," she squeaked out.

"Exactly," Em said. "Karma's a bitch—or, really, three bitches. Called the Furies."

Skylar nodded. "The ones you warned me about. I told them I was sorry," she said. "I shouldn't have . . ." She trailed off, staring anxiously past Em into the front yard.

"Listen, Skylar. I'm sorry too. But they don't care. None of that matters to them, so I'm hunting down a way to get rid of them. Forever. But I need to speak to your aunt," Em said, shifting her weight restlessly from one leg to the other. "She knows something. About the Furies. I'm sure of it." She couldn't tell her *why* she was sure of it—then she'd have to admit what was happening to her, what was growing inside her.

"She's not . . ." Skylar started to say.

"Look, I know your aunt isn't crazy about . . . unexpected visitors," Em jumped in, doing her best to keep her voice steady. "But I'm . . ." *Running out of options,* she thought. "I'm pretty sure she knows something *important.*"

"My aunt's out of town," Skylar offered apologetically. "She's down in . . . Well, she's gone for a few days, anyway."

"Where is she?" Em asked, hoping to be invited inside.

"She had to go down South to deal with some family stuff," Skylar said. "That's all."

Em looked down at her feet and tried to conceal her

disappointment. Even this, a relatively minor blow, seemed to strike deep into her gut. She was running out of time. She knew this, could feel it, could already sense the change.

"I should have listened to you," Skylar said in a whisper. "When you told me—about Meg and her cousins, or *whoever* they were." Skylar twisted her thin fingers together. "I—I didn't want to believe you. I wanted a friend, you know?" She looked up at Em, her eyes wide, pleading, and Em felt a pulse of pity for her.

"I know, Skylar," she said, and placed a hand on Skylar's arm. "But those girls weren't your friends." She thought of the multiple times she'd attempted to find out more about Skylar's relationship with the Furies. At the bonfire, at her house, at the hospital . . . rebuffed, every time. Still, there was always the chance that by warning Skylar in advance, Em had saved her from being targeted for the Furies' continuous wrath.

"I know that . . . now," Skylar said. Her green eyes were focused on something just past Em, into the now driving rain, and they looked filled with pain. Em could see that the girl standing in front of her was nothing like the mini Gabby of recent past. Her clothes were plain—medium-wash jeans and a gray shirt—and her face had the dull pallor of someone who hadn't been getting enough sleep or enough sun. Still, Em noticed that without any makeup on, her eyes were big and childlike. She was cute. If it weren't for the ever so slightly crooked wig and all those angry scars . . .

Em wondered whether they would ever go away—Skylar's scars and her own, invisible but no less real.

"I'm sorry," Em said, and it was true. "I should have tried harder." She felt a sea of hopelessness well up inside of her, threatening to drown her. The days were ticking away. No one would help her. And her fate would be much, much worse than Skylar's. What was happening to Em . . . it was unthinkable.

It was death.

And it wasn't fair.

Em was suddenly exhausted. Slightly dizzy, she leaned against the porch railing and closed her eyes.

"It's okay, Em, I know it wasn't your fault." Skylar spoke in a whisper. "If—if you want to talk about it . . . Do you want to come in, even though Nora's not here?"

Em knew she must look pathetic. Weak. Desperate. Which she was.

"Look, just for a minute or two." Skylar managed to smile. "We can talk things through. Maybe then we'll both feel a little better."

Em seriously doubted it. If it really was true that the evil was slowly taking her, nothing would make her feel better. Still, maybe she'd find some clue at Skylar's place—something she'd missed before.

She wiped her wet shoes on the doormat and stepped inside. The place was a mess—nothing like the tidy home Em had seen last time she was here. Someone, presumably Skylar, had set up camp in the living room, with a sleeping bag laid out on the sofa and a microwave-dinner tray on the coffee table.

As if reading her mind, Skylar moved toward the couch and gathered the sleeping bag in her arms. "I wasn't expecting visitors," she said as she hurried out of the room.

"I'll help," Em yelled as she took her jacket off in the front hall. She couldn't stand awkwardly by the door, and she couldn't just watch as Skylar ran around cleaning. Surveying the room, she figured the best place to start was the coffee table. She began gathering things to take to the kitchen: a microwave dinner tray, a bottle of hot sauce, used silverware, and napkins. Despite her exhaustion, it felt calming to do something so normal. There was a tube of ointment that Em swept up in her cleaning, turning it over to read the label. *Wig Adhesive: water-based and waterproof, for the strongest hold that dries clear.* Skylar returned and strode straight to Em, grabbing the glue out of her hand.

"I'll manage," Skylar said quickly. Her wig had been adjusted and now looked perfect. If Em hadn't known it was fake already, she'd have been completely fooled. "You sit down and I'll take all this to the kitchen."

Em thought to apologize, but nodded instead, handing her the things. She did her best to ease into the couch. Her sense of calm had all but disintegrated.

Rain drummed on the windows.

When Skylar came back and took a seat on the far side of the couch, Em cleared her throat.

"Look, I'm sorry to drag all of this up," she said. Talking about the Furies still felt crazy, surreal. "But it's important, okay?"

Skylar nodded, mute.

"The orchid. You were marked." Her heart was beating very fast, keeping time with the rain still pounding on the windows and door.

Skylar hugged herself. "Marked? What do you mean?"

"You were marked by the Furies. That's how they indicate their targets," Em said. She took a deep breath. "It happened to me, too." Saying it made her feel instantly a little better, as though a fraction of the weight in her chest had been released.

"What are they?" Skylar said in a whisper.

"I don't know," Em confessed. "But they're evil."

Skylar stared at her, wide-eyed. "How did they find me? How did they find *us*?"

Em shook her head. "I don't know that, either. All I know is that those girls—Meg, Ali, and Ty—they're sick. They seek revenge. They try to make people pay for their mistakes. But it's worse than that. They don't stop. They want to make people miserable. Insane. And . . . and they're willing to kill, too," she blurted out.

"An eye for an eye . . ." Skylar said. A clock *tick-tock*ed in the background. Rivulets of water ran down the windows. "They were there when I found that body," Skylar said suddenly. "That teacher who died."

She knew it. Mr. Landon.

So the Furies *had* been involved in his death in some way. Maybe they'd marked him, too. Maybe that explained why she became so furious when she heard Portia and Andy talking about him the other day. "What do you mean?" Em pressed. "What did they say?"

"That's when I first started to feel like they were . . . off," Skylar said. "They just showed up at the exact right time and their reactions were so weird. I was freaking out, you know? And they were like, *Oh, whatever, there's a dead body.*"

Because they knew about it already, Em thought. Of course.

She could picture it. Ali's icy smile, Meg's permagrin, Ty's sneer. "Did they do other things that seemed 'off'?" Maybe together, she and Skylar could pinpoint a weakness—a flaw in their strength.

Skylar seemed to shrink back a bit. "Well . . . there was . . ." Her voice faded.

"Spill it, Skylar," Em said. She was running out of time.

"Ty always scared me the most," Skylar said in one breath. "She was just . . . weird. Like, when she dyed her hair—"

Em held out her hand and interrupted. "You were there when she dyed her hair?" About a month ago, Em noticed that Ty had exchanged her fire-red locks for a shade that was much closer to Em's hair color—deep, dark brown. Almost black.

"She did it upstairs in my bathroom," Skylar said, and they both reflexively looked toward the stairs. "But the weird thing was that after she did it, there was no, like, evidence of it. No mess. It was like she magically transformed or something."

Transformed.

Her fingers started tingling. Em had the foreboding sense that Ty's "magical transformation" was more than just a parlor trick. It was a sign. A signal. A mirror of Em's own transition.

You're becoming one of them. Em heard the refrain in her head. It was increasingly clear that Ty was changing too—becoming more like Em.

"Don't you want answers?" Em said, as much to herself as to Skylar. "Don't you want to know who they are?"

"I guess so. . . ." Skylar didn't sound convinced.

"They messed with you—hurt you, disfigured you—but at least they've left you alone since that. For now," Em added. Skylar took a quick breath. Em knew she was being harsh, cruel even, but Skylar needed to know the truth. "What if they come back?"

Skylar's eyes practically bugged from her head. "What are you saying?" she whispered.

"Sky, you have to help me," Em said. "We'll never be safe unless we get rid of them for good."

"But how do we do that?" Skylar asked. "I don't know what to do!"

"Your aunt," Em said flatly. "She knows things. We need to talk to her. I think she might be able to tell us some things about the Furies. Don't you see it? Don't you think she knows something?"

"She's not here," Skylar reminded her. "But . . ." Her eyes drifted toward the ceiling and she bit her lip.

Em pounced. "But what?"

"There are a few things in the attic," she said. "Like, an old box . . . I dunno. Do you know what you're looking for?"

She didn't, of course. She had no clue what she was looking for. But her heart leaped. Because she had a feeling she'd know it when she saw it. Em envisioned a velvet diary with a tiny padlock, or an old-fashioned safe hidden behind an Impressionist painting. Something in which to hide dangerous, black secrets.

"This is crazy," Skylar added, "but Nora was always really weird around Meg. Like, even worse than she was around you . . . It did almost seem like Nora knew Meg was . . . bad. I guess it's possible she knew something about all this. It wouldn't surprise me. . . ."

Skylar stood and Em followed her into the kitchen, where they got a flashlight from a drawer, and then up two flights of stairs to the third floor, and helped her pull on a string that hung from the ceiling in the hallway. Down came a short, creaky ladder that led up to a drafty attic. Em watched Skylar ascend, then push up a trapdoor and disappear in the darkness. Em followed once it was clear, testing out her weight. The ladder was old but seemed reliable enough. When she got to the top and heaved herself onto the wood floor, the trapdoor sprang down and closed behind it.

"Freaky," Em said in the darkness.

"Yeah, me and Nora couldn't find the rod that's supposed to keep it propped open."

"So there aren't there any lights up here?"

"That's what the flashlight is for," Skylar said, clicking hers on.

Em found herself squeezing in between headless dress forms and boxes of old clothing. There were hatboxes on every surface, and an empty baby carriage sat in a corner. A row of masks was hung along one wall. The effect was freaky—Em felt like there were a dozen sets of eyes boring into her no matter where she turned. When her shoulder brushed against one of the dress forms, she involuntarily jumped.

"My aunt used to be a costume designer," Skylar offered as explanation. "That's why she has all this theater stuff. She's going to do the costumes for Ned's play."

"I heard you were in that," Em said, relieved to speak about something normal, everyday, even if only for a minute. It helped distract her from the creeping anxiety she felt, and from the weirdness of all those pale masks mounted on the wall.

She was tempted to add that she'd also heard that JD was doing the lights for the show. She felt a fluttering in her chest when she imagined him stringing lights, sleeves rolled up, brow slightly furrowed, as it always was when he worked on his car.

She loved that about him—that he knew how to do things with his hands, that he was so smart but also such a guy. Part of her was dying to ask Skylar for any crumb of a detail—what JD wore, what jokes he made onset, if he talked to other girls—but another part of her was too proud to even mention his name, and too afraid that if she did, everything would come out.

Em felt a draft and turned to find its source. There, in the slightly open attic window, she saw a creepy porcelain doll. It was missing half its hair, and in the moonlight, it almost seemed as though the doll was watching her. "Here it is," Skylar said, pointing to a wooden trunk with the name NORA inscribed on the top. "We were up here earlier this week looking for Greek robes, and Nora freaked when I tried to open the trunk. She practically jumped down my throat." She added, "It's locked, though."

Em dug into her pocket for a bobby pin. "I've never done this before," she said. *But I have broken into a school locker using a library card. . . .* She was becoming quite the cat burglar.

They kneeled down in front of the trunk.

At first, the pin did nothing. It twisted loosely, uselessly, in the keyhole. Em jabbed and jabbed, licking her lips with concentration, feeling her throat get hot with frustration.

"Here, want me to try?" Skylar asked. Em willingly gave up her tool in exchange for flashlight-holding duties. With pursed lips, Skylar bent down and jiggered with the latch for a few seconds. Then it snapped free. "My mom used to lose her keys a lot," she said by way of explanation.

The trunk's heavy lid creaked as they eased it up and open. The stream of light from the flashlight's bulb illuminated, at the very top of the chest was a gold snake pendant lying on top of a lacy piece of white fabric. Without thinking, she reached out and touched it. Pain shot through her palm, all the way up to her shoulder. She gasped and shrunk backward, hand throbbing, as if from an electric shock.

"I've seen that before. . . ." Skylar said, frowning, as though trying to remember. Then she nodded. "My aunt tried to give it to me. Or at least, something like it. I lost it in the woods the night of my bonfire party in the Haunted Woods."

"Drea had one. . . ." Em said, struggling to get the words through her strangled throat. "Sasha had one. I had one."

Skylar picked up the pendant and twirled it in her hand. "What's it for?"

"I think . . . I think some people believe it helps to ward off the Furies," Em said. Her hand still stung, but it was worth the pain. This was a clue. Surely this was a sign that she was right, and that Nora did have information about the Furies. "I'm not sure how well it works. Let's see what else is in here." She breathed a sigh of relief as she watched Skylar put the snake pin down.

They sifted through the next few layers in Nora's trunk. Several antique books about flowers, and one about mythology—

Em recognized it as a title she'd seen in her research. A few pieces of clothing, a shawl, a silvery top, a pair of ladies' gloves. There was a stack of photographs wrapped in ribbon at the bottom of the chest.

"That's my aunt," Skylar said, directing the light onto the photo at the top of the pile. It was a picture of three women smiling.

Em peered closer. She definitely recognized Skylar's aunt, but she also knew one of the women next to her: it was the angry librarian from the Antiquities Library at the University of Southern Maine. Em and Drea had had an unfortunate run-in with her; once she learned that they were researching the Furies, she had kicked them out unceremoniously.

"I know that woman," Em said.

"That's Hannah Markwell." Skylar took the picture and held it near her face. "She's a librarian, I think. She's a friend of my aunt's. They geek out over books together." Skylar rolled her eyes and for a second, Mini-Me Gabby was back.

The third woman was also a brunette. A pretty smile, a strong nose, striking features, but there were worry lines around her eyes. She looked so familiar. Em turned over the picture to see if there was more information on the back. Just three names—*Nora, Hannah, and Edie.*

Edie. The name rang a faint bell. . . . Em sat there for a moment, puzzling over the photograph. Looking at it seemed to spark an inexplicable feeling of déjà vu. She stared into the static eyes of the third woman, willing herself to remember. And then it came to her, so obvious that she was appalled that she hadn't seen it immediately. This woman was the spitting image of Drea.

"Oh my god," she said softly. "Give me that," she said, grabbing for the flashlight.

Skylar looked up from a pile of yellowing papers and handed it over. "What is it?"

"This woman, Edie . . . She was Drea's mom." Em licked her lips. Her mouth felt suddenly dry. "Drea believed she was a victim of the Furies, years ago. And Nora knew her." Em looked up. "I was right, see? Nora must know about them." Her heartbeat picked up again. "We need to talk to her as soon as possible. When does she get home?"

"If she knew how to stop them, don't you think she would have already?" Skylar asked softly. Her wig was slightly off-center, exposing her cheeks and her scars: fine and fissured, as though her skin had been covered in spiderwebs. Hearing the hurt and abandonment in Skylar's voice, Em felt ashamed.

She reached out impulsively and squeezed Skylar's hand. "She might not know how to stop them," she said, "but any help is better than none."

Skylar nodded. "Okay. I'll call you when she gets back."

Em slipped the black-and-white photo into her purse. She

felt the impulse to keep it as a token. An unspoken promise to Drea that she would win this fight.

Em looked up as she got to her feet, panning the flashlight back and forth. As she did, the light fell on a doll's face and Em swore she saw the doll blink at her—the eyelids lowering once over those dark, glassy eyes. There was a distant sound of silvery laughter and a gust of wind that came through—suddenly, violently—and made the doll propel forward and fall facefirst onto the floor. Em's heart rate surged as the flashlight slipped from her hand and the light went out once it hit the floor. Her muscles turned to jelly. They were in complete darkness.

"Oh my god!" Skylar screamed, groping for the flashlight. "Where is it? Where's the light? I can't find it!"

Was the doll *moving*? It was hard for Em to tell in the pale moonlight. The slumped figure seemed to shift ever so slightly, causing Em to recoil. She backed up into the standing dress forms, all of which teetered on their bases from the impact. "Never mind the light," Em said. "Find the door. Where's the door?!"

Em tried to pull Skylar to her feet but she wrenched away from Em's grip—reaching blindly into the dark spaces between boxes. "No, no, I see it!" Em watched Skylar's tiny frame practically disappear behind a box, only to reappear with the flashlight in hand. But it wouldn't turn on, and Skylar stood there, shaking it violently as if willing it to work. Em kept her eye trained on the lifeless doll, which seemed to inch closer every moment she wasn't watching it

"Let's *go*," Em said, yanking on Skylar's wrist and leading her through the makeshift aisle between boxes—many of which were knocked over in their panic. The attic was so cluttered. Em stopped short, approximating where the door should've been. Then another gust, even stronger than the first, followed by a splintering crash. Em screamed and dropped to the floor, running her hand over the wood planks.

"Skylar, is it here? How the hell do we open this?"

"There's a round handle that looks like a knocker."

"I need the light!" Em said. She couldn't control her voice and could feel it rising.

"I know, but I can't get it on!" Skylar yelped. The wind blew through again and Em's hair whipped around her head—getting into her mouth and eyes. She grabbed the flashlight and shook it violently. Finally: a beam of light. She panned the floor and found the handle—wrought-iron and ornate. Skylar dropped to her knees and pulled, but it wouldn't give.

"It's stuck. Oh god. We're trapped!"

"Let me try," Em said, pushing her aside. With one hand she pulled and it sprang open with a thud. "Go!" she yelled at Skylar, who tumbled through and nearly fell rushing down the ladder. Em followed closely behind, glancing once more at the doll, whose head was cocked on the floor at an awkward angle, one eye wide open, staring at her.

Back at her house, Em forced down a few bites of late-night chicken and pasta with her father, struggling to pay attention as he discussed the pros and cons of hiring an SAT tutor and some hilarious sketch he'd seen on *The Colbert Report*. Her senses were on high alert and her heart still hadn't stopped racing since she'd fled Skylar's house. Every scrape of knife against dinner plate, every drip from the faucet into the sink, she heard like it was being blasted in stereo next to her ears.

"Not that hungry, huh?" he asked, noticing her practically full plate.

"I ate with Gabby," Em lied. She'd barely been able to take a sip of her milk shake.

He cleared his throat. "Listen, Emily, while it's just the two of us . . . I wanted to let you know . . . you can talk to me."

She couldn't take this now—not more pity. Not more empty promises. She picked up her plate, brought it to the sink, and scraped a gob of cheesy pasta into the garbage disposal. "I'm fine, Dad—don't worry. I'm feeling better every day," she insisted.

"Your mother and I were thinking about taking a little trip, a long weekend in April or something," he said hopefully. "Maybe down to New York, or up to Montreal. Are you up for it? Just the three of us, a little change of pace? I think we could all use a recharge."

"A recharge," she repeated. "That sounds . . ." She felt a hard rock of sadness lodge in her throat, and had to force out the final word: "Nice." Then she headed upstairs to her bedroom.

Alone again, she stood in front of the mirror for a long time. She could practically see through her own skin. Her eyes were dark and dewy. *So this is what a dying person looks like,* she said to herself, bringing an unsteady hand up to her face. She stayed like that for a moment, unable to move.

In the shower, she made the water lukewarm, then tepid, then downright cold—trying to ease the feverish heat that enveloped her body. The droplets felt like they were falling onto skin that wasn't hers. Em let herself collapse against the white tile wall. Her tears mixed with the shower water and it all went down the drain.

She tossed and turned again that night. Hot. Tangled. Sweaty. On her stomach and on her back and on her side. Nothing allowed her the sweet relief of rest. Every time Em closed her eyes, the terror seized her all over again, and all she could see was that fallen, lifeless doll, staring—unblinking—in the darkness.

CHAPTER NINE

It's not like he was spying.

JD was running late, tearing apart the house for his American History notebook that he needed for an open-book quiz. He was studying in the den the night before and finally found it there under one of Melissa's sweaters. Nearly flying out the door, he stopped short when he saw Crow, cupping his hands against Em's kitchen window. Ducking back onto his porch, JD scanned the area and spotted Crow's truck, just past Em's driveway, halfway hidden by trees.

JD squinted. *What the hell?* Was Crow seriously stalking Em? How long had he been there?

First he gets all cozy with Ascension's bizarre mystery girls and now this?

No one was home to witness Crow's creepiness—he could see that both of Em's parents' cars were gone, and he'd seen Gabby pick Em up this morning while he was eating breakfast. Should he call the cops?

Without thinking much at all, he started striding across the lawn. JD had the right to tell Crow to get the hell off the Winters' property. And while he was at it he would tell him to leave Em alone, that he wasn't good enough for her in any universe. JD trusted Crow about as far as he could throw him, and for the first time in his life, JD was itching for a fight.

But before he got too far, he saw Crow turn and go back to his truck, moving stealthily across Em's lawn. In an instant, JD decided that he wasn't going to school after all, at least not right away. He sprinted back to his Volvo, waited a moment so that he wouldn't be right on Crow's tail, and followed the red-and-silver pickup truck down the road. Even if he got a black eye in the process, JD was going to finally tell Crow what he thought of him. He was going to find out how he knew Ty. He was going to prove—to himself, and then to Em—that Crow really was bad news.

Behind the wheel of his Volvo, trailing Crow out onto the main road, JD felt a momentary twinge of *What the hell am I doing?* But recalling the sight of Crow peeping into Em's windows, JD's feelings of paranoia flooded back.

When Crow put his blinker on to indicate that he was

turning into the cemetery, JD was mystified. A strip club, sure. The seedy motel by the highway where everyone knew out-of-town drug deals went down, okay. But the cemetery? JD eased up on the gas and pulled back to a distance where he hoped his presence was less obvious.

JD stopped the Volvo by the entrance of the graveyard. He got out and closed his car door carefully, peering down the lane to see that Crow had parked just next to a big oak tree in the new section of the cemetery.

JD crept closer. The grass made soft squishing sounds below his boots. Here among the gravestones, the air seemed cooler. There was a fine mist swirling through the graveyard, low to the ground, and the heavy smell of wetness, of damp dirt, hung around him. Only a few trees stood on the property, and they were still without their leaves, lending them a stark quality against the grayish sky. JD wasn't superstitious in the slightest, but there was no denying that this place was creepy. He had the same feeling here he'd gotten walking through the abandoned warehouse with Ty—as though he were being watched. If he believed in ghosts, he'd definitely expect to find them here.

He grimaced a little, thinking of the last time he'd visited this burial ground: a few weeks ago, when he'd followed Em to this very spot and found her hunched over Sasha Bowlder's grave with a knife in her hand and a dead snake by her feet.

A dead snake—just like the one in that creepy book he'd found on Em's bed. It had said something about the Furies under the picture. . . . He shivered and pulled up the hood of his jacket. He hated thinking about Em like that—not just vulnerable, but teetering on crazy. He'd never seen her so shaken.

JD stopped and hid behind an oak tree, watching as Crow approached a newly dug grave and kneeled in front of it on the freshly packed dirt. Crow bowed his head for a moment and for the first time seemed human, like he wasn't putting on a show or trying to be all anti-establishment. He just . . . was, and JD felt a prang of sympathy. Then, just as quickly as he'd come, Crow stood and brushed off his knees—then turned and headed back to his truck.

For a split second JD thought to confront him; out of principle he didn't want his anger to dissipate. But what was the point? *Let him go,* JD thought. It suddenly seemed wrong to start a fight surrounded by headstones.

As soon as he saw Crow's truck pull out of the cemetery, JD walked down to the grave. When he read the words on the headstone, he felt like he'd been punched in the gut.

> *Drea Feiffer*
> *Beautiful daughter, friend, individual.*
> *Gone from us too soon.*

The sight of it gave him chills. It seemed somehow like an offense that she would be here. This didn't do justice to the person she was: unique, curious, brilliant. No. Drea's ashes should've been shot into space, floating across the universe—or scattered in the ocean to move with the currents. Something . . . bigger. Just not here, buried in this old, crumbling place under layers of soil.

He stooped down and ran his fingers over the cool stone. His chest ached. Gone forever.

"I'm sorry," he said out loud. And he was. He was sorry for almost kissing her, for not kissing her, for not being a better friend. For not saving her from the fire in the gym. For choosing Em. Who had not chosen him back.

He hung his head, lost in his thoughts—but pulled away when he heard something nearby, a voice. A faint murmuring. He jerked upright.

"Hello?" he called out. The fog seemed to consume his words; they dissipated almost as quickly as they'd left his mouth. "Is someone there?" Had Crow seen his car and doubled back to confront him?

No response. JD squinted down the row of graves, focusing on keeping his breath even and quiet. He strained to hear the voice again, to try to place where it was coming from. Took a few steps in the other direction.

Then the sound came again, traveling like leaves caught in a swirling gust of wind, fading in and out in a spiral. He caught fragments of words, and the high trail of someone's laughter. He stood weighted down, like every ounce of his blood had turned into a liquid metal. *Move,* he told himself. More snippets of a girl's voice, melodious, as through from a music box. Otherworldly. JD had seen his share of scary movies, but nothing could have prepared him for the way his heart was pounding in his chest right now.

"I can hear you," he said, a bit louder. He balled his fists and turned in a circle, unsure what direction it was coming from. Every headstone seemed to grow taller, the sky grayer. As far as he knew, he was the only person in the cemetery now that Crow was gone. *If* Crow was gone. No other cars had been parked when they got there, nor had any arrived in the past few minutes.

And then he spotted her, not ten yards away. A girl, sitting with her back against a huge, bare-branched maple tree that towered over a white-stone mausoleum across the way. How long had she been there? She was in navy-blue sweatpants and a white T-shirt, and her hands and feet were covered in dirt. Her blond hair was stringy and her body looked gaunt. JD made his way toward her.

"I see you," she said in a singsong voice. She pulled at the grass around her but didn't look up.

He stopped short and waited for her to say more, but nothing came. He took slow steps toward her and finally, she raised her head, startled—as if she hadn't called out to him just moments ago. She scrambled to her feet and he could see that she was about his age, with dirty-blond hair and a blank gaze. He could tell she'd been beautiful once. Her eyes were green, but blood-shot. JD swallowed hard.

"Are you—are you okay?" he stuttered. He saw a long, angry scar along her hairline and his stomach went tight.

She turned away from him again, staring intently at a patch of grass for seemingly no reason. She whispered something, to herself or to him, he couldn't be sure. But he took one more step closer, straining to hear what she was saying.

"From blood the seeds are borne and from blood they will be buried," she murmured as though reciting something—a poem, or a spell. It was eerily similar to the words in the book he'd seen on Em's bed.

"Hey . . . Hi. Are you all right? You must be freezing. Can I get you some help?" In the pocket of his Windbreaker, JD closed his fingers around his cell phone.

The girl swiveled again, but this time her expression was different—softer, more lucid, like she somehow recognized him. She reached up to tuck her hair behind her ears, smearing dirt on her cheeks in the process. "I'm sorry," she said, looking embar-rassed. "Did you say something to me?"

JD looked around; it was an empty graveyard at nine o'clock in the morning. "I asked if you needed help?"

"Oh, well, now that you mention it, I think I should call my aunt." She smiled a wide, toothy smile—the kind you'd see in some sort of beauty pageant—and cocked her head slightly. It was weird how quickly she had shifted from Crazy Girl in the Cemetery to Miss America at a Dinner Party.

JD fumbled for his phone. This girl could be on drugs or insane or maybe she was just a wild hippie chick, but whatever she was, he didn't know what to do with her. "Sure," he said. "You can use my phone."

But when he handed it to her, she just held it limply in her hand—looking at it like she'd never operated a phone before. It fell to the ground. Her arms were shaking, like she was starving and weak, or didn't have complete control over her muscles.

"I'm supposed to call her whenever I hear them," she said, blushing deeply. A single tear ran down the side of her face, leaving a pale rivulet in the dirt. "They're so loud. They're laughing. They're—"

"Who?" he said, grabbing his phone out of the dirt.

"The Furies." She looked at him matter-of-factly. "I can hear them. It's getting worse. Henry was just candy to them. That's what they said. Just easy. Easy, easy, easy. Easy prey." She spoke evenly—like they were talking about the weather—but her words were totally out-there. JD was completely mystified.

He stared into her eyes then for the first time, feeling a current run up his spine, raising all the short hairs on the back of his neck. *The Furies.* Those words again. He didn't know what to say. "Listen, do you need me to make the call for you? Who's Henry? Do you want to call Henry?"

"We can't call him," the girl said, suddenly desperate and shaking violently. "He's dead. . . . Dead, dead, dead, dead—"

"Look, just hold on, okay?" JD punched 911 into his phone, praying the signal would be strong enough to connect.

"They're just waiting for the next one. The next mistake. They're everywhere. They're watching." He could hear a hysterical tremor in the back of her voice. She covered her ears and shook her head violently.

"It's going to be okay," he said. *Shit.* His phone call wasn't connecting. *Come on, come on.* He could run to the road and try calling from there, but he didn't want to leave her.

All of a sudden, female voices shot across the grounds, loud and jarring. "Lucy! *Lucy!*"

It took a moment for JD to realize that the voices were coming from the little cemetery road, where a sedan had come screeching to a halt. Two figures got out of the car, leaving the engine running as they came toward JD and the girl. As they got nearer, JD was shocked to see Skylar McVoy and the older woman who had accompanied her to Drea's memorial service.

Meanwhile, the girl—Lucy, apparently—had calmed down. Her eyes were dull and her limbs now hung at her side. "She wants out," she muttered to JD under her breath. "The others want blood, but she wants *out*."

The gray-haired woman immediately went to Lucy and wrapped a blanket around her shoulders. "Sweetie. Are you okay? We were so worried. . . ."

"I'm sorry, Aunt Nora. I had another episode. I got . . . confused."

The woman nodded as if this was a familiar routine. "Let's just go home, then."

"Aunt Nora—" Skylar started to say. But she cut herself off when she saw JD staring at her. She just stood there, motionless, her eyes veering from JD to the two women and back. She looked down at herself; she was wearing flip-flops and pajama pants.

"We realized she was missing at five this morning. . . ."

"Oh," JD offered, not knowing what else to say. Clearly, Skylar had been hauled out of bed. He opened and closed his mouth several times. None of the questions in his brain were able to make it to his mouth. The older woman, Aunt Nora, began to shepherd Lucy toward their car.

"Thank you so much for finding her," Nora said with a pasted-on polite expression. "We're so sorry. She's not well."

"I'm sorry if I scared her," JD offered, wanting to help. "I didn't know what to do. . . ."

The woman gave him a warm, sad smile. "She'll be fine. This

just happens every so often. She's still recovering." She turned and began to walk away.

He saw that Skylar was about to follow her. "Wait," he croaked. He had to say *something*.

He came up to her and tried to meet her eyes. "She said . . ." He licked his lips nervously. "I'm not sure if it matters. . . ."

"What?" Skylar refused to look at him. Even though she kept her head down, so her hair swung forward, he could see her scarred cheeks were flaming red.

"She was talking about something—or some people—called the Furies," he said. "She sounded pretty freaked out."

The word seemed to jolt Skylar back to awareness. She stiffened and raised her face, which was transformed into a glare. "Forget it," she snapped. "She's out of her mind. Brain-damaged. Broken. Forget everything you heard."

"Who is she?" JD asked helplessly. There was a pause, in which every one of his senses seemed to be at high alert. Blood pumped around his joints and insects hummed in the woods that bordered the graveyard.

"She's my sister," Skylar spat, before spinning around and stalking off into the fog.

You can't call him. He's dead.

JD knew one dead Henry, though it took him a little while to remember who he was. Henry Landon, Ascension High

School's handsome, smart, deceased English teacher.

Henry was just candy to them. Easy prey.

And hadn't Skylar McVoy been the one to find Henry Landon's half-frozen body in the reeds deep within the Haunted Woods?

The Furies. I can hear them. They're laughing.

JD checked the clock in his car. He'd already missed first period. Why not go crazy and skip second period too? He pressed on the gas and made a U-turn, feeling something like lightness in his chest as he drove out toward the Behemoth. He turned up the volume on WMPG, the Portland radio station he loved. He felt surprisingly free, not being where he was supposed to be. A light rain began to tap against his windshield as he drove.

Something was happening, something strange. And JD wanted to understand what it was.

Easy prey . . .

For there to be prey, there had to be a predator. JD recalled how Ty had referred to Ascension's recent deaths as murders. At the time, he'd written it off as bad word choice, but maybe it wasn't a coincidence. Was the spate of recent deaths really just bad luck?

Or was there something more sinister going on?

Once he'd parked and locked his car, JD set off into the woods. He was pretty sure he knew where he was going—past the charred spot where AHS kids held their bonfire parties, past the odd clearing with the brown, scratchy grasses just on the edge of the lake. He knew the chances he'd find any indication of the exact spot where Landon had died—or of what had killed him—were next-to-none. The police had been involved. A body didn't get hauled out of a pond every day. And Landon's body was discovered weeks ago—he wasn't about to find a preserved footprint in the mud or something.

Still, he kept walking, compelled by something he couldn't name: a drumming sense of unease, a foreboding flickering at the edges of his consciousness. A sense that he was being given clues to a puzzle he was barely even aware of. A light spring mist was falling from the sky, hovering in slow motion before sliding onto the leaves and bark and roots. The soft *shhhhh* of rustling branches mixed with drizzle was all around him, creating a veil of sound into which he walked deeper. He trudged through the forest, sidestepping muddy patches and stopping occasionally to break off a fresh branch—like Hansel with his bread crumbs, JD wanted to be sure he could find his way out.

The ground grew spongier and JD knew he was getting close to the small pond tucked into the trees. The drizzle turned to full-on rain. There it was. Surrounded by short reeds and cattails and bushes that would be rainforestlike in less than a month. He took a few steps nearer, wondering where exactly Mr. Landon's body had been found. *Squish.* Was this where he'd died? *Squish.* Was this?

Was this where Henry Landon had been marked as easy prey?

A bird called from the trees, a harsh, mocking cry. JD had the sense that he was very out of place. He looked behind him and squinted into the trees up ahead. Raindrops and fog settled on his glasses, obscuring his view.

Something glinted in the mud. Right there, just past that rock. JD squatted down, thrusting his hand into the wet dirt and pulling out a gold pendant.

His fingers went stiff. It was a snake charm, similar to the pin Drea had always worn.

They're everywhere. They're always watching.

A delicate chain dangled from the pendant. It was broken, like it had been ripped off instead of removed deliberately. He held it in his hand and ran his thumb over its engraving. The snake's scales were intricate.

He'd seen Em kill a snake in the cemetery. There had been a snake carved into the hilt of Ty's knife.

His glasses slipped down his nose. His sweater was heavy with moisture. His shoes were soaked and the lake looked gray and angry. Suddenly all the nature around him seemed tinged with malice. Spring was a time of growth and chirping and flowers, but here it seemed darker. More parasitic, creeping, clinging. He felt as though the muddy ground he stood on were sinking—it let off a faint hissing sound. Sinister. He had the sudden sense that if he stayed too long in this spot, he might never get out.

CHAPTER TEN

On Friday afternoon, Em dialed Skylar's number as soon as she got home from school. It was still light out, but barely. "Is your aunt back yet?" Em said.

"She got back this morning," Skylar replied. She sounded exhausted. Em thought about reminding Skylar she'd promised to call the second her aunt returned, but decided against it. "Do you want me there when you talk to her?"

"Yes, yes, absolutely," Em said. "She won't talk to me otherwise. I'll come right over."

"Don't come here," Skylar responded quickly. "We're, ah, doing some renovations and everything is a mess. Meet me at the Connor Greenhouse—do you know where that is, in the nature preserve off Rambling Brook Road? My aunt volunteers there some evenings."

Em did know where it was—she'd driven by it a few times on her way to and from Drea's house. She confirmed and hung up; as she crammed her feet into her muddy boots and threw on a light jean jacket, she could feel her blood buzzing in her veins.

She was getting closer to the truth—she knew it.

Nora had to have some answers. The picture of her with Hannah and Edie meant something—it had to.

The time passed in a blur as Em waited for Nora's return. She'd exchanged a few random texts with Crow, but his normally permissive parents were freaked out by his recent brush with the law—his court date was coming up in a couple of weeks— and were keeping him on house arrest. And on some level, she was relieved, because it meant someone was watching him. She hadn't really realized how worried about him she was, until now.

Still. She'd been at a complete standstill for the past twenty-four hours, and every day she could feel the darkness, the anger, the evil, surging more powerfully in her veins. Her skin felt tight and ill-fitting, like she was on the brink of shedding it for good.

But no. She wouldn't let that happen. She couldn't give in to the transformation. She had to stop it somehow. She had to save herself.

It was almost five by the time Em pulled up at the greenhouse, which sat glowing yellow-green against a dusky sky at the end of a winding driveway, just past Drea's neighborhood. The preserve encompassed marshy fields and a small arboretum, all of it pulsing with new life. As Em got out of her car and walked toward the glass-domed structure, her shoes sucked in the mud. It had been a wet spring.

The rusty door creaked open to reveal a warm room, abundant with lush greenery and vibrant flowers. Had she been there under different circumstances, Em might have marveled at the beauty. But tonight, she felt claustrophobic. The air seemed heavy and close, like she was stepping into an open mouth. Moisture clutched at her bare skin.

There was a round wooden table in the middle of the greenhouse, paint peeling off it like snakeskin, and Skylar was sitting there with two other women. As Em got closer, she recognized not only Skylar's aunt Nora, with her silvered hair and arched brows, but also the woman next to her—Hannah Markwell, the university librarian who had shunned Em and Drea during one of their research missions. Em stiffened involuntarily.

"Well," Nora said finally. "Here we are."

"Thank you for agreeing to meet with me," Em said. Her voice sounded loud and overly formal to her own ears. She felt the sudden inappropriate urge to laugh. They looked like they were all about to start a séance.

"I didn't want to at first," Nora said.

"I know," Em said.

"But Skylar told us that you tried to warn her. About . . . *them*. To talk sense into her while she was under their spell. So,

I'm willing to give you a chance." She folded her hands on her lap. Only her fingers, which were trembling slightly, betrayed her anxiety. Em looked around at Skylar, who was tearing at her cuticles, her hair curtained forward over her face, as always. Ms. Markwell was sitting ramrod straight, as though preparing to bolt. Em pulled back a chair and took a seat.

Silence built on silence, and Em swallowed, tried to choke out the words she so desperately needed to say. Finally, she managed: "I know you knew Edie Feiffer. And she knew the Furies. I need to find out what happened to her. I need to find out what you know."

A shadow passed over Nora's face. Sadness. She exchanged an almost imperceptible glance with Hannah, who nodded.

Nora cleared her throat. "We were best friends," she said, looking down at her hands. "The three of us were inseparable. Edie, me, and Hannah."

"Edie Feiffer." Em confirmed softly, thinking of the creased photo in her purse, of the stooped woman she had seen in her vision—or memory—earlier today.

Hannah nodded. "Your friend Drea's mom."

Em nodded. Drea's mom, who had been a victim of the Furies. Em remembered the first time Drea told her: *She was being haunted. I'm sure of it.*

There was no time to waste. "Why was she marked?" Em asked point-blank. "And did she fight back?"

Nora and Hannah exchanged another look. Nora toyed with a gold bracelet, twisting it endlessly around her wrist.

"She wasn't marked." Hannah spoke up now. Her voice was surprisingly deep.

"I don't understand," Em said, frowning. "So she wasn't being haunted?"

Nora looked as though she was on the verge of tears. "Edie was the one who summoned them in the first place," she said, her voice a hoarse whisper.

There was another second of silence. Em felt a yawning pit in her stomach. Edie had summoned them. Em shook her head, confused. That didn't make any sense.

Hannah jumped in, pursing her lips before starting to speak. "We all grew up together," she said. "And Edie was a wonderful woman. Full of life, and so passionate. But she had her share of problems, too. Her first husband was just awful. A drinker. He hit her too, more than once. A twisted man. Played all these mind games until she almost broke. She had these . . . blue periods. Just stretches of sad, sad time. She'd withdraw."

Just like Drea, Em thought.

"When she remarried, she seemed to get better," Nora said. "Especially when Drea came."

"But *he* was always lurking in the shadows," Hannah said.

"Her first husband, you mean?" Skylar piped up. Em had practically forgotten she was there.

The women nodded, and when Nora looked up Em could see that the tears were starting to overspill her eyes.

"We'd all heard stories growing up about three women who haunted the woods, taking revenge on people who had sinned," Nora said. "My grandma—your great-grandmother, Skylar— used to call them 'Dirae.' Some said they were ghosts, or demons. This is New England. People are superstitious."

That was true. No matter how many malls were built or iPhones were sold, people in Ascension, Maine, would always like to tell stories: about ghosts and witches and things that went creak in the night. Em had been, what, five years old the first time she heard the legend of the Haunted Woods? Ghost stories were like a rite of passage around here.

"I never actually believed all that stuff," Nora continued. "But Edie—she *believed*."

"Well, she was always looking for something to believe in," Hannah said authoritatively. "Whether it was crystals and healing stones or witches in the woods, she wanted something *external* to fix things. I don't think she thought she could fix them herself."

Em took a deep breath. She hadn't anticipated how hard it would be to sit here and listen to the truth, to hear about all of this old pain and old blood, dredged up and restored. She didn't want to rush Nora through what was obviously a traumatic retelling. But it was more than that—some part of her didn't want to hear, or know.

Blinking back the sudden desire to cry, she looked around the greenhouse. An explosion of color and green: plants growing up and out, stretching their way along the interior of the glass. They so clearly wanted out. All this life, condensed into this one artificial structure. Protected from the cold and the snow, but aching for fresh air.

"It's beautiful, isn't it?" Nora asked, watching Em's eyes roam the building.

"Yes," Em said shortly. She cleared her throat. She couldn't waste any more time. "Can you—can you tell me more?"

Nora sighed. "Edie found out about three women who burned to death in the Ascension woods, and she started gathering what she considered to be evidence of dark forces—unsolved crimes; murders and accidents that went unexplained; mysterious fires. And then she found the book. . . . *Conjuring the Furies.*"

A jolt went through Em and she sat up straight. "I have that book," she blurted out. Hannah looked at her sharply. "I—I found it. In Sasha Bowlder's things."

"We never thought she would do anything with it," Nora said, rushing on. There were red splotches on both her cheeks. Guilt, or anger, maybe. "But when Drea was three, Jack—the first husband—came back around. He threatened her. Saying he would take Drea, make it so that she could never see her child again, do things to Drea."

Em shivered. Bad energy was whirling around the table.

Skylar dug her fingernails into the soft wood of the table.

"Edie was so angry," Nora said. Her voice dropped to a near whisper. "So scared, too. She . . . she wanted protection."

"So she tried to summon the Furies for help," Em said. She was beginning to understand.

"She didn't *try*," Nora said dully. "She did it. She succeeded. Last she heard of Jack was a month later. He'd been found dead in a house he was working on, his head split clean by a circular saw—"

"But they weren't done," Hannah interrupted. "That was only the start. Edie thought she could control them. But that isn't how it works. They wouldn't—they wouldn't leave her alone."

They won't leave me *alone either . . .*

"But she hadn't even done anything wrong," Skylar pointed out.

"They'd gotten their claws in her," Nora said. "They'd found their way into our world again. They didn't want to leave. They kept saying she owed them. . . ."

Em fought a surge of nausea. It was all too familiar. And now, finally, the pieces were all in front of her. Still, she was having trouble putting them together. When she spoke, it was to the floor. "So they killed her, right? Just for fun?"

Hannah surprised Em by shaking her head. "No. Not directly. They wanted something from her—she would never tell us what. All we knew was that it was something she would never give them. It was driving her insane." Hannah's voice broke. "And so she took the only way out she thought she had."

Skylar inhaled sharply. The four of them sat for a moment in stunned silence. Em turned over the information in her mind. So Drea's mom had killed herself, rather than give the Furies what they wanted?

What had they asked of her? And would they ask the same thing of Em?

"She left us a note," Nora said, breaking the spell to dig into her sweater pocket with shaking hands. "I've kept it all this time." She locked eyes with Em and handed her the paper; it was old and had been folded and unfolded hundreds of times.

I did a terrible thing, it read. *They are eating me from the inside out. I can't stand it. It isn't just about me anymore. I have to save her.*

The words felt like tiny sparks showering over Em, making her skin burn. This was a message from someone desperate.

Someone just like her.

"They put their darkness in her," Nora said, as if she was reading Em's mind. "Just like they've put their darkness in you." For once, she didn't look terrified or disgusted when she stared at Em. It was pity Em saw in Nora's eyes.

They see Edie in me, Em realized. *I am a reminder of their long-lost friend. I am the carrier of that.*

"But after she died . . . they just . . . left?" Skylar asked. Clearly she was thinking of the next logical question: *How can we get rid of them?*

Hannah spread her hands. "That was the last we heard of

them. I guess they were . . . satisfied when Edie died. We thought they were gone for good, until . . ."

The sentence didn't need to be finished, but Em did it for her: "Until now," she said. "Until me." No one bothered to respond; they all knew the answer.

Em lungs felt like a pressure cooker that was about to explode. Was the only solution for her to do as Drea's mom had done, and do the Furies' dirty work for them? Is that what had happened to Sasha and to Chase—had they leaped from the Piss Pass, driven to suicide by Ty, Meg, and Ali?

Possibly. But then why had the Furies had stuck around, instead of fleeing as they had in the wake of Edie's death?

"There must be a way to stop them," she said, as much to convince herself as the people at the table.

Nora set her mouth into a grim line. "Of course, we all have our theories," she said, staring into the space behind Em, where the overgrown flora suffocated itself beneath heavily glazed panes. "I carry my snake pin. Never been without it since what happened to Edie. Some say that rituals of purity and sacrifice will mollify them, and Hannah once read there was a way to undo the curse if you've been poisoned by them—an antidote of some sort." She shook her head. Now Em could read the pity in her eyes again—the resignation, too. "But we tried all we could. I fear no mortal can stop them. And their game never really ends, you know. The Furies always win."

CHAPTER ELEVEN

"Only you would wear a suit to Fun Zone," Ned said as his ball ricocheted off the fencing behind them. Foul.

"It's not a suit," JD said, taking a few strong practice swings as he got into position. "It's my dad's blazer with pants that aren't ripped jeans. And stop trying to throw me off my game."

It was Saturday morning and they were at the indoor batting cage in the middle of a much-larger sports arcade near Ascension, a place made for kids' birthday parties and rowdy teenage boys. JD and Ned weren't the usual clientele—a few too many honors classes (not to mention years) under their belts—but it was a spring tradition for them to come here every year before opening day of baseball season.

JD was grateful for the chance to blow off some steam. The

interaction with Skylar's sister in the graveyard was etched in his mind, mingling with unavoidable image of Crow stalking Em, and of that snake pin buried in the mud. . . . And then there was Ty. Ty texting him, teasing him; Ty's laugh echoing in his mind. Like she'd implanted herself there.

He couldn't shake a bad feeling. He'd woken up from a nightmare only to forget the details but be haunted by the sense, all day, of darkness.

"Don't forget that Keith wants us to come over tonight to pick our fantasy rosters," Ned said, squatting in the corner of the cage and tearing into a bag of sour-cream-and-onion potato chips. Dressed in a T-shirt and army-green cargo pants, Ned looked ripped from the pages of an online gaming brochure. As for JD . . . well, it wasn't clear what type of catalog he was modeling for. His pinstripe pants, buckled boots, plain white T-shirt, and glasses . . . None of it suggested Sports Guy.

The first pitch from the machine came barreling toward JD and he let it go by. He liked to get used to the space, to the feel of the bat, to the speed of the pitch, before taking his first swing. "You'd be having a better time if you hadn't gotten off to such a crappy start," he said, and Ned grunted in assent.

"You gonna wait all day there, buddy?" Ned called out as JD let another one fly by his head.

"It's called patience," JD said, tightening his grip on the bat.

"It's called being a—" Ned cut himself off as JD swung at

the next pitch. Made contact. The ball soared straight toward the back wall, getting stuck in the netting that lined the rear of the cage. "Okay, beginner's luck," he said. "Nice one."

JD smiled, feeling the dancing sensation in his stomach that came whenever he did something well. Like when he aced a test, or figured out a complicated circuit. Like every time he beat Em at Scrabble.

"You call it beginner's luck; I call it having a good eye," he said, grabbing for the chips. "You're up."

On his next turn, Ned managed to hit another foul ball that shot straight up in the air above them. He had to scramble out of the way when it came back down. "I knew you had it in you, Nedzo. Next Coke's on me."

They went back and forth like that for a while, getting into a comfortable rhythm with the machine-thrown pitches and the weight of the bat in their hands. When he made contact, the wooden crack of the bat was the sweetest sound there was; it cut through the all the noise going on in his brain. The questions, the anxiety—they softened, faded somewhere into the background until he was ready to handle them again.

JD started to feel a little better. A little back-to-normal. He allowed himself to revel in the simplicity of it. The tiny routines he developed every time he approached the plate—brushing the bat against the floor before hoisting it over his shoulder, squinching his face, and adjusting his glasses.

"We should have gone out for baseball," Ned said after his first decent hit of the day.

"Yeah, we would have fit right in with that crowd," JD answered, rolling his eyes. But it got him thinking again. "Hey, dude, you ever hear anything about Chase Singer?"

"What do you mean? That he's dead?" Ned took a swig from his soda bottle.

JD winced. Ned didn't mean to be a dick, he just had all the subtlety of a Mack truck. "Obviously," JD said, tapping the bat mindlessly against the metal cage. "I meant *about* his death. About when they found him."

"Oh, yeah," Ned said. "Impossible to ignore that stuff. Like how people thought he was gay because he had that flower in his mouth or whatever? Come on. People in this town are so freaking homophobic. They see a dude and a red flower and all they think is . . ."

But JD didn't hear the rest. *Red flower.* His pulse quickened. All the mystery-girl stuff, and Ty's red flower, and the detail about Chase's body, and everything. His suspicion that Ty was somehow connected to Chase's death was getting stronger by the minute.

Beep-beep-beep. His text alert sounded, and JD went to grab his phone from the pocket of his blazer. As he did, something fell to the Astroturf with a thud. He looked down to see a silver Zippo, engraved with pine trees on one side and *To WF, with love* on the other. It belonged to Drea's dad, and it looked nice, expensive. He must have accidentally pocketed it after lighting Mr. Feiffer's cigarette at Drea's funeral.

What are you up to today?

Ty. Of course.

He should have been psyched that she was into him—she was definitely the hottest girl who'd ever even looked at him—but he couldn't shake the feeling that something about her was off.

She wasn't Em. How similar they looked only made it more obvious how different they really were.

JD pocketed his phone without responding, then turned the lighter over in his hand, flicking it open and lighting the flame once, twice. He recalled Mr. Feiffer and how distraught he'd been at the memorial service. How alone he must feel. He shoved it back into his pocket.

To return the lighter would mean going to Drea's house—potentially walking into an emotional minefield. Not to mention standing face-to-face with an unhinged, grieving man. But it would also mean doing something kind for the father of his dead friend.

He decided he'd pay a visit to Walt Feiffer after Ned dropped him off.

"You giving up?" Ned jabbed JD with the bat, looking at him expectantly.

"Sorry, got distracted for a sec," JD said, grabbing the bat and moving toward the fake home plate.

"Does your distraction have a name?" Ned asked.

JD raised his eyebrows. "I, ah, I . . . yeah," he said, lifting the bat into the air.

"You and Em talking again?"

"Ha, not quite," JD said. "It's a different distraction."

"Oh, yeah?" Ned said, perking up. "Do I know her?"

"Nothing to get all worked up about," JD laughed. "*I* barely know her myself. In fact, I'm not sure I want to be distracted by her anymore." Did he like Ty? Part of him knew he only liked her because in certain lights, when she tilted her head a certain way, he could pretend she was Em.

But another part of him suspected he was just trying to find excuses to keep hanging on to hope: that someday Em, the real Em, would realize they belonged together.

"Well, then cut her loose, Fount," Ned said with mock-seriousness. "You're the one who's always talking about honesty being the best policy."

Ned was right. Honesty was a point of pride for JD, and he didn't want to be one of those douche bags—stringing a nice girl along while he waited for something better. He'd just have to tell Ty he wasn't sure they should be hanging out. Besides, a beautiful girl like that couldn't be too disappointed. She'd bounce back in a few hours. Right?

This time at bat, JD didn't wait for the perfect pitch. He went for the first ball that came toward him, swinging hard, letting the weight of the bat propel his whole body forward. For the first time that afternoon, JD struck out swinging.

Once JD got home he texted Ty back.

Let's meet up, he wrote. *Coffee?*

Nah, she responded. *How about the hidden courtyard behind Town Hall? That's one of my fave spots.*

Random—but he should have known not to expect anything else from Ty.

Driving downtown, he rehearsed what he was going to say.

"You're great, but I don't think it's a good idea for us to be hanging out right now." His words echoed emptily in the Volvo. "You are obviously very pretty, but I don't think you're right for me." Ten times worse than the first one. He sighed deeply. How did you break up with someone you weren't even going out with?

She was waiting for him on a metal bench, wearing shorts, a tank top, and some sort of see-through flowy top that made her look like she was wafting in the breeze, not fixed to any one spot. He tried to smile as he approached, but his mouth wouldn't obey his brain.

"This isn't a good talk, is it?" she said easily as he sat down next to her. "I've seen that look before."

JD coughed. "Well, um, I . . . I guess not," he admitted. "It's just that . . . I know that we haven't really *labeled* this"—he motioned to the space between them—"but it feels like we might be, ah, headed in a certain direction . . . and I don't—I don't think it's a good idea. Right now. For me." God. He'd really mangled that one.

Ty sighed and turned away from him for a minute, squinting. There was that flash of vulnerability again, the part that drew him to her, just a little. "Is this about something else?" she said finally. "Because, it's just . . . We have a great time together."

Stay strong. This was what he had to do. "You're right. We do. We totally do. But things are crazy for me right now. With Drea, and Em, and school . . . it's just not a good time for me to be getting to know someone new. Someone like you."

"Someone like me?" Ty raised her eyebrows.

"I mean, of course I can see why you're . . . I mean, you're beaut—"

She cut him off, laughing, and stood up. "It's okay, JD. It's cool. Don't worry about it. . . ."

Relief washed over him. If he kept talking he'd just trip over his own tongue. "Thanks. Thank you for getting it."

He stood there for a minute, feeling a thousand times awkward, then decided to lean in for a hug. As his sternum touched Ty's, she pulled back with a strangled gasp.

"Ow!"

She reeled backward, and JD saw that her chest was marred

by a swollen red mark. A burn. For a second, her eyes flashed practically black with anger.

"Holy shit, are you okay?" What the hell had happened? He leaned in to get a closer look but she sidestepped him, her hand flying up to cover the burn.

"I'm fine, silly," she said with a flat grin. "We must have shocked each other. I knew we had chemistry." When she took her hand away, the mark was gone. Nothing. Her skin was back to its usual milky pureness. She gave a final, flirty wave. "I'll see you soon."

He stood there stunned, watching her walk away. She'd recovered quickly, but not quickly enough. For a single moment, Ty had totally lost it. Confused, he ran his hands down his sweater. What could have possibly hurt her so badly? His left hand caught over his chest.

And there, in his breast pocket, was the snake charm, the one he'd found in the marsh. It had been there since yesterday.

It didn't make any sense. That bad feeling—the one JD had been trying so hard to dismiss—came rushing back. But with it came a tremendous feeling of relief: He was glad that he had gotten rid of Ty for good.

Drea's house was dark when JD pulled up, except for a bluish television glow coming from the living room window. The place looked sort of wilted, as though the air had been let out from the inside. Weeds in window boxes seemed suctioned to the glass behind them; the roof was missing some shingles. Newspapers were accumulating in front of the doorway, a garish display of bright plastic against the dirty siding.

Squeezing the Zippo to remind himself why he'd come, JD walked up the steps and knocked tentatively on the front door. No answer. He knocked again, more forcefully the second time. He thought he heard rustling on the other side of the door, but he couldn't be sure. He debated whether to bang on it a third time. As he did, a loud crash came from inside, followed by a wordless cry.

Shit. JD inhaled deeply. He regretted coming already, but he knew there was no turning back now.

He tried the knob and when the door swung open he went in—through the dim entryway, where Mr. Feiffer's work overalls hung on a hook, into the dark hallway, where he fumbled for a light switch.

"Mr. Feiffer?" he said. "I'm sorry to just barge in like this, but . . ."

"Who is it?" a voice yelled.

"Mr. Feiffer? It's JD. JD Fount. Do you need any help?" He continued to advance toward the source of a flickering light.

It was only the second or third time he'd set foot there; the handful of times he'd been over, Drea had shepherded him directly down to the basement. Rounding the corner into the

Feiffers' living room, the first thing he saw were the photographs: hundreds of pictures, some of them ripped, on the table, the rug, the couch. There was a slowly creeping puddle of moldy water around an overturned vase of flowers on the floor. On the television was a twenty-four-hour news station, but the volume was turned way down and all JD could hear was a low drone of words. That and the sound of Mr. Feiffer coughing up a lung.

This sad squalor . . . It made JD want to turn and run. He was intruding. He shouldn't be seeing this.

"Mr. Feiffer, I'm so sorry," he said, wondering how long it had been since Mr. Feiffer had been here, in this house, in this room. How long it had been since he'd gone to work at the docks. The ashtray was overflowing, and there was a pile of pizza boxes underneath the TV stand. The stench of stale cigarette butts and old food drifted into JD's nose.

Mr. Feiffer looked up with empty eyes. JD could see Drea in his features—his wide forehead, his striking nose.

"I just came by . . . to drop this off," JD said feebly, holding up the lighter. "But is—is there anything I can do for you?" His eyes went to the empty beer bottles on the coffee table and then to the door to the kitchen, where JD could only imagine the state of disarray.

Drea had often mused about how lost her father would be without her around to cook and clean. It wasn't that he was lazy, she'd said, or even selfish. Just that he wasn't used to having to do things for himself. He needed someone to look after him.

"It was my fault," Mr. Feiffer said, his voice breaking. "My fault she went after them, my fault she died. It was my fault they *both* died."

"It's not your fault," JD said automatically. That was what you were supposed to say. Mr. Feiffer was shaking his head. JD took a tentative step toward him. "It's going to be okay," he said.

With unexpected force, Drea's dad reached out his hand and swiped his arm across the side table, knocking over a couple of bottles. JD watched as stale beer seeped onto a pile of photos. He took a step back, wondering if he should call his parents, or someone else. He wasn't equipped to deal with this.

"No it's not. Nothing is *okay*," Mr. Feiffer countered. "If I'd just gotten to them sooner . . . they wouldn't have gotten their claws in our baby. And now, no one will listen to me. No one will listen. Because I'm a drunk. Did you know that, boy?"

JD shivered, as though the temperature in the room had dropped. He tried to focus on the paisley pattern of the Feiffers' couch. "No, sir. I'm not sure I know what you're talking about."

Mr. Feiffer squinted his eyes. "The Furies," he whispered.

"Sir?"

"The Furies!" he yelled. "I've been whispering their name

for twelve damn years. I don't care if I scream it. I don't care if they hear me. They've taken everything anyway. There's nothing left for them to steal. Nothing left for them to kill."

JD couldn't believe it. There was that word again: "Furies." He felt like he had swallowed metal. There was a knife of fear lodged in his gut.

"I knew . . . I knew the moment I laid eyes on Edie," Mr. Feiffer said. "I had to protect her. It was my duty. I *saw* it." He convulsed into another coughing fit and the blotches on his face went white, then red.

"Let me get you some water, Mr. Feiffer," JD said, stepping toward the kitchen. He needed any excuse to get away. What did it mean? *The Furies.* Who were they?

"Crazy—they said I was crazy," Drea's dad said as JD began backing into the hall. "They said I'd get what was coming to me."

It reminded JD of what Ali had said about the man in the pizza place. . . . *He'll get what's coming to him.*

"I'll be right back, sir," JD said, but Mr. Feiffer kept talking even as JD went into the other room and filled up a water glass from the tap over the overflowing sink.

"The things I see . . . the things I've dreamed. It's enough to drive *anyone* crazy. That's why . . ." He trailed off as JD came back into the room.

"Drink this," JD said, handing him the water and clearing some photos off a spot on the recliner so that he could sit down and face the couch. As Mr. Feiffer took a few thirsty sips, JD took a moment to glance at the photos strewn about the room. Upon closer inspection, he noticed that while many of them were personal snapshots of Drea and her mother, others were images ripped from magazines—creepy pictures of flowers, fire, snakes. Like his snake pin . . . the one that had burned Ty. JD felt like he was swimming through murk. "I'm not sure I understand what you're saying, Mr. Feiffer."

Mr. Feiffer laughed. A laugh without humor or hope, it seemed to say: *What could you possibly understand about my misery?*

"She thought she could keep secrets from me," Mr. Feiffer said, and for a moment JD didn't know if he was talking about his dead daughter or his dead wife. "She didn't know how much I knew. That she'd conjured them. That we were all in danger. She didn't know I was trying to protect her, and protect Drea. I loved her. I loved them both." A cry gurgled from his throat, and JD looked away, uncomfortable.

"I'm sure you did," JD said softly, helplessly. "Drea loved you, too." *Conjured them.* Em's book was called *Conjuring the Furies.* Was that why she'd been so weird lately? Had she been messing around with this all this crazy stuff?

"I didn't know they'd come back," Mr. Feiffer said. "I thought I'd gotten rid of them. . . . That they'd gotten what was coming to *them* for a change. But then . . . that boy off the bridge. The flowers. My girl . . . It must not have worked. Not permanently."

"What didn't work?" JD repeated, hoping for a further explanation.

Creak.

They both heard it. A footstep. And was that the sound of laughter, from the other side of the living room window?

Walt's eyes widened in terror. "We can't talk here," he whispered. "It's not safe. I'm being watched."

"By the Furies?" JD ventured.

"They're killers. Once I break my vow . . . They've killed before, and they are going to kill again. I have nothing to lose."

Killers. The Furies. The flowers. It was all connected. Somehow.

Then Walt was on his feet as well, lunging forward and grabbing the collar of JD's flannel shirt. JD stood frozen, breathing in the man's fetid breath and trying not to look into his watery eyes.

"They're here," Walt said menacingly. "Get out of here, while you can. We have to meet in the open. In public. For your sake."

For his sake. JD racked his brain for a meeting place. "How about the football field at AHS? First thing tomorrow morning?"

"I'm an early riser," Walt warned.

"I'll be there by eight," JD said.

Walt nodded in assent and JD was secretly relieved. He'd rather meet Walt in a place where, if he had to, he could call out for help. He still wasn't really sure what he was getting himself into. . . .

CHAPTER TWELVE

The stream water slid around Em's feet, cooling them as it rippled around moss-fuzzed rocks. Eventually it would reach the ocean. With her face turned toward the sun, Em wondered if she would ever see the beach again.

The Furies always win. She'd replayed that conversation in the greenhouse over and over, but nothing came of it except more questions.

She was glad to be out of the house—here with Crow, sitting in the grass at the edge of the stream at Devil's Run, a small park off a back road where water had cut a deep canyon through rocky banks over the years. He'd called her there. Another vision to report. His yellow-green eyes were intense and serious, like a cat's. Against his torn gray T-shirt, they somehow looked even greener.

"I've been . . . feeling the Fury in me," Em said. She slouched forward, looking at her hands. "The anger. And also—the strength. It's growing."

It was terrible to say it all out loud. Every part of her wanted to scream and beg and *hurt* something the way she was being hurt. Birds flew from branch to branch in the trees nearby, oblivious.

She wished he'd put his arm around her, or scoot closer, or do something to act like he cared—like he'd protect her the way he said he would. Instead, he was just staring at her, biting his lower lip as though holding himself back from speaking. He couldn't sit still, kept shifting his weight and fidgeting like he were a little kid.

"Thank god I'm out of that house," he said finally.

"Were your parents really pissed?" she asked. Em had never known Crow's parents to punish him—when there were no rules to break, it was impossible to get in trouble.

"They've been watching me like a hawk," he said. "They know something's up. I think they're . . . I think they might be scared for me. Or *of* me. Who knows. The only reason I was able to escape today is because they went on some epic shopping trip." As he spoke, Crow rubbed his forearm absentmindedly. Following his fingers, Em noticed Crow's hands pass over a cluster of thin scars. Stripes on his arm, like a body bar code.

"What are these?" she asked, grabbing him.

They locked eyes for a moment, and in that second Em felt as if he wanted to devour her. Then he looked down and pulled her arm back, then tugged his sleeve down over the marks. "Nothing," he said. "Just a little scrape."

"Don't. It's not 'just a little scrape.'" She'd seen it; four or five lines all about an inch long. Em stared for a moment at the bags under his eyes. She suddenly felt very thirsty, and even more exhausted than she'd been in weeks. "Crow, talk to me. Are you okay? What's going on?"

"Listen, princess, I really can't handle this right now. There's something more important. . . . The reason I called you here . . ."

She swallowed hard. "Fine," Em finally said. If Crow didn't want to talk about the cuts on his arm, she wouldn't make him. Not yet.

"I had another vision," he said, looking forward at the running stream. His jeans were rolled up and his feet were in the water. For some reason, she found it hard to look at his ankles. They made him seem bony, human, weak. She wanted him to be strong, to have some kind of magic ability to change everything.

The stream gushed past them happily. It wasn't warm enough for what they were doing, not really, but the sun was shining and the ice had melted and this was what Mainers did after long, cold, wicked winters. And anyway, she never got cold. Not anymore.

"Happened this morning." He dipped a cupped hand into

the stream and let the water sift out through his fingers.

She lifted her toes out of the water and hugged her knees to her chest. "Okay. Tell me."

There was a flash of discomfort in his eyes. "I saw a woman in a dress. Or not a dress, exactly. Like a robe or something—long and white and flowing," he said, staring across the stream into the trees, the dappled patterns of sun and shadow. "I couldn't see her face. Or, well, I could, but it was dark, and the light caught something on her face that wasn't human. Her face had these pale lines across it, like stripes. It was like she was a tiger. A white tiger woman. I have no idea what it means."

Em plunged her feet back into the water, barely noticing how the icy water sliced into her skin. She was unconsciously balling her fists. "A tiger woman? Seriously?"

"It's hard to explain," he said defensively. "It's like a bunch of images and, I don't know, a certain *feeling*. She was saying something. About a prophecy, I think. *Someone is plotting vengeance.* Then I saw you—" He cut himself off, staring into the distance. His skin looked pale. The shadows of leaves played across his face.

"What? What about me?" Em urged.

He looked at her anxiously. "You were . . . on fire. *In* fire. It was almost like you were swallowed into the smoke and flames and then, and then . . ."

"And then?"

"And then you were gone, and I snapped out of it."

The words were even colder than the water. They carved straight through her heart.

"It's useless," she said. She cleared her throat, willing herself to stay calm. "They are taking over. Spreading through my life. *Everywhere.*"

She lay back onto the muddy grass, willing herself not to cry. The blackness she was feeling inside crept over her in a thick blanket, making it hard to breathe. She felt she'd never be able to stand up again. How many times had she lain here next to Gabby or JD, when the woods were warming and the world was shaking off its layer of ice? How many days had she taken for granted, days she could never have back?

"I understand," Crow said in a low voice. "But I'm not just giving up. I have a plan."

He picked up her hand, massaging his thumb into her palm. She had to admit it felt good. Em stared down at their intertwined fingers. He had nice hands. His nails were clipped short. His knuckles were rough. She tugged her hand away.

"Okay, so what is it? What's your brilliant plan?"

He leaned even closer, as though he were about to cuddle up next to her on the grass. She didn't move away. "I can't tell you," he said.

"You . . . *what*?" She struggled to sit up. "What do you mean? Why the hell not? What if I can help?"

Crow shook his head. He smiled, but his eyes were black,

expressionless. "Sorry, sweetheart. You're too stubborn. Like a mule. You'd try to get in my way."

"So you have a plan, and you won't let me help—much less even *tell* me about it. And I'm just supposed to trust you?" she asked, feeling her voice rise. She wasn't sure she could, not sure if he could even trust himself.

"Looks that way." He raised an eyebrow at her. "Believe me, you don't want to be part of this. You're in deep enough already."

"But I *do* want to be a part of this. It's my life—and yours. We're supposed to be here for each other."

Crow cocked his head, like he was really thinking about it. "Well, all I'll say is—I've gotten nowhere ignoring them. So maybe instead I need to study them," he said.

"Study them?" she repeated incredulously. "Who? The Furies?"

"Not exactly," he said. "The visions. I have to let myself listen . . . and give in to them."

"Are you kidding?" she asked, jerking her hand away from his and sitting back up, a little dizzy. "You're saying you're going to surrender to them? Try to get closer? Whose side are you even on?"

"I'm not even going to answer that," Crow said with a hint of bemused humor in his voice. "You think I'm a Mr. Fury?"

"This isn't *funny* to me. And the fact that you can joke about it makes me sick. I'm scared, Crow. And I'm worried about you too." All she felt was sadness and worry, but her words were coming out so angry. She couldn't control herself.

"I don't need a babysitter," Crow fired back. "And I sure as hell don't find this funny either." She felt him drifting back into the abyss.

"I know," she said, trying to reel him back in. But it was too late. He was on his feet, leaving wet footprints on the warm rocks in his wake. Already, she regretted her reaction. But she was terrified by what he wanted to do. Submit to his visions? Give in to the darkness? It was too dangerous, too awful to consider. And yet, a chord was struck deep within Em. Would Crow's strategy work for her, too? If she played Ty's game, did she stand a better chance of winning?

Impossible. She'd lost so much of her old self already—she couldn't risk letting go of the last threads holding her to this life.

On her drive home from Devil's Run, Em got a text from Gabby: *Excited for the movie—glad you called this morning. See you in a few!*

Her stomach plunged all the way down through her toes.

She hadn't called Gabby this morning. She wasn't going to meet Gabby at the movies.

But she had a feeling she knew who had, and who was.

Instead of going home, as she had intended to do, Em headed straight to the theater. Rage began to overcome her. Ty was impersonating her—that much was clear. The dyed hair. And now this. She gunned the gas petal with her foot and felt the car groan in response. She kept reminding herself to keep her eyes on the road. It had to be the work of Ty. But *why*? What was she hoping to achieve?

The only rom-com currently playing—the only movie Gabby would agree to see—was in Theater Five. Em paid for a ticket and stalked across the lobby, deliberately avoiding looking at the new girl working the concession stand—the girl who'd taken Drea's place. Only a few short months ago, she'd come to the movies with JD . . . sitting in the front row, like always, craning their necks up to the screen and sharing popcorn out of a jumbo-size bag. . . .

It seemed like a memory from someone else's life.

She made her way past the EMPLOYEES ONLY velvet rope. There was no way she could just barge right into the theater itself—if Gabby saw her and Ty together, she'd be completely confused. No, Em needed to figure out a way to get Ty out of there, to confront her privately.

She hated to believe that Gabby, her best friend in the world, would ever confuse Ty for Em. Not up close, anyway. But if Ty met her in the darkness of the theater, it might be possible. . . . And what other explanation was there? Unless Em had made the plans and somehow forgotten. It seemed anything was possible these days, including the fact that she might be completely going crazy.

Perhaps that was all Ty was after—threading her way deeper into Em's life, confusing her, spinning different realities.

As Em moved up the back stairs, she felt like she was coasting on her anger. She was invincible, as though a bubble of protection had formed around her—as though, like a character in one of JD's video games, she was suddenly infused by a volcanic force, and could do anything.

She pushed open a door that said DO NOT ENTER. The projection booth was tiny and dark and the guy running it was small and pimply. He whipped around, clearly shocked.

"Hi," she whispered.

"Um, you can't be—be up here," he stammered. His eyes were wide and he looked Em up and down nervously; Em felt power radiating from every pore. She felt like she owned this boy. She felt . . . like Ty.

"There's a problem with the film in Theater Two," she purred. "I thought you might be able to help us figure things out? I can stay here and make sure this one runs smoothly."

"Theater Two?" He seemed hypnotized by her words. This was so easy. He didn't even question her.

"Theater Two." She nodded, slithering forward. "I'll stay right here until you get back." He was gone in seconds. As soon as he left, she peeked through the small glass window down into the audience. It took a minute to scan the darkened room, but her eyes seemed to adjust quickly—too quickly. Bingo. There were Gabby's blond ringlets, and next to them, a head that could be hers—a pile of messy dark hair, big gold hoops. Ty.

Slowly, languidly, as though her head was not attached to her neck, Ty swiveled around and stared directly into Em's eyes. With a gasp, Em stepped away from the window, feeling like she had just jumped into Galvin Pond in the middle of February—her breath had been swept away. Pinpricks of terror ran up and down her body.

Just a few seconds later, the door to the booth swung open. There stood Ty, smirking. Her loose white T-shirt and tight gray jeans were practically identical to Em's own outfit.

"What are you doing here?" Em said, trying to keep her voice steady. Whenever she stood next to Ty, she was overcome by a frigid sense of blackness. Almost like drowning. She refused to look at their reflections in the projector window. The double vision would only make her dizzier.

"Seeing a movie with my friend Gabs," Ty said, as though it were the most obvious thing in the world. She trailed her fingers casually along the equipment in the projection booth. "I love a good rom-com."

"She's not your friend," Em said coldly. She looked Ty up and down. "Why are you . . . wearing that? How did you know what I'd be wearing? Why are you trying to look like me?"

"How did you know what *I'd* be wearing?" Ty countered. "Maybe you're copying me, not vice versa. Did you ever think about that?" She did a quick spin in the small space, like a model on a runway, and laughed.

Em's eyes caught hers in the window's reflection, and her vision swam. It was in fact hard to tell who was who. Her breath hitched in her throat and she willed herself to turn away from the glass.

"You can feel it inside you, can't you?" Ty whispered. "The heat. The power. The anger. It's exciting, isn't it? And scary. Scary how evil feeds on itself."

"Why me?" The words came out hoarse and quiet. "Why now? Why don't you just kill me, like you've done with all the others?"

For a moment, Ty's taunting look vanished, and Em detected something else, almost—*almost*—like sadness. The way an animal might pity its prey, right before devouring it. "You were in the wrong place at the wrong time," she said, and that brief glimpse of empathy was gone. She smiled. "Don't you see, Em? I just want to be good. Like you."

"Good?" Em repeated. It was disgusting to hear Ty even say the word.

"Let the darkness take you," Ty said, taking a step forward, more seductively now. "Time is running out, you know. It's almost over. And then the pain will be over, and the transformation will be complete." It sounded almost like Ty was saying a prayer. "Anyway, I've gotta get back to the movie—I don't want to miss the best part! See you at the party later." She winked.

And then, before Em could question her or respond in any way, Ty whisked herself out of the small room. As she brushed by, it was as if they shared the same slice of air. As if their molecules mingled for a split second. Two wisps of smoke, twirling around each other.

And the mirrored glass reinforced the sensation—in the vacuum of Ty's wake, as Em leaned over, resting her hands on her knees and trying to regain her balance, her reflection wavered in and out, like a shifting hologram. Was the girl in the mirror "good," like Ty had said?

She barely knew herself. *There I am. There I'm not.*

Back and forth. In and out. No matter how hard she blinked, she seemed translucent.

Holy shit.

She tried to tell herself to keep breathing, but panic roiled inside her, making it hard to grasp on to a lifeline.

I'm disappearing, she thought.

Then aloud: "I'm disappearing." Saying the words seemed to break the spell. Like waking up from a dream, she clicked back into herself and saw a normal reflection in the glass. She brought a hand to her face and touched her skin, making sure it was there. Making sure she was real. There was little relief, though; instead, she felt like she'd dodged the bullet that would surely get her eventually.

CHAPTER THIRTEEN

Less than a mile from the Feiffers' house, JD parked on the side of
the road. When he pulled out his phone, his hands were shaking.
Within a couple seconds of online research, he was quickly able
to nail down two solid pieces of information:

1. The Furies were mythological goddesses of
   vengeance.
2. They usually appeared in groups of three—
   and their names were a mouthful: Tisephone,
   Alecto, and Megaera.

Ty, Ali, Meg.
His stomach rolled and he kept scrolling through webpages,

hunting for information. What he read about the Furies put a bad taste in his mouth.

JD's unsettling interactions with Ty, Lucy, and Mr. Feiffer only served to heighten his unease, not to mention the snake charm he'd found. It was difficult to separate the truth from the madness—it seemed like crazy stories and wild behavior were becoming the norm around here.

But what was he supposed to believe? That three storybook characters had leaped from the pages of Greek scrolls to the streets of Ascension? And that Ty was one of them, along with her cousins?

Meg, Ty, even Ali—all of them were pretty, but off. JD was reminded of the open casket funerals he had been to, and how the bodies looked after they'd been drained, stuffed, and powdered. That's how these girls were: perfect on the outside but empty and rotten on the inside. You could sense it.

It was definitely weird that the mystery women who had recently entered his life had names that were remarkably similar—just a little more pronounceable—to the mythological goddesses'. And that Lucy and Mr. Feiffer had both dropped hints that connected the Furies with recent happenings in Ascension. But coincidences were not evidence.

And then there was the possibility Em was somehow entangled in this mess. After all, the first time he'd ever heard of the Furies was in the book on her bed. . . . Sweat prickled his forehead. He punched down the window, taking deep breaths of cool air. The wind whispered through the trees outside, as though passing along its secrets.

I can't believe you're even considering this, he chastised himself.

JD had always liked order. Gears, circuits, electrical flow: stuff you could categorize, understand, process. But more and more, he felt as though he was entangled in something he couldn't understand—plagued that he had somehow placed himself in danger. And that other people were in danger.

Three people—four, including Sasha Bowlder—had already mysteriously died this winter. And Ty seemed to be connected to at least two of them.

Could *that* be a coincidence?

Driving home, he found himself compulsively checking his rearview mirror and craning his neck to see around every bend. He felt jumpy, electric, like he used to as a kid playing hide-and-seek—as though at any second someone might pop up and grab him.

And when he got out of his car, he practically sprinted for the front door, making doubly sure to lock it behind him.

Moments later, he settled onto the living room couch with his laptop, but it was impossible to concentrate.

"Can you turn that down?" JD asked Melissa. She glared at him, but turned down the volume on whatever reality TV show she was currently watching.

As Melissa punched the remote control, JD noticed her nails were literally neon green. Why were girls so weird?

"Is that color called I Fell Into a Nuclear Reactor?" he asked.

"Bright colors are in right now, idiot," Melissa said. "Ali put the same color on her toes."

JD tried to stifle the alarm bells that began ringing in his head. "So? Then her toes are radioactive too. And when did you see Ali?"

"This afternoon," Melissa said, plunging her hands into a bag of popcorn and eating the kernels one by one. "She picked me up while you were out with Ned and we did mani-pedis at her house."

"I'm glad stranger-danger really made an impression on you, Mel," he said, trying to keep his tone light.

She rolled her eyes, tucking a strand of strawberry-blond hair behind one ear. "Ali isn't a stranger, dummy. She's a friend. Remember?" She looked genuinely disappointed.

He reminded himself not to overreact—there were no facts on the table, only insane theories. "I know, I know," he relented. "But we just don't know her very well, and with everything that's been happening around here—I guess I'm just feeling a little overprotective."

"Well, don't be. You don't need to worry about me."

"Says the girl who almost broke her ankle last week," he said.

"Almost." Melissa smiled. "Anyway, all we did was go to her

house—which is incredible, by the way—and do girly stuff. Ty was there too. They say I'm practically like family."

"Oh, yeah?" JD shook his head when Mel held out the bag of popcorn. "So what's the rest of their family like? Moms? Dads? Sisters?"

Melissa shrugged. "I'm not sure exactly. They don't talk much about that kind of stuff. It seems like, I don't know, maybe something bad happened in their family that they don't like to think about."

"Where does Ali live?" JD asked, realizing that he'd never gotten a straight answer to that question.

"It's a *huge* house out in the Haunted Woods," Melissa said. "All rickety and old, like something from a movie."

JD was surprised. "I didn't know there were any houses back there," he said. "I thought that was just where Ascension kids went to party." *And where Henry Landon went to die.* The snake charm he'd found out there was still in his bedroom upstairs.

"Not like you'd know," Melissa teased.

"All right, all right. I get it. I'm antisocial." He nudged her. "And Em always hitched a different ride to those parties."

The joke fell flat, and a cloud of guilt passed over Melissa's eyes; she more than anyone else understood the connection between Em and JD. "But the craziest part," she said, trying to change the subject, "was this amazing garden they have out back. It's not even a garden, really—more like a field. Of flowers. Here, come here," she said, grabbing his hand and dragging him off the couch, nearly upending her popcorn bowl in the process.

"Come on, Mel. I have to work," JD protested, but, keeping a firm grip on his hand, she tugged him out of the room, up the stairs, and into her own bedroom, which was painted a deep shade of purple.

She plucked a bloodred orchid from her dresser, where she'd placed it in a mason jar just next to her jewelry box. "Check it out." She twirled it in front of his nose, and he instantly began to feel nauseous.

"Did Ali give you that?" he asked. The flower. It was too red, somehow. Unnatural—just like Ty and her cousins. And he'd been seeing it in all the wrong places. First at Drea's funeral, in Drea's hands. Then in Ty's hair. In the torn pictures strewn around Walt Feiffer's living room. And now here, in his baby sister's bedroom.

It was the same flower—he was willing to bet—that they'd found in Chase's mouth on the night he died too.

Melissa's embarrassment was practically palpable. "She didn't say I couldn't have it," she said.

"You *stole* it?" He grabbed the flower out of Melissa's hand. Was it his imagination, or did it make his skin start to burn?

"What's your problem?" she demanded, following after him as he left her room and started heading downstairs. "What are you doing?" Her voice got louder as he ignored her.

It's just a flower, he told himself. But he couldn't help it. He was gripped by a sense of dread. He felt instinctively that with Ali, Ty, and Meg, things weren't what they seemed to be. He was increasingly convinced they were dangerous, and that Melissa's minor indiscretion might have consequences far beyond the ones that made sense. JD flipped on the kitchen light, feeling the flower's weight in his hand. It didn't have thorns, but he was still scared the thing was going to somehow slice him open.

"You're such an asshole," Melissa cried out. "What are you *doing*? *God.* I hate you sometimes!"

He didn't want to just get rid of it, he wanted to *destroy* it. He walked straight to the sink and shoved the flower down the garbage disposal, ignoring Mel's hysterical tone. "You have to stay away from Ali," he warned. "She's not as nice as she seems."

"Just because you don't have a social life, doesn't mean you can destroy mine!" Tears were welling up in Melissa's eyes.

It was awful upsetting her, being screamed at—but the relief he felt when the final red petal got swept into the crunching gears seemed worth it. He'd be fine if he never saw one of those flowers again.

"It's not my fault your friend died," Melissa yelled before storming out of the kitchen. "It's not my fault Em doesn't give a shit about you!" Her final jab echoed throughout the house.

And that's when it hit him, where he saw the first red orchid—not at Drea's memorial service; no, it was before that.

208

When Em wore one clipped to her bag for a few days, right around Christmas. Right before they went down to Boston together. Right before she started acting truly batty. Right before Chase died—with a red flower *in his mouth* when he was found underneath the Piss Pass.

He leaned over the sink, bracing himself with locked arms against the counter. Something was happening here, and it was way bigger than JD could comprehend.

Red flowers . . . and people who died.

Evil forces that Drea's dad blamed for the deaths of his daughter and his wife.

Em acting crazy, like someone he'd never met.

Walt and Lucy raving about the Furies.

It was all adding up to something terrible, something JD didn't want to face, but he was beginning to believe that he had no choice. He'd have to meet with Walt tomorrow; Walt had claimed to know how to get rid of the evil for good.

The Furies were in Ascension, they were killing people he knew, and somehow, he'd ended up right in their crosshairs.

CHAPTER FOURTEEN

Where did u go??? Gabby texted.

You are crazy, girl, Fiona wrote.

Em's phone was blowing up before she even got to Noah's house. Noah Handran's annual shindig marked the start of the spring sports season—the lacrosse team had their first game tomorrow afternoon. It happened every year, and everyone went. Gabby had made Em promise that she'd at least make an appearance tonight.

See you at the party, Ty had said earlier, at the movie theater. Em had a hunch she knew why she was getting all these texts.

Until a few hours ago, Em had still been going back and forth about showing up—if she had limited time left as Em Winters, did she want to spend some of it at a keg party?

And now, clearly, Ty had gotten there first. And everyone thought she was Em.

It was time for major damage control.

Sean Wagner was the first person she saw as she approached the front door. He was smoking a cigarette on the front stoop, his signature baseball cap worn backward. His eyes lit up when he saw her. There was a bottle of whiskey on the step next to him.

"Back for more, huh?" He curled her in for a one-armed hug and she ducked her head automatically to avoid the smell of smoke. "I thought this was going to be a tame night, but you never fail to surprise me, Winters. Although I gotta say, I preferred your clothes from before. Way sexier."

Em looked down at her outfit—the same one she'd been wearing earlier—and wondered what the hell Ty had changed into. "Sorry to disappoint," she said. But really, even Sean's typical asshole comments, the way he scanned her body up and down (and the different ways in which she planned to subtly reject him . . .) they all felt sad in their familiarity. In their everyday-ness. This was just one more thing she would never experience again, one more thing to say good-bye to.

She leaned down and grabbed the whiskey, blindly hoping that alcohol might diffuse her rising panic. The glass felt slick against her lips, and the whiskey burned as it slid down her throat. She clamped her lips shut to keep from coughing.

"That was far from disappointing," he said with a laugh.

Then he stubbed out his cigarette and opened the door, ushering her inside and to the basement, where jam-band music came from the speakers and Ascensionites lounged and leaned on every available surface.

Em didn't know what kind of welcome she'd expected, but this wasn't it. As she stood at the bottom of the staircase, scanning the room for Gabby and the rest of her friends, she felt a million eyes on her, and not in a good way. The room seemed to tilt ever so slightly to the left, and she shook her head to clear it. The drink must have gone straight to her head.

There were some snickers coming from the makeshift "bar"—a card table with bottles on it—and a weird wink from a senior named Jack who she'd spoken to maybe once in her life. She tried to keep a smile on her face, but her insides were rattling with discomfort, like there was nothing in her stomach but splinters of wood.

Someone passed her by and handed her a red cup sloshing with beer. She took a long sip. It was cold and harsh and flavorless. She shifted on her feet, dancing like she had to pee. Suddenly, her shirt was too revealing; her body was on display. Dizziness gripped her and the music danced curlicues behind her eyes. She realized with horror that she was swaying with the music now, that she was putting on a show.

Stop, she willed herself. *Stop it.*

"I thought you'd left," Jenna said, coming up behind her and placing a hand on Em's lower back. "You were so drunk! What'd you do, take a cold shower or something?"

Em offered a weak smile. Her searchlight finally found Gabby, in a gray silk romper and leggings, perched atop a bar stool in the corner near Noah's pool table. They made eye contact and Gabby's eyes widened. She hopped down from the stool and quickly came to Em's side.

"A little much for a Wednesday night, don't you think, Em?" Gabby whispered, pulling her out of the line of fire into a quiet alcove that held the house furnace and water heater. Jenna crowded in behind them, and suddenly Fiona was there too, wanting to be in on the action. This part of the basement was muggy. Em didn't like it.

"I'm fine," Em said, casting a look back over her shoulder. Couldn't her friends tell who she was? Couldn't they tell the difference?

The girls looked back and forth at each other knowingly.

"Don't worry, Em," Fiona said. "Everyone gets wasted sometimes. . . ."

Jenna giggled. "Maybe not *that* wasted. By the time we got here, you were pole-dancing half-naked around the basketball hoop in Noah's driveway."

"You acted like you barely knew us," Gabby said, unamused.

"No, guys, really," Em said. "I just got here. It must have been someone who . . ."

Someone who looked just like me.

A chill slithered down Em's spine. She had that feeling again, the one like flickering. The one like smoke. "I wasn't here," she said again, more forcefully this time. "I'm here *now*." She dug her fingernails into her own palm, proving it to herself.

"Whatever, Em," Gabby said. "It's okay. We can talk about it later. I'm just glad you're okay. You just took off . . . like a total madwoman." She hooked her arm through Em's.

"God," Fiona said, looking at Em wonderingly. "You look good. . . . I mean, you sober up quick. I wish we could trade places. Whenever I get that messed up I look like a mug shot."

Em wobbled slightly and let herself lean on Gabby. With dread that loomed like shadows on a cave wall, she began to acknowledge exactly what type of bargain she'd made with Ty. From the hair to the sharpened senses to the cases of mistaken identity, a horrifying truth was starting to take shape. It wasn't only that Em was becoming a Fury. Ty was trying to take over her life at the same time.

They were going to switch places.

Em lied. She told her friends that her mom was coming to pick her up and that she was going to wait outside. Really, she just started walking. She stumbled through the basement toward the stairs, trying to keep her blinders on and see nothing but the path in front of her.

"You wanna show us again how you blow those smoke rings?" Alex got right in her face, but she pushed him away, hearing the thud as he hit the wall behind him. She'd pushed too hard. She'd forgotten how strong she was now, how powerful.

"What the hell . . . ," he snarled at her as he brushed himself off.

"Somebody's gotta get Winters into a ring," someone called out.

She shook her head, a frantic apology. "I'm sorry," she murmured. "I'm didn't mean to." She pitched up the staircase, twisting and turning her body to fit it through the spaces between people.

She kept walking when she got outside. Walking away. Down Main Street, away from Noah's house in the middle of town, past the library and the gourmet food store and the dusty old copy shop that had been open forever. Tears swelled somewhere at the back of her eyes.

She didn't have much time. Not much longer until she joined the ranks of the Furies. What did that even mean? She would seek vengeance for other people's crimes. She would grow bloodthirsty, drunk on the feeling of making the guilty pay. So intoxicated, in fact, that she would keep torturing them long after they'd paid for their sins.

No. That wasn't who she was. It would never be.

She looked up at the sky, not watching where she was going,

half-wishing she would fall into a hole and not be able to make her way out. Lost and not found.

Swish-swish-swish. The whirring of bicycle tires sounded behind her and Em moved over to make way on the sidewalk. But rather than passing her by, the cyclist skidded to a stop right next to her. Em looked over and saw Skylar, panting from exertion.

"I'm fine," Em said with an edge, wondering if Skylar had been sent to check on her. "Everyone can call off the rescue mission."

Skylar swung her leg over the bike seat to dismount. "I'm just coming home from the movies," she said. "Late show." She looked up at Em through long, light brown lashes; without heels on, she seemed tiny.

"Sorry." Em crossed her arms. She felt bad that Skylar was the innocent bystander caught in the crossfire of Em's foul mood. "I just had a bit of an . . . incident over at Noah Handran's house. It seems I have a doppelgänger. And she's ruining my life." She found herself choking a little on the words.

There was a moment of silence. The moonlight on Skylar's scars created white stripes on her cheekbones and forehead. Skylar shifted uncomfortably on her feet. Then she pointed down the road. "Well, we're right by my house. Want to come in for a minute?"

It was true; Nora's house was just down the block. And while it felt strange for Em to be accepting offers of comfort from Skylar McVoy, her options seemed pretty limited right now. Plus, if Nora was home, maybe Em could tell her about these symptoms and see if she had any advice. . . .

"I—I don't know who else to talk to," Em admitted, and they started walking, Skylar wheeling her bike alongside Em's steps. Their footfalls echoed on the empty street. Em focused on taking deep breaths to ease the tightness in her chest.

"You can survive very terrible things," Skylar said quietly.

Em didn't answer. She didn't know if she could—not anymore.

Aunt Nora's driveway was lined on both sides by well-maintained hedges and planters that would soon be full of flowers. Skylar stood hesitantly there, as if she was reconsidering bringing Em inside.

"There's something you should know," she said finally.

"Yeah?" Em asked.

"I've done stuff I regret too." Skylar hugged herself. "I—don't think I'm a good person."

Em looked up, sniffling. "We all do things we regret, Skylar," she said quietly. "That doesn't make us bad."

Skylar nodded and led Em to the front door of the big Victorian house. "We have to be kind of quiet," she said apologetically. "My aunt's probably asleep by now. She goes to bed at, like, eight."

Em didn't blame her. She would have slept through the darkness, if she could have.

The door was heavy, old, and squeaky, and the foyer was dim. Em didn't know how Skylar could stand living here—not after what she'd been through and seen. The very first thing Em saw when she entered was a long ivory-colored robe. It was just hanging there on a coat tree in the foyer. Gossamer and gauzy, billowing in the gust of wind they'd created just by coming in the door.

What had Crow said? *A robe—long and white and flowing.*

She pointed at it shakily, letting the door close behind her. "What's that?"

"That?" Skylar asked as she shrugged off her coat and hung it on a hook. "That's my costume for the play." She walked over and took it off its hanger. "I have to remember to bring it to dress rehearsal tomorrow." When she held it up to her body, it practically engulfed her. Its creases and shimmering ripples had the odd effect of mimicking Skylar's still-healing face. It probably looked incredible under the stage lights. Em wondered if Gabby was planning to put makeup on Skylar's scars. . . .

No. It couldn't be. Em stood there dumbstruck. The robe . . . the striped scars . . . This was her—the tiger-faced woman.

"Skylar," she said nervously, trying to recall the rest of Crow's vision, "have you ever heard the phrase, 'Someone is plotting vengeance'?"

"Of course," Skylar replied. Her voice got slightly deeper.

"'For this I declare—someone is plotting vengeance.' It's one of Cassandra's lines in the play."

"The play . . ." Em could barely speak. "When does the play start?" Em asked.

Skylar nodded. "Tuesday night—one night only. Just a reading. Do you want some water or tea or something?"

Tuesday. Three days away. Crow had seen Em consumed by fire just after hearing those words. Was it possible that Crow's vision did mean something? That it meant a *when*, a final date when Em's transformation would be complete? If so, Em would die in three days. She would be swallowed into the Fury world after Skylar's play on Tuesday night.

A pounding drumbeat began to thunder through her body. She hadn't taken one step since they'd been in Skylar's house; she knew Skylar had asked her a question but she couldn't remember what it was.

"Are—are you okay?" Skylar reached out tentatively to touch her arm.

Em's head felt uncomfortably light, and there were flashbulbs popping in her peripheral vision. She thought she might faint. And then, a momentary distraction—Em heard a faint, tuneless humming coming from another part of the house. She looked at Skylar, whose mouth was set in a grim line.

"What's that?" Em asked. "I thought you said your aunt was asleep."

Skylar opened and closed her mouth twice without saying anything. Then she said flatly, "It's . . . my sister."

"Your *sister*? I thought you were an only child." Back when Skylar was following Gabby everywhere like a lost puppy, she'd never once mentioned a sister. The humming started again, and Em sensed it was coming from upstairs. All of a sudden this place seemed more like a haunted house than ever before. She took a step or two away from the staircase, toward the hallway that led to the kitchen.

"Well, I'm not," Skylar snapped. "And she's none of your business."

Em caught the thread of a few words. She *wasn't* just humming. The girl was saying something that Em could hear only faintly. If she listened closely, she could even pick out a word here and there.

They'll never stop, she heard. *She's here.*

"I'm sorry," Em said. "I didn't mean to pry."

"It's fine. She's just . . . She's visiting, and she's sick, and I'm not used to talking about her." Skylar looked anxiously toward the stairs. The barely intelligible monologue continued from somewhere on the second floor.

"She's sick?" Em felt the strangest sensation that the girl was talking *to* her. The words she could hear stayed stuck in her head like wisps of cotton candy on a child's fingers. It was sticky-sweet and unsettling. Hypnotic even.

"It's brain damage. From a fall . . ." Skylar's fragile voice broke through the spell and pulled Em back.

"Oh."

"And it was my fault," Skylar's continued. She was shaking. "Her name is Lucy, and it's my fault she's like this."

So that's your mistake. Em turned to look at Skylar. She looked so young. And so sorry. That more than anything else.

"Is that why the Furies came after you?" Em asked. Skylar had babbled something along these lines when Em visited her in the hospital after her accident, but this was the first time she'd truly come clean.

Skylar was shaking. She opened her mouth and then closed it again. Then she nodded. "And they made me . . . They brought out the worst in me," Skylar whispered. "You would hate me if you knew."

"It's okay," Em said. The truth was, Em didn't care about the nitty-gritty of Skylar's mistakes—not as much as she wanted the key to saving her own soul. "We all make mistakes." *And some pay for them more than others.*

She could still hear strains of Lucy's babbling. God, it was creepy, yet melodic and relaxing. Em had to fight competing urges to run up the stairs or out the door. *Everyone wants to be good,* Em heard her say.

"Can I talk to her?" Em said suddenly. She knew it was forward, but there was something about that voice. Those words.

Skylar looked at Em suspiciously. "You want to meet her?"

"If it's okay with you," Em said, but she was already moving toward the stairs.

"Okay," Skylar relented. "But we have to be quiet. I don't want Aunt Nora to wake up." She motioned for Em to follow her up the creaky wooden steps, closer and closer to the singsong tune that emanated from behind a wooden door on the second floor.

The noise continued, high-pitched and repetitive, like a music box that refused to unwind. Em heard snippets of words; they seemed to be luring her forward. The song was somehow familiar, like a lullaby Em would have heard when she was little. And the way Skylar was reacting to the sound—all jittery, clearing her throat over and over—it made Em very nervous.

Skylar stopped for a moment in the hall. She took a deep breath, then swung open the door.

A girl was sitting on the floor in front of a full-length mirror. She had high cheekbones and she was thin, almost wiry. Her arms reminded Em of something you might see in a museum: all sinew and ropy muscle. Em could tell she used to be pretty, but it was hard to see her as such now. A prominent scar ran along her hairline. Her forehead was pale and sheened with sweat, even though it was cold in the house. Her dirty-blond hair, the same shade as Skylar's, was uncombed. She was in the process of applying maroon lipstick shakily across her lips.

She made piercing eye contact with Em in the mirror and stopped humming immediately.

"Hi, Sky," the girl said happily. "Want to try this new color I found?" She held up the tube of lipstick.

Skylar swallowed and offered a strained smile, obviously trying to regain her composure. "Lucy, this is my friend Emily," she then said, taking an unsteady step forward. She gestured for Em to follow her. The room was clearly an office that had been converted into a makeshift bedroom. An old computer and a jumble of wires and electrical equipment were heaped in the corner beyond the bed. It was small and musty and smelled, to Em, like ink cartridges.

Lucy continued to primp. Her eyes seemed to be locked into a wide stare.

"Lucy?" Skylar ventured.

"Yes?" Lucy turned around slowly, with an expression somewhere between confused and content. Then she smiled, like she was remembering a line from a script. "It's nice to meet you, Emily."

"You too," Em said. She wished Lucy would start mumbling again, now that she was close enough to catch every word.

But Skylar's sister seemed suddenly shy. She mashed her lips together, rubbing the redness into the skin around her mouth.

Skylar shrugged apologetically. "Sometimes she doesn't really say much," she offered.

"That's okay," Em said. Outside Lucy's window, the night was dark and starless. "What color is that, Lucy?" She moved closer, hoping to make the girl more comfortable.

Lucy turned it over to check, and as she did, her whole body stiffened. Without warning, she threw the lipstick away from her; when it hit the wall near Em and Skylar it left a sharp red smear on the wall.

"Lucy! What are you doing? Why did you do that?" Skylar shrieked, going to her sister, who had begun to rock softly back and forth.

"I'm sorry, Sky," she said, drooping into Skylar's arms. They won't leave me alone. Even the lipstick . . ." A single tear ran down her face, and when she swatted at it, she smudged her makeup.

Skylar stroked her hair. "Shhhh," she said. "Shhhh."

Something in Lucy's tone made Em's blood run cold. Made her want to listen more closely. She bent to pick up the tube, which had landed near her feet. When she turned in over, there was a little white sticker on the bottom of the silver tube.

DEEP ORCHID, it read. Em stiffened, resisting the urge to throw it across the room just as Lucy had. The color of the lipstick was Deep Orchid.

"Skylar . . ." Em started to say. But Lucy began talking again.

"The mouth . . . of the albino," she said, clearly finding it increasingly difficult to catch her breath. "It's the only way . . . to undo it."

Undo it. It couldn't be. . . . Did Lucy know something about the Furies? Was she one of the unlucky "patients" whom Em had read about, whose damaged minds made them susceptible to the Furies' evil ramblings?

"Undo what?" Em said. She moved into a squat. Skylar glared at her, clearly wanting the interrogation to end, but Em ignored her. Her heart was beating very fast. "What do you mean, the albino?"

"It's purity," Lucy said. "Clean slate. Purity. Clean slate. Purity. Clean—" The words gave Em goose bumps from her scalp to her legs.

"Okay, we hear you, Luce," Skylar said. Her eyes were wide with anguish.

"She knows about the Furies," Em said aloud. "She hears them."

"Ever since the accident, she gets riled up and I can't calm her down." Skylar shook her head, on the verge of tears. "You're right. She somehow knows about them. Will ramble about them for hours, then just stop. Like a switch has been flipped in her brain. But nothing she says makes any sense. You have to believe me. I didn't mean—I didn't want this to happen."

"I believe you," Em said quietly.

So the Furies brought this on too, Em thought. Em remembered the passage in her book about how sometimes the brain was damaged in such a way as to make patients "open" to the voices of the Furies. *They hear the Furies' chatter, but they cannot channel it. Unlike prophets, these troubled souls have no direct links to the Furies' energy. They are merely exposed to it and tormented by it.* Em had wondered many times whether this was her punishment, her terrible fate: to be driven mad by the Furies. But now she knew that *her* punishment would be even worse.

The albino—what did that mean? Who was she referring to? Em's breath came tight and fast. Whiteness. Purity. A clean slate, as Lucy had said. She tried to stay calm, even as a soaring sensation of hope fluttered through her chest.

Nora had said there might be a way to reverse it. A way to banish them. Something about purity.

Was there really some way to make the Furies think that their job here was done?

CHAPTER FIFTEEN

The early morning light shone hazily on the AHS athletic field, where the girls' field hockey team was warming up on Sunday morning. JD made his way toward the bleachers, expecting to see Walt Feiffer's pinched face staring back at him from the metal seats. As he climbed up the steps, he took in the expansive field, the smell of freshly cut grass and dew, and the sound of wooden sticks clacking against each other.

JD settled into a spot near the announcer's booth, where he could see both entrances and wait for Walt to arrive. He had a view of the school, up on a small hill just to the east of the field.

It felt surreal that this could be JD's life. It was like a film he'd once loved as a kid, but as he watched it now, everything felt forced—the script, the dialogue, the settings. As if everything he'd understood about the film no longer connected to the person he now was. Sitting there, feeling the cold metal through his jeans and overlooking the whole of his high school campus, JD thought about Chase and Zach, and how jealous he had been of that whole crowd. Of their clichéd high school experience, of the effortlessness with which it all came. He used to think he'd have to do something really freaking amazing in order to win Em's heart. To stand out amid all that perfect normalcy.

But now, here he was—waiting to meet Walt Feiffer, who still hadn't showed. And he was doing it *for* Em. To save her. All that crap from before . . . how he'd felt passed over. It was meaningless now. He could barely remember what it felt like to be that guy.

He rubbed his arms against his thick canvas jacket and checked his phone. 8:20. Drea's dad was twenty minutes late. There was no answer when JD tried calling the Feiffers' landline.

A whistle blast pierced the air and the field hockey girls moved from warm-ups into drills. The sun rose higher in the sky and JD stood up, craning his neck and wondering if he should go back out to the parking lot to look for Walt. Had he misunderstood their plan?

Mr. Feiffer had been drunk at both the funeral and his house. Had he drunk too much last night and passed out? There was a decent chance he had forgotten all about their meeting.

No, that didn't make sense—Walt was the one to have suggested the meeting in the first place, and now he was almost half an hour late. JD tried calling Drea's home phone again. Nothing. He had a bad, bad feeling. His boots clanged against the metal as he jogged back down to the parking lot. Seeing no sign of Walt, JD made the split-second decision to pay the Feiffers' a visit. He needed to hear what Drea's dad had to say.

The feeling of unease only got worse as he drove up to the Feiffers' house, his heart hammering in his chest. The place had seemed run-down yesterday, but when JD pulled into the driveway it looked as though it was on the verge of collapse. No one answered when he rang the bell (though he hadn't expected anyone to), and when he leaned over the stoop railing to peer into the front window, he didn't see any signs of life. Everything was still. Lifeless.

A sense of foreboding flickered in JD's stomach. The front door was locked, so he made his way around to the back door, which swung open. There was no sound in the kitchen except the faint buzzing of an invisible fly.

He knew instinctively that it was useless to call out, but he did anyway. An itching sense of fear tremored through his whole body. "Mr. Feiffer?" There was no one here. Nothing. No response.

Except for a sudden, loud, shattering *crash* just to JD's left. He jumped; his neck stung from twisting it so hard and so fast.

Jesus.

But it was nothing. A plate, slipping from the top of a pile of dishes in the sink and breaking into a hundred pieces on the Feiffers' tile kitchen floor.

His hands were sweating. He palmed them on the back of his jeans. JD moved through the kitchen, conscious of the tiny sounds his sneakers made on the squeaky linoleum. Just before he crossed into the living room, he grabbed a frying pan off the counter. Just in case.

"Mr. Feiffer?" he said again, pushing through the door onto the matted carpeting. Every hair on his body stood up straight.

The smell hit him first. Stale. Not yet rancid, but something like a trash can—like coffee grounds and wet newspapers and a dog's breath mixed together. He gagged, brought his hand to his nose.

Oh god. The reeking odor of the place was making him delirious as he stepped cautiously down the hallway—he almost thought he heard the distant sound of shrill laughter. He tightened his grip of the handle of the frying pan.

Another step.

Another.

"Mr. Feiffer?" he tried one last time. "Are you—"

But the words were ripped from his throat.

Because there was Walt Feiffer.

Sitting upright in his recliner. Eyes open, but unseeing. His face red and twisted and completely frozen. Pinned to his shirt, right above his heart, was a red orchid.

"Oh shit. Oh my god, oh shit, Mr. Feiffer, oh god." JD's voice sounded wild and strangled even to his own ears.

Walt Feiffer was dead.

JD stumbled backward into the hall, his legs like heavy blocks he had no control over. And then a wave of dizziness hit him and he hunched over, gagging. He was on his knees now. His face was burning from the feeling of having to puke or cry or in some way get what he had just seen *out*.

Another one dead.

He heaved, trying to catch his breath in the wretched air.

Slowly, his breath started to get to normal. He tried to steady his mind. *What do I do what do I do what do I do . . .*

Call the cops. Of course. Of course.

Unable to take his eyes off the body in front of him, he called 911. It seemed to take forever for someone to pick up.

"I'm calling to report . . . a man. A dead man." JD ran a hand through his hair. "Sixty-one Hanover Way . . . Yes, I'm certain he's dead. . . . Yes, I'll stay here."

He hung up and headed down the hall toward the front door, avoiding the living room entrance. Just then, a figure—in the window. There. Someone's face. He could have sworn he'd just seen eyes, shining against the glass.

Had Mr. Feiffer been murdered? Was the killer still here?

"Get out of here," he told himself. "Get the hell away."

But he knew deep in his blood. He knew what kind of killing this was.

This was the work of the Furies.

There was no longer any doubt: The Furies were real, and they had done this. That awful red flower bloomed just next to Mr. Feiffer's heart, like an enormous spot of blood.

He'd missed his chance.

Mr. Feiffer was gone. And with him, JD's chance of learning about the banishment ritual.

Drea was gone.

There was a good chance that Em, too, would soon leave him. Gone.

He had to talk to her. Had to find out who—or what—was doing this.

JD stumbled to the front door and opened it, taking deep, grateful breaths of fresh air. He collapsed to a seated position on the stoop.

It wasn't until the police cruiser pulled up that he started to think about what he would say to them. JD stood up and steadied himself.

"Drea Feiffer, Walt's daughter, was a friend of mine," he told them when they asked. "I've been visiting Walt now and then. Just checking in. He's been having a tough time. When I came by today . . . this is what I found."

"Had he seemed different to you at all recently?" A female officer named Breton was talking to him while her associates milled around inside.

JD stared at her. "His *daughter* just died. Yeah. He seemed different."

She blinked. "So . . . changes of mood? Appetite?"

JD exhaled. "I don't know. I didn't really know him that well."

"And did he seem depressed?" she persisted.

It occurred to him that the police must suspect he'd committed suicide. But how? By suffocating himself? There were no marks on his body—that, JD had seen. It was almost like he'd been . . . scared to death.

But what could JD say to convince them differently? *He'd mentioned something about mythological goddesses who really had it in for him. . . .* Not so much.

"I saw him yesterday," JD said, hearing his voice get thinner with anxiety. "He was fine. . . . He was *alive*."

"Uh-huh." She scribbled a few notes. "Well, we'll keep looking. Let us know if you think of anything that might help. Did you notice anything strange about the house when you arrived?"

He shook his head. "Not really. . . . The front door was locked and the back door was open, but that's not too weird." Should he mention the flower? Should he mention the Furies? Should he tell the cops that he suspected this was a homicide? That this death—and several others—were all connected to the same three girls, and that he knew how to find them?

"Well, we're going to try to find Walt's next of kin and do some investigating on our own," Breton said. "But we'll probably call you down to the station for a more official statement sometime in the next day or so. In the meantime, get yourself home."

Before he left, JD stole one last look at Drea's father. *I'm sorry,* he thought. *I'm sorry I didn't come sooner.*

He parked in a short gravel driveway right by the Behemoth, off Silver Way. His hands were still shaking. For the first time in his whole life, he almost wished he was a smoker. He could use a cigarette.

As he opened the car door and stepped into the gravel-dust-filled air, he tried not to think of the last time he was here, but his hand involuntarily went to the scar above his eyebrow.

Why had the Furies killed Walt Feiffer? Was this a vendetta against Drea's whole family? He wanted answers, and he was going to find them in the only place he could think to look.

Melissa had said Ty's house was back here in the Haunted Woods.

The gray-red sunlight was waning; twilight would be falling soon. The woods were deep and after a minute or two, he could no longer see the Volvo when he turned back in the direction from which he'd come. He popped the collar on his jacket and continued walking.

He'd gone maybe a mile in—around a cluster of birch trees and over a fallen oak—when he saw something moving in his peripheral vision. He whipped around . . . but there was nothing there. Just thick, heavy trees, practically dripping with fog.

Another few steps, another fleeting shadow out of the corner of his eye. His skin prickled. But it was another false alarm. It was just him, alone, in this dark labyrinth of forest. JD stood still for a moment, listening. The rustling around him became a cacophony—insects, leaves, wind, and birds—a marching band with an indecipherable beat.

And then *bam*, just like that, Ty was right there, right in front of him.

A twist of fear seized him; he willed himself to stay calm. Where had she come from?

"Well, well," she said, stepping over a mossy log. Her thigh-high boots, black leggings, and silver tunic were incongruous against the natural backdrop. She looked more like Em than ever, and yet there was something *not-Em* about her, something hard and superficial. "I didn't know if I'd ever see you again."

Could they read minds? Had she already figured him out?

"I, ah, I asked Melissa where your house was," he said sheepishly. "Thought maybe we could hang out tonight."

"Lucky me," Ty said brightly, smiling her polished smile.

"And lucky *you*. No one wants to get lost in these woods. Trust me. Want to come in for a bit? I can show you, we found these crazy old maps of how the town used to look. . . ."

He squeezed his eyes shut for a second, blinking hard to clear a feeling like honey that was entering his consciousness. Despite himself, he was drawn to her. *Remember why you're here,* he reminded himself. *For answers.*

He nodded and began to follow her along a path covered in dead and decomposing leaves. JD tried to pay attention to details along the way; he might need to come back here. A left at the craggy oak tree, the one with a disc of fungus growing out its side. Slight right after the huge rock covered in a carpet of deep-green moss.

His heart rate picked up as the house appeared suddenly before them, in a clearing that JD could have sworn he'd passed through on his way to the ice pond where Mr. Landon died. Except the other day, it had been empty. Well, almost empty. There had been three ancient stone markers in the center of it, and dry grasses rustling at the edges. Now, however, he faced a big, old, decaying house with a clapboard roof, a house that had history in every nail, in every brown shingle. It was boxy and big, with a stone chimney and black shutters framing the windows. It stood tall with energy—like it was somehow alive. Granite slabs lined the walkway to the front door, which was adorned with an ornate gold door knocker.

"Here we are," Ty said. "Home sweet home." Her voice was a sing-song but had a cutting edge to it, like syrup poured over a knife.

Inside, the whole place smelled of flowers. Cloying, sweet, and overpowering—like one of those girls who poured a bottle of perfume on herself before leaving the house.

Ty showed them into a living room filled with Victorian furniture. The color scheme was oppressive—all reds and maroons and browns. JD stood stiffly, not sure where to look, where to sit, or what to say. There was a feeling that all this stuff was frozen in time—that to sit down would mean getting stuck in another era. This place was sucking the air right out of his lungs.

"I'm not sure if Ali told you, but this place used to be in our family," Ty explained. "All this stuff isn't quite our style."

"It's incredible," he said, just to stay something. He had to get her out of here. Had to look around. For what, he wasn't sure. "Could I have a glass of water?"

"Of course." Ty laughed. "What a terrible hostess I am. I'll be back in a minute. I'll get us something to drink and I'll dig up those maps I told you about."

JD watched her walk down the hallway. When she came back he would ask her again how she knew Drea. Why she was at the funeral. Whether she'd ever met Drea's dad. He was going to force her to show her hand.

He moved over to a large bookcase that stood near the bay

window in the front of the house. It was filled with leather-bound tomes and glass-encased knickknacks. A curvy hourglass lay on its side on one of the shelves, its white sand forever suspended. Next to the bookcase, a gargoyle bust. Then a floor-to-ceiling window that looked into a giant backyard garden bursting with those hideous crimson orchids. Against the barely blooming branches of early spring, the flowers looked out of place and foreign. Just like these girls in Ascension. JD thought back to Mr. Feiffer's words: *It must finish where it began.*

He moved through the room slowly, feeling as though he were swimming through something thick and dark.

Next to the window, tucked away in a back corner, there was a small display case with several items on a swath of red velvet.

He stooped to get a closer look, trying to understand why these seemingly ordinary items were being showcased. A worn copy of Shakespeare's *Othello* with the initials *H. L.* inscribed on the cover. An earring, simple and silver, sitting on top of a ripped piece of paper, one marked by heavy charcoal smears. Two small pink oyster shells. A tin of Altoids. A stamped envelope. A patch, meant to be sewn to a backpack or a jacket, in the shape of a football. JD was so close that his breath fogged up the glass. He paused for a moment, listening for footsteps in the hall. Nothing. The house was eerily silent, every room cloaked in soundproof sheets of velvet.

There seemed to be hundreds of items in the case, but the

next one on this shelf made his breath catch in his throat. He would have recognized it anywhere. A gold squiggling-snake brooch. Where its eyes should be, two tiny pieces of red stone. He'd seen it hundreds of times—pinned to Drea Feiffer's clothes.

He shrank back from the case, his mind racing, certain now that he was in a bad place—that this house, and its inhabitants, were evil. It was all starting to make sense. The football—Chase Singer. The charcoal drawing—Sasha Bowlder. The pin—Drea. Now that he thought about it, he wouldn't be surprised if that copy of *Othello* was connected to Mr. Landon. JD's blood went cold. What was he looking at? Prizes? Trophies?

Pieces for some kind of demented scrapbook?

These girls were the killers. JD steadied himself against the mantel above the fireplace, trying to get his thoughts to come one at a time, rather than all at once. The current was fast and there was no jumping to shore.

Before he turned away, another item in the case caught his eye. Up in the right-hand corner was a pen. Not just any pen. The fancy one, embellished with silver swirls, that he'd given to Em as a gift two Christmases ago. It was the kind of pen you kept—refilling it with ink when it ran dry, using it only to write down your most important secrets. He remembered how she'd looked at him when she opened the box on Christmas morning, still wearing her striped pajamas.

This is for a real writer, she'd said, her eyes glowing shyly.

239

That's why you should have it, he'd responded.

And there it was, lying lost in the Furies' case of terrible triumphs. He balled his hand into a fist and raised it high above his head, compelled to smash the glass, retrieve the pen, and get the hell out of this haunted house.

Suddenly, Ali appeared right next to him, close enough to make his arm hairs prickle. "I wouldn't do that if I were you."

He stumbled backward, knowing that his face betrayed a look of both shock and fear. JD tried desperately to appear unfazed. "Hi! I, ah, didn't know you were here. I was just . . ." He trailed off, unable to come up with an excuse.

"I heard you two come in," she said, smiling coyly. "I thought I'd come say hello. I've got to keep a pretty close watch on her these days."

On Ty? *Me too,* he thought.

"Yeah, I ran into Ty out there in the woods. . . . She's just in the kitchen," JD said, pointing vaguely. "I think." His mind was racing. Should he excuse himself and make a break for it? Being here with Ty and these trophies was bad enough. Now he had two of them to deal with? And what if Meg was home too . . . ? There was a seesaw tipping back and forth in his stomach, and JD felt vaguely seasick.

Ali's eyes narrowed. Her lashes and eyebrows were so light that her eyes appeared as pricks of black on a white canvas. The room hung with silence as heavy as the drapes. "You know, you should be careful," she came right out and said at last. "If Ty's paying attention to you, that means she wants something. And when she wants something, it's never good."

A wave of cold broke over him. "What does that mean?" He wondered if he should say something about the trophies, call her out on being connected to the murders, or simply run.

"It's a warning," Ali said. "If things don't go according to plan, it'll be worse for everyone."

"Well, I don't know what the *plan* is," he said. "In case you hadn't noticed, I'm a little late to this party."

She smiled brightly. "And it's been such a fun one. . . ." Then her face clouded over slightly. "Until Ty got carried away. She doesn't understand. We're family. We're supposed to stay together. . . ." She trailed off and looked past JD at the trophy case.

"She doesn't understand what?" JD asked. He knew he should leave, but he needed answers. His frustration and fear were mounting, and he felt like he might bubble over at any second. If there had been something to throw, he would have, then. He wanted to break something. To see it shatter into a million pieces.

"Well, I can't tell you *that*," Ali said. "We have a lot of secrets. I just want to make sure no one was spilling them." She looked pointedly toward the kitchen.

"I know your secrets," JD bluffed.

Another tinkling laugh. "Oh, no you don't," she taunted. She sidled right up next to him and whispered the next bit into his ear, making him shrink away. "If you did, the past few months would have been *very* different. In fact, someone's been keeping secrets from *you*."

She was like a cat, batting him back and forth between her paws. He was at her mercy. His brain might as well have been rattling in his skull. "I don't know what you're talking about," he said tonelessly. But he desperately wanted to know.

"Aw, that hit on the head must have confused you," Ali cooed, reaching up to trace a finger along the scar on his forehead.

It felt like a hot poker being dragged across his skin. He jerked away. "What do you know about that?"

Ali tossed her hair over one shoulder and reached a pointy fingernail up to tap her lips in an exaggerated expression of thought. "I seem to remember a construction site . . . a pipe . . . a *terrible* accident . . . and a girl who was so in love that she did whatever we asked her to do in order to save you."

The seeds. Em. That night at the Behemoth.

He'd had it all wrong.

Em. *Oh god, Em.*

"So all that stuff about Crow . . ." JD trailed off, recalling how convinced he'd been that he'd seen her kissing Crow at the construction site. How he'd believed Crow was the one responsible for knocking him out. Now, in a flash, he knew otherwise. It wasn't Crow—it never had been. It had been the Furies all along. They'd tricked him. Possibly even messed with his mind somehow.

"We like telling stories," Ali said with a shrug. "And we're pretty good at it, huh?"

The sensation of cold gripped JD even tighter. "Leave us alone," he said, inching sideways toward the front door. "Leave us the *hell* alone. What are we, some sort of sick little game to you?"

"A game? Hardly. You know as well as anyone that this is *dead* serious," she said. With that, she stepped aside with a flourish, gesturing to the foyer. "Now get out, before Ty gets any more ideas."

He didn't wait for her to change her mind.

CHAPTER SIXTEEN

I wade waist-deep into a red sea. Above me, the moon cuts the sky with its sharp sliver. . . . Is the sky bleeding? Is this blood I'm marching through? No. Not blood, not sea . . . flowers. Swaying their scarlet petals. Tiny seeds eyeing me. Elegant stems reaching upward. A sharp sweetness all around me. A whole garden of them around my ankles, like children pressing toward their mother. I can feel their cool breath. Exhaling. They are alive. They are evil.

Em was swimming somewhere between the darkness of dreaming and the clarity of wakefulness.

I know this place, I know this hunger. I'm looking for something, something . . . What is it? I stumble through the sea of red, suffocating in its power. Dizzy. My whole body shaking.

Evil. Evil is everywhere. This is my last chance.

"Fire!" someone yells. "Fire!"

Suddenly all the flowers are on fire. The garden has burst into flames in front of me. The air is yawning with smoke and I am no longer alone. It is hot, hotter than hell. Hotter than . . .

"Fire!"

The sounds become more and more frantic. The yelling, the sensation of being choked by smoke and heat. The moon is raining fire. A high-pitched wailing, deafeningly loud . . .

Then, hands were on her—on her shoulders, shaking her fully awake. Someone was screaming.

"Emily! Wake up! Emily! Fire!"

She looked fuzzy-eyed into her mother's face, etched with worry and fear, yelling into her ear as she tugged Em from her bed. The wailing pierced her ears and the smoke made her eyes water. She coughed, feeling the air come up raw through her throat. Was this it? Was the transformation happening already? Was she dying?

Panic tore through Em's body and she snapped wide-awake, tingling with fever. She sat up, breathing hard, letting her mom pull her across the room.

"There's a fire, Em—we've got to get out," her mom said as they made their way down the hallway, which was slowly filling with smoke, coiling like dark snakes.

The fire was real. In her house. That was a fire alarm she was hearing. That was real smoke she was breathing in. It was sticking

ELIZABETH MILES

to her. To her face, to her skin, to her sweatpants and tank top. This was real.

Fire.

"Come on! Get out!" Em's dad met them at the bottom of the stairs, wild with panic. "Susan! Grab her!"

And just as Em and her mother slipped out the front door, she saw flames licking around the corner of the kitchen door.

Out on the lawn, the fresh air bit cleanly against her lungs. She gulped it down gratefully. It was damp and surprisingly humid outside; it contrasted with the dry smoke inside she had just escaped. She followed her parents to the shelter of the oak tree near the end of the driveway and turned to survey the scene. Here, the wailing was even louder. Two fire trucks were already zooming down the street, screeching to a halt in front of the house.

Seeing them reminded Em of Spring Fling, of Drea's death, and made her stomach turn in terror. She crouched down, feeling too unsteady to stand up straight.

Her mom kneeled beside her and rubbed her back. "Are you okay?"

"Yes," she said. She cleared her throat. "Yes," she said again, a little louder.

There it was the slipping, desperate sensation then—she'd woken from a dream and felt it instantly fading into the backstage of her consciousness. She squeezed her eyes open and shut as if she could seal in the memory.

246

In a trance, she watched the firefighters, heavy with gear, run toward the house with thick hoses. She watched her father put his arm around her mom and lead her across the grass. Watched the Founts, all four of them, come flowing out of their house. Watched JD scan the crowd and stop when his eyes fell on her. Watched the police car pull up behind the firemen and start asking her parents questions.

She saw it all, but couldn't process it.

Her house was on fire. She could barely see any flames from her vantage point, but she could see smoke billowing off of it like steam rising from a teakettle.

There was movement on the side of the house and Em turned, expecting to see another firefighter emerge from the bushes. But it wasn't a man in uniform who rounded the corner.

It was Crow, unmistakably—wearing a leather jacket and beat-up jeans—stumbling toward her. Ignoring the quizzical looks that followed him as he crossed the lawn, he came straight to her.

She stood up to meet him.

"You're not hurt," he said.

"I'm fine."

He swept her into a hug, and she didn't resist. She felt like a spectator, standing outside herself.

"I had another vision," he whispered into her hair, and now she could smell the alcohol—whiskey, or maybe rum. "I saw smoke. . . . I had to come here."

She pushed away, fully seeing what was happening from the outside. "Why are you here?"

"I told you," he said, annoyed at having to repeat himself. "I saw this. I came." Once again, she smelled alcohol on his breath. Beer.

"Hey—hey you." A police officer approached. Em prayed he wouldn't come too close.

Crow disengaged and turned to face the officer. "What?"

The police officer was staring at him suspiciously. "What's your name, kid?"

"Colin," Crow answered, shoving his hands into the pockets of his jacket. "I'm—I'm a friend."

The officer, whose brass nametag read D. GOUDREAU, glanced to Em for confirmation.

She nodded, still in a daze. "It's true," she said. *Please cooperate,* she begged Crow in her mind. *Please don't make things worse.*

"And why are you here?" Goudreau's pencil was poised above a small notebook. Em's senses started to kick back in, one by one. The air was tinged with the chemical scent of firefighting foam mixed with acrid smoke.

"I was—I was just dropping by," Crow stuttered. They all heard how feeble the excuse sounded. Em shifted uncomfortably from one foot to the other, feeling the night breeze whisper along her bare arms.

"You two boyfriend and girlfriend?" Goudreau asked.

Em sensed eyes on her; she looked up to see her parents staring at her and Crow from where they were standing in a clump with the Founts.

"No," she said quickly. "Nothing like that."

"Uh-huh?" The cop wrote something down in his little book, seemingly unconvinced.

"No, sir," Crow said, speaking in a clipped tone Em had never heard come out of his mouth. "We're just friends, and I was just coming over because . . . just to visit."

The officer looked Crow up and down. "You were coming over in the middle of the night? Strange timing, huh?"

It *was* strange timing, that much was true. Em didn't want to consider the implications of what Goudreau was implying.

"What do you mean?" Crow's eyes narrowed.

"Just what I said. It's a pretty good coincidence that you *stopped by* while there was a fire going on."

"Look, you want to accuse me of something?" Crow took a menacing step forward.

"Crow, stop," Em said, putting a hand on his arm. A snap of electricity went through her fingers. "Officer, Crow—Colin, I mean—Colin is just my friend. And he stopped by. That's all."

Mr. Winters appeared behind them. "Is everything all right here?"

"I'm just trying to figure out why this *friend* of your daughter's is skulking around in your yard in the middle of the night,"

Officer Goudreau said. "Right before a fire almost takes down your whole house. Reeking like he just came from Eddie's Tavern."

"Well, I think the morning is as good a time as any to figure that out," Em's dad said, giving Crow a quick—and disapproving—glance. "I think we'd all like to go inside and warm up. Our neighbors have offered us their guest room for the night."

Em turned to see her mom walking in the Founts' front door, looking curiously in their direction.

But Crow wanted to have the last word. "Sorry to disappoint, *Officer*," Crow sneered. "But I wasn't at Eddie's. But maybe you just came from there yourself?"

Goudreau reared his head, pissed off. "Don't mess with me, boy," he said.

"How about you not call me 'boy'?" Crow countered. As he spoke, he pitched slightly to the left, like he'd been pushed by an invisible force.

Em's father cleared his throat and Em dropped her head, mortified and angry. Why did Crow do this all the time? She wanted to slap it out of him—and pray he'd just shut the hell up.

"These goddamn kids," Goudreau said, more to Em's dad than to anyone else. Then, to Crow: "I'll be in touch." He stalked off into the night.

Once he'd gone, they made an odd, awkward trio—Em, her dad, and Crow, standing silently on the lawn. Firefighters milled around the yard, shouting to one another and trudging back and forth between their trucks and the house.

"Well, the fire seems to be out," Mr. Winters said. "Didn't get upstairs, thank god. Just the kitchen and the laundry room, mostly. Dryer lint, they said."

"That's lucky," Crow said. His voice was back to normal—slow, disinterested, and slightly slurred. He nodded quickly at Em and her dad, barely lifting his eyes from the ground. "Sorry for the trouble, Emily. You too, sir. See you soon." Without another word, turned to leave. She was terrified he'd find more trouble tonight. Was he driving? What if he just wandered off to find another fight?

"I'm not even going to ask, Emily," her father said as they watched Crow stumbling across their front yard toward the street. She felt like he was spiraling away from her, and had the powerful sense that she was on the brink of losing him to something terrible. The darkness was eating away at him; it was obvious. And Em couldn't help but feel it was her fault. If she'd managed to get rid of the Furies, maybe he'd be getting better instead of worse.

"There's been enough excitement tonight," her dad went on, putting his arm around her shoulders and leading her toward JD's house. She stole one final look behind her, but Crow had already been enveloped by the shadows of the woods.

The adrenaline was wearing off slowly. Inside, Mrs. Fount

fluttered around the kitchen, making tea and clucking about *the terrible luck*. JD, in sweatpants and a cardigan, had hopped up to sit on the kitchen counter. Em leaned in the doorway and tried to avoid eye contact with him, which was next to impossible. Every time she looked up, he was staring at her—and every time, she shifted her eyes away immediately.

She couldn't get the visions from her dream out of her mind. How realistic they'd been—the flames, the smoke, the sense of panic.

"Thank you so much for the hospitality," Em's mom said. "We won't really be able to assess the damage until tomorrow."

"Don't mention it, Sue," JD's dad said, coming into the kitchen with a pile of extra linens in his arms. "I'll set up the guest room for you two down here. Em, Mel's already gone back to bed, but you can have JD's room."

"Oh no, that's fine," she said hurriedly. "I'll be fine down here on the couch." No way was she going to boot JD out of his own bedroom. No way was she going to fall asleep on his sheets while he sat down here, probably hating her. No way in hell.

"I already set things up for myself down here," JD said, cocking his head toward the den. "You look exhausted. You'll get a better night's sleep upstairs."

She was too tired even to be offended by the fact that he said she looked tired. Of course that didn't mean she would be able to sleep. But at least she could lie down and think. For the first time that night, she allowed herself look him straight in the eyes. "Thank you," she said. "I think I'll head up now, actually."

JD jumped off the counter. "I'll make sure you have everything you need."

Once they were out of earshot, Em turned to him and said in a low voice: "You don't have to do this. I'm fine."

He kept following her, up the stairs and into his bedroom. "We need to talk," he said, closing the door behind him. "I'm glad you're okay. But now that I've got you here, there are some questions I need you to answer. Not about the fire."

"Does it have to be right now?" Em's voice was trembling. "I'm so tired—I've been dealing with so much. . . ."

"Yes," he said, pushing his glasses up his nose. "I've noticed." The way he looked right now . . . so focused, so concerned. It made her want to burrow into his arms and stay there forever. "And I think I know what's been going on."

No, you don't, she thought. *You can't.*

"But I want you to tell me," he said.

She sat on the bed with a thud. "What do you mean?" She looked down at her hands.

"You've been keeping things from me. Big things." He stood in front of her and took her face in his hands. They were bigger than she would have thought they'd be; his fingers spanned the length of her cheek. He smelled like something spicy. Like

Christmas. She couldn't take it. His kindness. His hands. How good it felt to sit in his room.

The tears rolled up her throat like a bowling ball coming full-force toward its pins. She clapped her hand over her mouth to stifle a sob. Hot tears began to fall from her eyes. *Yes.* She nodded wordlessly. *Yes.* She leaned over against the pillows, cries smashing through her body. Her body curled in an effort to control the spasms that shook through her.

He sat down next to her. She felt his warmth. When he placed his hand on her shoulder, soothing her, stroking her, it was like her skin was melting beneath his touch.

What did he know? What *big things* was he referring to? Was he in trouble? How long would she be able to lie straight to his face?

She wanted to ask. But the tears—and the deception—were so exhausting, they were taking her into a cloudy zone of half-sleep. That empty feeling in her stomach, the one that came when she'd cried all the tears she had in her, was making her nauseous.

"Shhhh," JD said. "I know. We'll get through this. You'll get through this."

"I can't—I can't tell you. . . ." she murmured, sniffling into the pillow.

"You're going to have to," he said, not letting up. "But you don't have to right now. Just rest. I'll stay until you fall asleep. We'll talk tomorrow."

"It's too late," she said.

JD squeezed her arm and leaned down to whisper into her neck, so close that she could feel the movement of his lips against the soft hairs at her nape. "It's never too late." She felt his warmth.

And there was the growing crevice in her heart, threatening to crack the whole thing to pieces. Because he was wrong. She had two days left, two days as Emily Winters, the person she'd been for almost seventeen years. The person who loved mac 'n' cheese, and her grandma's murder-mystery paperbacks, and old musicals. Who couldn't stay awake during long car rides—not even with caffeine—and didn't like zucchini no matter how it was prepared. Who first met Gabby Dove in Girl Scouts when they were eight, and who won the All-Maine Spelling Bee when she was in sixth grade. Who loved JD Fount, loved his flannel shirts and his sensitivity and the fact that he knew how things worked, things like airplanes and DVD players.

These things were all she had left to hold on to. The things that made her Emily Marie Winters. Those last, swirling bits that made her wholly *her*.

Soon, even those intractable things would be lost, forever.

CHAPTER SEVENTEEN

JD woke to someone screaming. He jerked upright, sweaty, tangled in the flannel sheet he'd thrown over the couch. For a second, he was totally disoriented. He reached for his glasses on the bedside table, before remembering that he wasn't in his room but downstairs on the couch. They were somewhere on the coffee table just out of reach. He got up, fumbling in the dark, bumping his shin, cursing.

And upstairs, Melissa kept screaming—high-pitched, senseless.

Finally he found his glasses, and as he raced upstairs, he heard his parents' bedroom door open. His father's heavy footsteps slammed down the hall, with his mom's flapping slippers not far behind. Melissa's screams continued, growing more hysterical.

He thought he heard the word "help." He thought he heard the word "no."

Fear was like a drill, beating out all logic, all sense. They were after him. They'd found out what he knew. Ty and Ali and Meg. They were here.

By the time he reached the top of the landing, the door to his room was open too, and Em had stepped into the hall. He caught a brief glimpse of her bare legs, so thin beneath the enormous T-shirt she was wearing. It made him shiver.

"What is it?" He stopped in Melissa's doorway; his father was hovering over his sister's bed, shushing her, while his mother sat at the foot of the bed, rubbing Melissa's feet through the blanket. She wasn't screaming anymore, just whimpering, sitting with her arms wrapped around her knees and her chin buried between her forearms. The clock on her nightstand read 4:34.

"There's no one out there, honey," Mr. Fount said, leaning over Melissa's bed to look out her window, where a purplish dawn was just starting to break. "I promise."

"You're just overexcited because of the fire," JD's mom added, stroking her daughter's sleep-mussed hair. "Nightmare," she mouthed to JD.

Melissa shook herself free. "It wasn't a dream," she said. "I saw someone. I'm sure of it. Right there." She pointed to her window frame, staring at the glass with wide, tear-glassed eyes.

JD's stomach knotted up. He thought of Mr. Feiffer's face,

frozen in death. But he tried to stay calm. "That's impossible, Mel," he said, trying to shake any doubt from his voice. "How would someone get all the way up to your window?"

"Someone was there," Melissa insisted. "I *know* someone was watching me. I could feel it." Her parents exchanged a hopeless look over Melissa's head.

"I have an idea, Melly." Suddenly Em was in the room behind him. She'd pulled on her sweatpants. Her long dark hair was piled on top of her head in a messy ponytail. JD thought she had never looked so beautiful. How could someone be here, so close, and yet so untouchable? "Why don't you keep watch from up here, and I'll go downstairs and make sure no one is out there?"

Mrs. Fount gave a nervous laugh, making *You don't have to do this* eyes at Em. "I don't think that's necessary, sweetheart. . . ."

But Melissa nodded slowly. "Okay," she said. "Just to make sure." She squeezed her knees tighter, and said defensively, "I *didn't* imagine it."

"Let's make sure they're gone, then," Em assured her. "I get it. It's no big deal," she said, more to the Founts than to Melissa. And then she was gone, headed downstairs and for the front door.

"I'll go with her," JD said hurriedly. What was she thinking, going out there alone?

He followed Em into the front yard, shivering as his bare feet hit the dewy grass. Em had passed into the front yard already, making a great show of looking up, down, and all around. The sky was charcoal, lit by hazy stars.

"You're a great actress," he called out to her as she turned to give a thumbs-up to Melissa's bedroom window. They watched as Melissa waved to them, hugged her parents, and turned off her light.

"I'm not acting," she said quietly. She'd been beaming at the window. Now her smile faded. "I was worried."

As the words left her mouth, a gust of wind blew through the yard, rustling the branches, the new leaves. He tried to ignore the prickling feeling on the back of his neck—like there really was someone, or something, out there with them.

"Did you feel that?" Em asked.

"Yeah. Just a breeze." He tried to keep his voice light. But he felt urgently that they had to get inside—away from the dark, and the night, away from all the places someone could hide. "Let's go back in."

Em was standing rigid, her face suddenly contorted with fear. He wanted to put his arm around her, but the six inches between them felt like an abyss of awkwardness, unable to be spanned. He wished he could tell her that he knew the truth—about Crow, about the Furies. But would it help? Would it change anything? He wasn't sure.

"What? What is it?" JD took a step toward her, then stopped. She pointed wordlessly at the oak tree. There, tangled in a branch about eight feet off the ground, was a strip of shiny red ribbon.

Meg.

JD turned a slow circle. The lights upstairs had gone dark. The only light came from a porch across the street—it lit a bare circle of new grass. Was it his imagination, or did he hear someone laughing?

They're here.

"I'm scared," Em whispered.

"Come on," he said, grabbing her hand.

She did, and together they started to run toward the house—covering the distance in fewer than ten swooping paces. JD felt like he was moving in slow motion. There was something behind him. Someone chasing them. And then the laughter got louder—a cackling, rushing up behind them. About to engulf them. Taunting them, pursuing them with outstretched fingers.

They burst through the front door and shut it quickly, and stood with their backs pressed against it, nearly out of breath. He listened. Everything was silent.

"I don't think I'll be able to sleep," Em whispered into the half-darkness. "Can I stay down here with you?"

He didn't want to push her. But he had to, if he was going to help. "Only if you'll answer some questions," he said, motioning for her to follow him into the den. "I told you I wouldn't give up."

Even though she hadn't been over in months, they automatically assumed their regular positions on the couch—facing each other with feet just barely touching. He felt that ache in his chest again. Where had she gone? Was she really with Crow? Did she love him?

"We haven't done this in a while," Em said, staring at her feet.

"Yeah, I've noticed the absence of your tiny hobbit feet in my life," JD teased.

"I do not have hobbit feet!" Em insisted. Just like always. For a moment all that sadness, all that misery, was gone from her face, and she was there, beautiful and shining and *his*.

"I want this back," JD said suddenly, not even knowing that he was going to speak until the words were on his tongue. "I want the old Em back."

Em inhaled sharply, as though his words were a physical hurt. "I do too," she said finally. "But I don't know how to find her." She looked away, and he could tell she was trying not to cry.

Silence built around them. JD knew that this was his chance. He pressed his lips together, took a deep breath.

"Em, what are the Furies?" His question seemed to echo in the quiet room.

Em flinched. Her eyes were huge, and her face drained of color. "How—how do you . . . ?" She trailed off, stricken.

"Who are they?"

She still didn't answer.

"Em, who are Ty, Ali, and Meg?"

Her hand flew to her mouth, muting a yelp of shock and fear. She shook her head back and forth.

"They're the Furies, aren't they?"

As he spoke, Em's eyes grew bigger and bigger. She opened her mouth, then closed it. Opened it again. "No," she said pleadingly. "No. I won't tell you. Please. Just leave it alone."

"Why are they here?" he persisted. He took a deep breath. "Why were they just outside my house? And why are they after you?" Not until he said the question did he realize how clear it was that Em was being haunted, pursued. That she had been pursued for a long time.

"You need to stay away from them. All three of them." Her voice was as sharp as a razor.

JD threw his head back against the couch cushion in frustration. "You can't keep secrets anymore, Em. You're going to get hurt."

"Going to? I already did." She let out a frantic, false laugh.

JD leaned forward again. "I know," he said. "And so did Chase, and Drea, and Drea's father. . . . You need to tell me what's going on so we can stop this."

"What do you mean, Drea's dad? What does Walt Feiffer have to do with this?"

"Shit," JD said. Of course she didn't know; she couldn't have. . . .

"JD, what does he have to do with this?" she persisted. There was an edge of hysteria in her voice.

"Mr. Feiffer is dead." He was too tired to mince words.

The color drained from Em's face. "No," she said. "No, that's . . . You're wrong. That can't be true."

He could see how badly she wanted it to be false. Death was all around her now—and by extension, it was all around him, too. "I'm sorry, Em," he said. "I found him. I found him just this morning. And that's why I want to help you. I need to. I know you're in danger and if they did that to him—"

"You can't," she interrupted. Em looked up at him with eyes as big as quarters. They were glossy with tears and there was a smudge of makeup below her right eye.

"What did they do to you?" he begged. Why didn't she see he was trying to help her?

"They offered me something," Em said. Her eyes were focused on a faraway spot. "In return, I had to do something for them. It was worth it, though. You have to believe me, JD."

"What did you do?" he asked, afraid of what the answer might be.

"I . . . I bound myself to them." She glanced up at him. "I know it sounds crazy, but I . . ."

"It doesn't sound crazy," he said, coaxing her to continue. "Tell me."

"I swallowed five seeds," she said in barely a whisper. Her

eyes told him she was one hundred percent serious.

"Seeds? What kind of seeds?"

She shook her head. Tears were rolling down her face. "I don't know. Red ones . . ."

"But why?" It didn't make any sense.

"They said if I took them, they'd give me what I wanted. But ever since then . . . I'm changing. Drea warned me—" She cut herself off and turned her face toward the window.

JD tried to keep calm, even as he felt the heat rising into his face. The room felt like it was melting. The real world, the world he'd always known—where there was no magic but no monsters, either—seemed to be dissolving like sugar in water.

"I'm not supposed to be telling you this," Em said tearfully. "I shouldn't be putting you in danger."

"Em, it's you who's in danger," he said. "I was at their house the other day. I saw—"

She exploded. "You were *where*?" All of a sudden she was on her feet. He could see her chest heaving up and down. When she continued, she made a point of lowering her voice, and it came out as a strangled whisper. "What the hell were you thinking? You can't go there, JD. You can't go back there. Jesus. You have to stay out of it. Promise me. Promise me you will."

"Why? I get that you're scared of them," JD said, "but I know how to stop them."

"Impossible," she said. "They can't be stopped."

"They can," he insisted. He swallowed. This conversation had been far easier in his head. "Mr. Feiffer knew how to banish the Furies." He remembered what Mr. Feiffer had told him—he knew how to get rid of the evil for good. JD felt his throat constrict. How might Mr. Feiffer have helped him, if he'd had the chance?

"Mr. *Feiffer*?" For a second, she stared at him. "He couldn't have known anything about them. If he did, do you think his daughter would be dead? Do you think *he'd* be dead? No. They're ruthless. And powerful." Suddenly she turned a full circle—wide, panicked. "I get it. They're tricking me. They— they want me to break my vow. They want to hurt you. I won't let them."

"Em, calm down."

"I won't let them," she repeated, her voice rising shrilly.

They both jumped when they heard someone on the stairs.

"JD?" It was Melissa coming downstairs. Nothing good would come of scaring her. They looked at each other.

"Yeah, Mel? What's up?" JD called out. Em swiped the tears from her face. They looked at each other again and a silent agreement flowed between them: No more. Not now.

"Do you need anything? You okay?" he asked Mel once she appeared at the foot of the stairs.

"Yeah, I'm okay," she said, looking back and forth between him and Em. "Are *you guys* okay?"

"We're fine," Em said. "Just had a little trouble sleeping and came down here to see if your brother was awake. . . ."

"I couldn't sleep either, really. And it's already seven o'clock. Gonna be exhausted today. . . ." Mel said as she disappeared into the kitchen.

"This isn't over," he whispered once Mel was out of earshot. He reached for Em's hand. It felt small and cold.

"Not yet," she said. Her voice was resigned. "But soon."

I bound myself to them, Em had said. The words stayed with him, crawling under his skin and scalp, all day. *I'm changing. Putting you in danger. This will be over soon.*

Her premonitions played and replayed in his mind all day long. Stuck on the idea of the "red seeds," he was making his way through the school parking lot that afternoon when he heard someone call his name.

He snapped his head up and saw Crow leaning nonchalantly against JD's Volvo. He looked like shit, all scruffy and sloppy, in a big gray T-shirt and ripped jeans. Even now that JD knew that Crow was most likely *not* responsible for wounding him at the Behemoth, he still hated the guy.

Anger flexed inside him. "Get off my car, man."

"Listen, I don't like seeing you any more than you like seeing me," Crow said, straightening up. "I just came to talk to you about something."

"By *something*, do you mean Emily? She has a name, you know." He gripped his keys in his left hand, squeezing them so hard that their jagged edges pressed into his skin.

"You're in over your head, Lover Boy," Crow said in the same infuriatingly calm tone. JD could smell cigarette smoke on him, and sweat. "Don't drown."

JD took a step forward, so he and Crow were only a few inches apart. "Or what? You'll start following me like you've been following Emily?"

"Whoa, whoa," Crow said, holding up his hands. "Calm down, Romeo. You're really bummed that Em and I have been hanging out, huh?"

"Oh, is that what they call stalking nowadays? *Hanging out?*" JD flashed back to Crow peering into the Winters' dining room. "I saw you outside her house, spying on her—looking in the window."

"Wow, man. Ladies and gentlemen, he's cracked the case," Crow announced loudly, holding his arms out and spreading his chest wide. "Or maybe, just maybe, Fount, you knew that because *you* were stalking her."

JD's head was spinning. Black was eating at the edges of his vision, anger pumping through his blood. "Don't screw with me. I saw you on Thursday. I could have called the cops. I should have."

"So I needed to talk to her," Crow admitted. All traces of his smirk were gone. His eyes were just slightly unfocused. "But I wasn't following her."

"You're a liar," JD said.

"I've been called a lot of things, but I'm *not* a liar," Crow pressed his finger into JD's chest in response. JD pushed his hand away. "Jealousy must be messing with your head."

"Jealous of *you*?"

"Sure." Crow said. "I mean, I *did* make a move on your girl. But I don't need to sneak around to make it happen. She's willing to be seen with me in public."

Something snapped inside JD. Em wasn't his girl, and Crow knew that, and him saying it made the whole thing worse. JD barreled into Crow full-force, pinning him against the car with his forearm pressed forcefully against Crow's chest. They were face-to-face, just inches apart. JD's adrenaline was flowing hard; he had never hit anyone before in his life.

"Shut up," he spit. "Stay away from Em. Stay away from me."

"Back atcha, asshole," Crow said, pushing back against JD's weight. He was weaker than JD expected. "You're going to mess things up. Stay out of this."

"Or what?"

"You don't want to find out."

With disgust, JD let Crow go. They glowered at each other for a few wordless seconds, both of them breathing heavy. Then Crow stalked off toward his ugly pickup truck. JD watched him go. He got into his own car and sat there for a minute, shaking. Finally he turned the key and drove away.

On the ride home, JD was jumpy and wired. He'd never come that close to hitting another guy, at least not since he was four years old on the playground near Sebago Lake. It felt shitty, like he'd accomplished nothing. But a part of him liked it too, this feeling of blood rushing right below his skin.

There were two pieces of mail waiting for him on the kitchen table: the latest issue of *Rolling Stone*, and an envelope with a handwritten label and no return address. It had some uneven bulk to it, like there was something inside. He tossed the magazine on the counter and ripped into it. He couldn't remember the last time someone sent him actual mail—even his grandmother had sent an e-card last year.

The handwriting was unfamiliar and boxy, and as he pulled the note out, written in a heavy hand on lined paper, he saw it was dated just yesterday. But the date wasn't what threw him. It was the gold snake pin that came tumbling out of the envelope. And the sender.

Walt Feiffer.

The letter in his hand was from a dead man.

ACT THREE

WHAT LIES AT THE HEART

CHAPTER EIGHTEEN

Being exhausted at school was nothing new, especially on a Monday.

But being exhausted at school with her hair still smelling like smoke, despite the fact that she'd taken a shower at JD's house *and* spritzed on some of Gabby's secret-weapon locker perfume? Being exhausted at school while still fending off creepy glances from guys who thought she'd been pole-dancing at a party on Saturday night? Being exhausted at school while knowing that she was racing toward some terrible fate—and that her supposed friend Crow might be greasing the wheels? These were new lows.

The day dragged. She ignored a million calls and texts from Crow, who said they needed to talk. Probably to explain his behavior last night—and presumably, why he'd shown up at the exact moment her house was on fire. She spent English and chem wondering what was going on at home, whether she'd be able to sleep in her own bed that night. And now she had a new nervous tic: pulling strands from her ponytail around to the front of her face to make sure that they hadn't turned red in the last five minutes. By the time the school day was over, Em was feeling manic with fatigue.

"I'm heading home," she said, pulling Gabby aside after the final bell. "I want to see if there's anything I can do to help my parents. Thanks for everything this morning."

Students flowed around them, chatting and laughing, but Em was so tired that she barely heard them. They were just a low drone in the background. She couldn't believe that once, not so long ago, this had been her whole life: what had happened over the weekend; who'd hooked up, who'd broken up.

Gabby reached up for a hug. She'd met Em in the gym locker room that morning with a fresh set of clothes—leggings and a denim tunic—plus coffee and a carrot muffin. "Of course, sweetie," she said, giving Em a squeeze. "Let me know if there's anything else I can do. And how about this weekend we go out for Thai? My treat."

Em felt a pang somewhere deep inside her. *I don't think I'll be here this weekend,* she thought. She ran a hand nervously through her hair and contemplated spilling it all to Gabby. This could be her last chance to tell the truth to her best friend. . . .

"That would be awesome" was all she said. She felt like her heart was snapping in half.

Before they parted ways, Em was compelled to reach out for Gabby's hand. There was an underwater-type whooshing in her ears. Everything else seemed to melt away except for the two of them, leaned up against the cold brick wall of the Ascension High hallway. A locker slammed somewhere down the hall. "Listen, Gabs, before you go . . . I just wanted to say—thanks. Thank you so much."

"It's no problem," Gabby said, tilting her head. "It's the least I can do—your *house* was on fire last night."

"I'm not just talking about the clothes and stuff," Em pressed. "I'm talking about *everything*. With . . . with Zach and all that. I was a terrible friend. And you were there for me anyway." She felt her throat closing up. "You have to know how sorry I am. How sorry I've been."

The words hung between them and Em thought she felt her heart stop beating for a few seconds. Gabby picked at a bit of pearly pink nail polish. When she looked up, her eyes were bluer than ever.

"I know you've been torturing yourself," Gabby said, tucking a blond tendril behind her ear. "But you've got to believe me. I'm over it." She managed a smile. "Look, I dodged a bullet, right? He was a total zero. And we both learned from it."

"You deserve better," Em said. For the first time, she realized it was possible that she judged herself more harshly even than Gabby did.

"It's over," Gabby said, wrapping her arms around Em's neck for another quick hug. "Really. And we have each other. That's what counts. Best friends for life, right?"

"For life," Em echoed, attempting a smile. But she knew that this—Gabby, the halls of Ascension, the gossip, and the blur of people—might never be her life again.

Bing-bing. Her phone beeped in her pocket and Em straightened up. The text was from Crow, again. His message was terse: *Meet me at the Dungeon.*

Okay, she wrote back. She couldn't avoid him forever. *See you soon.*

Was meeting him crazy? There was a chance that he'd gone completely off the deep end, that his reasons for being at her house last night were, in fact, less innocent than he'd have her believe. These were the thoughts that gripped her as she drove to the coffee shop.

"Hold up," Crow said, intercepting Em on the sidewalk in front of the Dungeon. "Come back here." He jerked his head toward the alleyway behind the coffee shop where smokers usually congregated.

"Why?" she asked.

Crow looked haggard—like he hadn't slept in days. He definitely hadn't shaved this week. And there was a new, red scrape on his jaw. "Privacy," he said shortly.

She followed him warily into the alley, which was dim despite it being broad daylight. The ground was littered with cigarette butts, and a few upside-down milk crates were set up as makeshift seats. "Well? You gonna tell me what happened last night? What did you see?"

"It was the worst one yet—like it was really happening," Crow said. He fumbled for a cigarette. Em had never even seen him smoke. "You were lost in a swirl of smoke. You couldn't get out. You were burning to death."

"So you saw the fire before it happened?" *And did you get drunk before or after you had the vision?* she silently added.

He slumped against the Dungeon's brick wall and crossed his arms. "Not quite," he said. "It wasn't your house. You were outside. And it was . . . It was JD who *put* you there."

"JD?" she repeated. Putting her in danger? He would never. She nudged a milk crate with the toe of her sneaker. "What are you talking about? He's not involved in this." But she felt a flicker of doubt. JD knew things—she didn't know how, but he did.

She'd told him last night to stay out of it. She prayed he would listen.

Crow's eyes narrowed. "That's what you think," he said. "He's been going around behind your back trying to save the day. I tried to warn him off, but he practically punched me."

"What?" Em looked up, her cheeks blazing. "When did you even see him?"

A muscle in his jaw flexed. "Look, Em, I'm just trying to warn you. He's going to do something. . . . I wouldn't make this up. He's . . . It's a trap. You have to be careful."

Em's chest constricted. She put her hand against her neck to stop herself from getting too warm. "He wouldn't do that, Crow. Leave JD out of this," she said.

When he turned to her, his eyes were cold. Dull. "I get it. You don't want *your boyfriend* to get hurt." He laughed, but there was no humor in it. "But not me, huh? You don't care about what happens to me."

There was a bad taste in her mouth. Was this a war of jealousy, or was there truth to what Crow was saying?

"First of all, he's not my boyfriend," Em said. "Second, I warned JD to leave it alone—I told him that they were dangerous. That I was taking care of it." *And I do care if you get hurt,* she thought, but couldn't say it.

Crow moved away from the wall and took several steps closer, backing her against the bricks on the opposite side of the alley. He reached down and grabbed both her wrists, pinning them up next to her shoulders. It was rough and urgent. It was scary. There was a look in his eyes that came from somewhere else, somewhere bad. She thought she'd be able to overpower him—she was stronger than she'd ever been, despite feeling so weak all the time. But she couldn't. Where was he getting *his* strength from? The thought terrified her even more.

"But it's not just *you*, is it Em? It's *us*. I'm supposed to help you. We're in this together, aren't we?" He leaned into her. She felt the bricks grinding into her back.

"You didn't confront JD to help me," she said, ripping her arms from his grasp. "Not that it matters. Not that any of it matters. You can't help me and neither can he. I can't even help *myself*. It's over—it's too late."

Crow looked at her with raised eyebrows. "You're giving up? Are you kidding me?"

"I don't have any other choice." She took a deep breath. "Look. Just calm down. I don't get it. JD would never hurt me. Ever. So your vision? Whatever it was, it was wrong."

He stared at her for a long second, his eyes black and full of a need she couldn't identify. Then he released her, and shoved a hand through his hair.

"I told you. They aren't, like, how-to manuals—they're not totally literal. What I see . . . What I sense . . . They're more like . . . puzzles," Crow said, pacing on the asphalt. "I don't understand it any more than you do. All I know is what I saw—and felt. JD is dangerous. The details may be fuzzy, but the feeling is never wrong, Emily. I *knew*." His voice got lower. Rougher. "I knew there would be a fire the night of the Ascension dance. If I had said something sooner, Drea might still be alive. Okay? So you'd better listen to me when I say stay away from him. You *have* to listen to me. You have to, Emily. I'm *not* going to lose you." His voice started breaking. "I'm not going to *fucking lose you, too*." His voice was almost a whisper, and Emily didn't know what to say. He went on, quieter, pleading now. "Just—for a few days—till we figure this out. Stay away from him. *Please.*"

"But I don't *have* a few days," Em whispered back, feeling the full weight of the truth pressing in on her lungs, making it hard to breathe. She swallowed hard. "Remember your vision about the tiger girl? About when the transformation would happen? Well, I've figured that one out. And it's *tomorrow*. Skylar is the tiger lady. Or she will be, the night of the play. Tomorrow night. I only have twenty-four hours left."

"*Tomorrow?* It can't be—not so soon. . . . I need more time." He stopped pacing to stare at her. "I haven't figured out how to . . . channel them. Those bitches won't give an inch. They won't tell me anything. So I have to get closer. You have to get as close to the heart of evil as you can, if you want to strike it down."

How could he even think about getting *closer*? She wanted to be as far from the Furies as possible. "That's not a plan, Crow. That's suicide."

He let out a harsh laugh. "Listen. Don't worry about me. All you need to know is that I'm going to keep you safe."

"How? It's not like you're gonna sit down over tea and have a chat. They're crazy. And dangerous, and—"

Something passed across his face, an expression of uncer-tainty or fear, but it was gone too quickly for her to decipher. "Maybe I'll make them an offer they can't refuse."

"What could you have that they want?" she asked.

He stared at her hard. There was a pop of electricity between them. She could feel his eyes boring straight into her.

"You just let me handle the details," Crow said quietly.

"I am *not* some damsel in distress. Whatever it is you're plan-ning, it's too dangerous."

"I'm supposed to save the princess, though. At least that's how it works in the movies. . . ."

"Don't fucking joke about this, Crow."

"I'm not joking, princess." He took a step toward her. His voice was softer than she'd ever heard it. "You still don't get it, do you?"

Her pulse quickened. "Get what?"

His eyes, those yellow-green cat eyes, flared with emotion. He sighed deeply, as though he was reluctant to even say the words that came out of his mouth. "That I love you."

Her stomach dropped and she was mute, unable to respond, terrified of her own pounding heart.

"I know you care about me," he said, staring at her as if he were doing mental arithmetic. Then he offered her a thin smile.

"And maybe you don't love me, not the way I love you. But that doesn't change the fact that I'm going to protect you."

And then he was gone, Em's feet glued to the ground while Crow's boots scuffed away. She wiped a tear from her cheek, whispering a good-bye he would never hear.

Driving home, she realized that she hadn't yet told Skylar or Skylar's aunt about the fire—or about Crow's visions, or about Mr. Feiffer being dead. What would Nora and Hannah Markwell make of Walt's death? It would be the final blow, tying the Feiffers' tragic history together for Edie's two friends.

She grabbed her phone and pulled up Skylar's number. It didn't ring—straight to voice mail. Em didn't like that. She called the landline; it rang and rang. Something didn't sit right; something was wrong. She decided to take the long way home, which would take her past Skylar's house. If someone was home, maybe she'd just stop in. . . .

Nora's tan Camry wasn't in the driveway, but there was someone kneeling in the flower bed on the side of the house, where Skylar's aunt planted her perennials.

"Mrs. McVoy?" Em called out her open car window. The hunched figure didn't turn. She got that now-familiar swing of fear, almost like vertigo. "Nora?" Em said even louder.

But by now she was close enough to see that the person in the dirt wasn't Aunt Nora or Skylar. It was Lucy, Skylar's sister.

She was humming again, that same tuneless drone that Em had heard the other day. Her face was practically buried in the plants.

"Lucy?" Em parked and stepped out of her car, wondering if she should call Skylar, or try to get Lucy back inside the house. "Do you remember me? I'm Emily."

The girl turned around slowly, revealing a toothy smile. Em drew back unconsciously. Lucy's arms were smeared with dirt, and in one hand she held a crushed white geranium; on closer inspection, Em saw that a piece of white petal was stuck to her lips. Had she been *eating* the flowers? And were geraniums poisonous?

Em looked over her shoulder, hoping in vain that she would see Nora's car pulling into the driveway. She took a deep breath. Lucy was damaged, and probably scared, but she wasn't dangerous. Em came closer and motioned to the flower in Lucy's hand. "Doing some gardening?"

Smiling one of her bright, pageant smiles, Lucy nodded eagerly. "The albinos like shade, not sun."

That again. *The albino.* "I . . . don't know much about flowers," Em admitted. "Are your sister or your aunt home? I just have a few quick things to tell them."

The deranged garden show was apparently not over. With the same TV smile—one that did a poor job of hiding the blankness in her eyes—Skylar's sister continued to describe her prized plant. "The albino. It will make the voices stop." As if she were discussing what sort of fertilizer to use, Lucy continued her lesson. "It kills the darkness. They tell me it will. They *promised*."

Em looked down and realized that Lucy's fingernails were digging into her skin.

"Who promised?"

"They're trying to protect the seeds," Lucy said sadly.

"What seeds?"

"The seeds bloom inside a heart of evil," Lucy intoned, as though she was reciting a child's nursery rhyme. "Shhhhhh."

Heart of evil. That was the exact phrase Crow had used, talking about his visions, talking about the Furies. To hear the words come out of both of their mouths made Em more sure than ever that there were clues hidden in Lucy's nonsense talk.

The seeds. A heart of evil. Could Lucy *know*—truly know?

"Who tells you these things, Lucy?" Em asked.

Lucy looked at Em with one final remark. "When the light brings up the albino," she said, "the darkness stops." Then something happened, a flicker across her face, and Lucy's demeanor changed. She grew suddenly quiet.

"Did the Furies tell you this?" Em wanted to snap her fingers in front of Lucy's eyes. "Did they?"

But Lucy was taciturn now, silent, sullen.

"Please. Listen to me." Em's hands were on Lucy's shoulders and then she was shaking her, back and forth, like a rag doll.

It took just a second for Em to realize what she was doing.

She cried out and let Lucy go, snapping her hands behind her back. *Jesus.* What was wrong with her? She backed away quickly when she heard wheels turning into the driveway.

Aunt Nora emerged from the car and her linen skirt billowed behind her as she walked toward the flower bed.

"What's going on? What's going on here?" She looked back and forth between Lucy, who had retreated back into her private universe, and Em, who tried to explain. She prayed that Nora hadn't seen her turn momentarily violent.

"I came over after school, to tell you . . . I thought you should know that Walt Feiffer is—dead," she blurted out. "And Lucy was here, outside here, and she started talking. I think about the Furies. She was saying something about seeds, and a light. . . ." Em trailed off, not knowing what else to say.

"Emily, I'm sorry," Nora said after a long pause. "I really am. But we've had enough tragedy here. She doesn't know what she's saying. And I can't help you any more than I already have."

"Nora, I need your help," Em pleaded, but Nora ignored her. "I don't have much time."

"Let's go inside, Lucy." Nora said as she started guiding Lucy toward the front door. When she reached the entryway, she looked over her shoulder at Em.

"Please don't come here again. You're not welcome." Then she slammed the door before Em could sputter out a response.

Em's head was spinning. *Flowers. Seeds. The albino.* Could the answer have been in front of her all along? For the first time in days, she felt a surge of hope. Maybe, just maybe, she had one last chance to save herself.

"You're home earlier than I expected," Em's mom said when Em pulled into the driveway. It was dusk on Monday evening and Mrs. Winters was in the yard, scrubbing their kitchen curtains by hand in a huge soapy bucket on the lawn. "I thought you were going to try and catch up on some homework with Gabby today."

"I couldn't really concentrate," Em admitted. "Thought I'd come home and see what was going on around here."

"Em, honey, we've got it under control. . . ." Her mom leaned back on her heels and sighed.

Sorry, Mom, homework and lab reports have been taking a backseat to fighting the bloodthirsty witches who want my soul.

"I'll get everything done," Em promised. "We barely got any sleep last night and I have a lot on my mind. I didn't know how bad it was, you know?"

"Well, the damage is worst in the laundry room and the kitchen," her mom said. "Your father took the day off—he's in there now, ripping up what's left of the linoleum. We'll have to get new cabinets and patch up the walls. But it's nowhere near as bad as it could have been. Nowhere close. Plumbing works."

"Can we, like, still live here?" Em looked up at the house and felt a wave of nostalgia. She just wanted to curl up on her bed and smell her family's laundry detergent. What if Lucy's words held meaning? What if Em actually had a fighting chance?

"Yes," her mom said. "Things are going to be in shambles for a few weeks, but it's safe. We'll be able to sleep in our own beds."

That was a relief.

"What caused it?" Em asked, even though she thought she knew. The Furies were egging her on. Teasing her. Daring her. Turning this into a game.

"Something with the wiring," her mom said, waving her hand vaguely.

Em kneeled down in the cold grass next to her. "Mom," she said, reaching out to touch her mother's arm. "Thank you for waking me up last night."

"You think I would leave you in a burning house?" her mom responded. "Only if you forget Mother's Day." She nudged Em with her shoulder, then grew serious. "I'll always do what I can to protect you, sweetie. But I'll be much more effective if I know what's going on in your life. Like this Colin. Care to tell me who he is?"

"He's just an old friend of Drea's who's having a hard time right now," Em said. "He had nothing to do with the fire."

"I'm not accusing him of anything, Emily," her mom said, wringing out a curtain. "I just like to know the young men who visit in the middle of the night. Next time he comes over I'd like to meet him under more relaxed circumstances."

She tried to imagine Crow sitting on their living room couch, making small talk with her parents. . . . It was so absurd, she almost laughed out loud. "Sure, Mom, if that will make you feel better."

"It will," her mother said. "Thank you for humoring me."

Em started to get up.

"You're sure you're okay?" her mom asked for the thousandth time.

If her mother only knew—if she had even the slightest idea of what was going on—could she help? Would she be able to? It was tempting for Em to succumb to the childish notion: *Mommy will fix this.* But she couldn't bring herself to tell the truth. Not because she was worried that her mom would think she'd gone truly insane (though that would probably happen too), but because she was ashamed to admit the mistake that had bound her to the Furies in the first place. It was like light-years had passed since that fateful night when she and Zach shared their first kiss. She felt like a different person. She *was* a different person. And no one could fix things but her.

"I'm gonna be fine," she whispered, her throat hoarse with regret. She wished she believed it.

CHAPTER NINETEEN

Once I send this, it will be too late for me, Walt's letter read. JD lay in his bedroom, rereading the thin sheet of paper for what felt like the millionth time.

I started seeing the visions when I was young, the letter said. *Thought I was just overdoing it with the late nights and the partying. I used to see these three figures. Dark. Women. Snakes in their hair. I saw them coming here. I knew they would come even before they did. Because they'd been here before, just like they've been everywhere.*

And then my Edie summoned them because she didn't know any other way. There wasn't any other way to get rid of him. That's what she thought, anyway. I didn't know everything—not then. She thought he was coming after Drea.

They really got their claws in her. And so she made a deal with them, some sort of arrangement. After that, everything changed. She thought she was tied to them forever. She thought they'd never leave her alone. So I did what I had to do.

I offered a sacrifice. What else do the gods ever want? It's been that way forever. Greeks knew it. The Romans, too.

The gods and goddesses want sacrifice, plain and simple.

They want blood. Blood like the color of those orchids.

I saw that in my visions.

JD was starting to get pins and needles in his right arm. He flipped onto his other side and kept reading.

Edie kept talking about fire. About how there had been a fire here, in Ascension. That's when the Furies first infiltrated this place. I thought I could draw them back. With a fire. End it how it all began. I saw that in my visions too.

The way I saw it, I was offering Drea as a sacrifice. An innocent. The way it happened in my visions, I put Drea in the middle of a circle of sticks and a pile of those red flowers. She was wearing a gold pin—shaped like a snake. It was her mother's. I figured it was for good luck or something. I'd light the fire, watch it burn ... and then they'd disappear. Drea would always be safe. It was like they got cheated. It was like they got tricked. Because they got nothing.

Finally I broke down. I decided to try it. Follow the vision like it was an instruction manual. I brought Drea (she was still so little) into the Haunted Woods. Even back then, that's what everyone called them. Where Edie had seen the Furies' house.

That morning, I'd taken her mother's snake pin from its jewelry box. I stuck it to Drea's shirt for protection and then I built a fire around her. She just sat there the whole time, looking up at me with those dark eyes. So trusting. It almost broke my heart.

What could I do?

JD shivered and looked over to his bedroom window. It wasn't warm enough yet to keep the window open overnight. After closing it, he settled back down on his bed, holding the letter above his face.

The flames got higher and higher, until I couldn't see her anymore. They were getting so close and it was getting so hot. She started crying. My little girl started crying.

They weren't there, and then suddenly they were—they appeared out of nowhere. They were screaming. Like they were in pain. Through the smoke, I watched their faces melting.

And they left. Just disappeared into thin air.

I ran through the flames. I grabbed my little girl. She was untouched. It had worked. I came home, hid the pin, and prayed that I would never see them again.

I believed we were free of them. But it was too late. Edie had already done what she did. I was too late. I hope you're not.

—Walt

JD scoured the page, making sure he understood what Walt Feiffer was trying to tell him. He held the paper in his right hand; in his left, he ran his thumb over the contours of the snake pin. Almost identical to the one he'd found near Henry Landon's icy grave. The one Walt referred to in his note.

He stared down at the page until the words started to blur. He felt sick to his stomach. He thought of little Drea, behind a wall of flame. . . .

But if Walt Feiffer had done it, couldn't JD do it too?

Sprawled on his twin bed, he focused on each letter, trying to block out the sounds of thudding pop music bleeding through the walls from Melissa's room.

It was only a few hours later, but he'd already memorized certain lines.

Edie kept talking about fire . . . and we were free of them.

When he finished reading the note, JD's hands were shaking. The paper was crumpled from how hard he was gripping it.

He understood the banishment ritual. It had worked for Drea's dad. It could work for him. And maybe he wouldn't be too late. But he needed to find an innocent—someone who could serve as a sacrifice. Someone he would have to rescue at the last second, as Drea's dad had rescued her. From beyond the wall of smoke and flame.

The faint wail of a song seeped through the wall. Melissa always listened to her music too loud.

Melissa.

No.

The idea bled into his mind quickly.

No. I can't put her in danger.

But she would be safe. That's what Mr. Feiffer's note said. He could save her at the last minute.

She's my sister.

Drea had been Walt's daughter.

But what if it doesn't work?

What if it does?

What if I don't do it?

Em's eyes flashed before his own. Big, trusting, light with laughter.

With that, JD got up, marched out of his room, and knocked on Melissa's door. It was time to send the Furies back to hell.

CHAPTER TWENTY

SMASH.

The greenhouse window broke easily, several shards of glass spraying out onto the cement floor inside. Em looked down at her hand, amazed that it didn't hurt—not one bit. Not even that fresh laceration on her right knuckle, which was rapidly healing in the last of the moonlight.

Em reached her hand through and twisted the lock on the door, which squeaked open rustily. She looked around behind her at the quiet, dewy fields, the buildings with darkened windows, and the long driveway to the road. No one was around.

And so she slipped inside.

Just before the dawn of what was possibly her last day on earth as Emily Winters, Em was breaking and entering.

She was still shaken from Crow's confession and Lucy's odd insights. Shaken, shocked . . . and scared. For him, for her, and for everyone.

After Crow had left her outside the Dungeon, she had frantically reviewed everything she knew: Edie killed herself to save Drea from the Furies. Ty was trying to take over Em's life. Skylar seemed to be left alone now, but her sister Lucy could hear the Furies—likely a result of her brain damage turning her, as the book had put it, "mad." But then again, Lucy wasn't exactly a trustworthy source, babbling about albinos and mouths and seeds.

That was how she'd made the connection. Albino flowers . . .

Hadn't Nora mentioned rumors of an antidote, a way to clean the slate and become pure again? Something derived from nature, something derived from the Furies' source?

Em's heart started hammering and she stood up, pacing the alleyway.

She wondered if the secret was in the seeds. If it was possible that she had literally ingested the Furies' evil, and if it was possible that the white flower held an antidote. Was it feasible, even, that the same seeds had properties of both evil and good?

Ty had said that evil always contained the power to destroy itself. That she wanted to be "good." What if the very thing that symbolized the Furies' evil was the key to their undoing?

She had practically flown to the greenhouse. She couldn't even remember the drive. She knew that if there was any connection between the plant world and the Furies, she would find it at the greenhouse.

Once she was inside, the atmosphere was claustrophobic; shining her flashlight around the space, Em noticed the yellow-white film that had accumulated on the inside of the glass panes. The plants looked more cooped in than they had before.

"Hello?" Her voice echoed thinly off the walls. On her tip-toes, shining the blue light in front of her feet, she made her way slowly down the center aisle of the greenhouse, toward the wooden table where she'd sat with Nora, Skylar, and Hannah Markswell the other night. Her shoes clicked against the cement. To the left was a rickety metal shelving unit filled with books about gardening, landscaping, and botany, some of them ancient and some brand-new. She positioned herself so that she could see both the front and the rear doors, and leaned over so she could read the books' spines. *Plants of the Northeast. Growing Annuals Indoors. Victorian Horticulture.* She ran a finger down the row. Next to those was a set of black three-ring binders, each labeled with a name. Nora's was one of them.

Em pulled the binder from the shelf and opened it to find loose-leaf papers marked in Nora's neat cursive. Notes. Each of the gardeners kept notes on their plants, on their findings. Nora's appeared to be arranged alphabetically by type of plant: helio-trope, ivy, violets. The largest section, however, was labeled with a simple *F.*

Em flipped quickly to those pages and found exactly what she'd expected to find: Nora's observations about orchids. The terms were scientific, but Em's breath hitched. Nora was attempting to breed what she referred to as the "albino orchid."

I am starting to believe that the red orchid turns white only during a full moon, Nora had written. *It has happened to me twice now. There must be some significance. The moon must be at its peak in order for the flower to open its petals and reveal the seeds inside. The seeds can be good or bad—they can yield new plants, or shrivel in the dirt. It wilts almost instantly—usually within one hour of having bloomed. The flower is extremely rare, extremely sensitive. As yet, I have not succeeded in keeping it in bloom.*

Em read the passage several times. As she closed the binder, she realized her hands were shaking. It was starting to make sense. If the flower was special, then its seeds must be unique too. *The seeds can be good or bad.* Just as the red seeds from the Furies' evil flowers had launched her transformation, the seeds from the albino orchid could counter their effect. When the seeds were bad, they were very bad. And when they were good, they were saviors.

"You were right, Lucy," she said into the silence.

When the light brings up the albino, Lucy had said.

Good or bad.

Ty wanted those seeds too. They'd make her good, make her human again.

The red orchid turns white only during a full moon, Nora had written.

Em pulled her phone out and clicked over to her mariners' calendar—the one JD had downloaded to her phone one night when they were hanging out. It listed high and low tides, what time the sun would rise and set, the phases of the moon. A combination of humidity and nerves made the phone slick in her hands. What was the date? She could barely remember.

And when she pulled up today's date, Em's heart leaped from her chest. The full moon was tonight. It all made sense: the same night as the play, just as Crow's vision had predicted. She had one final chance to save herself. And Ty had to be thinking the exact same thing. Those seeds would save her, or, in the wrong hands, condemn her forever.

The school day had been itchy, like wearing a wool sweater with nothing on underneath. She'd spent half of fourth period shaking in the corner of the girls' bathroom by the cafeteria, even as everyone bustled around her, psyched to see buds blooming on the trees, looking forward to spring break. She wanted to say good-bye to everyone one last time, but couldn't stand to even look at them. Just like she couldn't bring herself to pick up Crow's insistent calls and texts. Just like she was avoiding seeing JD, and Gabby, and Skylar, who were all going to the play.

And now she was back at home, hiding in her room, trying

to stop her whole body from trembling. Because it was tonight.

Do or die.

Her last chance.

"Thank god it's finally calmed down out there." Her mom poked her head into Em's room. "Remember how terrified you used be of thunderstorms?"

Em did remember. The smallest bolt of lightning, the thinnest roll of thunder, would send her shrieking into her parents' room, into their bed, under their covers. That was before everything else got scary. Even now, a part of her wished she could just run for their bed as she used to, and hide. Instead, she was curled up in her own, pretending to do homework and staring at her laptop at the foot of the bed. Thank god the Winterses had been able to keep living in their home after the fire—if Em were stuck in some bland hotel, she'd probably lose her mind completely.

"Are you sure you don't want to come?" asked Mrs. Winters, breaking into Em's thoughts. They were going to see the school play with the Founts; her parents saw every performance at Ascension, even the ones Em wasn't in. Weirdos.

"I'm sure," Em said. "I'm just not feeling all that well. Tell JD I said congrats." She kept her eyes on her computer screen, afraid to look at her mom. She was scared she might start to cry. She'd been home from school for hours and all she'd done was leaf sadly through last year's yearbook and rifle through a wooden box filled with special letters and mementos. She wanted to hold everything in her hands—not just the pieces of paper and scraps of tickets, not just the photographs and shards of beach glass, but the feelings that came with them. The hilarity of one of Gabby's disjointed notes, passed between classes, unfolded in secret. The excitement of her first trip to Portland without her parents. The peacefulness of summer days spent on the sand and in the salty ocean. Would she never feel those things again?

Mrs. Winters nodded, then came into the room and ran her hand once over Em's head. "Everything will be okay, sweetie," she said.

Hot tears pricked the backs of Em's eyes. *But will it?* She turned and gave her mom a weak smile. "Thanks. I love you."

Right before her mom left the room, Em spoke up again. "Mom? Also? I wanted to ask you . . . Can you make homemade mac 'n' cheese tomorrow night?" If she was still here, and still Em, there was nothing she'd want more.

Her mom tilted her head quizzically and then smiled. "Sure, hon, if that's what you're craving. We can have a nice family dinner, the three of us."

"That sounds awesome," Em said. She kept her game face on until her mom closed the door.

As soon as she was alone again, she pulled out her notebook and started to write. There was one more person she needed to say good-bye to. She scribbled furiously. And when she was done, she folded up the note and left it on top of the coiled, broken piece of string on her windowsill. She'd kept it there, through all this craziness. On the outside, she wrote *JD*.

The sun had set. It was time to go.

It was easy to find the house this time. Making her way through the Haunted Woods, with ashen birches violently waving their scraggly fingers in the sky, she had the feeling that she was floating, skimming the ground. She had a mission, and she would not be drawn off course.

The house stood shadowy in the inky-blue twilight, towering up to paint a black silhouette against the sky. Em crept through the clearing, trying to sense whether the Furies were around. She pulled the hood of her black sweatshirt over her head to hide her braid and part of her face; in dark skinny jeans, sneakers, and the sweatshirt, she felt kind of like Drea. Kind of badass.

Crickets whined in the tall weeds around the house, clicking off whenever she got too close.

She peeked into a downstairs window and saw nothing. Nothing moving. All dark. She put her toe against the front door and pushed lightly. The door creaked open.

No one was home. Where were they?

The house looked different than it had in the past. Where it had once appeared charred, empty, it was now opulent and decorated. The Furies had been here long enough to transform it. As their power increased, so did their presence. Em's stomach flipped. Squinting her eyes to adjust to the dim lighting, she saw curved pieces of furniture, a golden chandelier, and a glass case under a tall window. She was drawn to it. Using her flashlight to guide her through the room, she made her way to the cabinet.

There, she saw trinkets that she knew were sick trophies: a ripped piece of one of Sasha's drawings, Drea's treasured brooch, and . . .

She inhaled sharply.

Her pen. The pen JD had given her.

Right next to it was a long beaded dangly earring. Just like the one she'd lost on the night of Noah's party. And next to that, a tiny shred of paper with one word written on it. She practically gagged as her stomach turned over. She recognized that handwriting. JD's. She knew that note. The word was: *Always.*

"Get out of my life," Em whispered. Although she had spoken quietly, the words seemed to echo in the vast black chamber of the room.

Once again, she wondered where the three Furies had gone.

She looked out the window, and at first all she saw was her own pale reflection staring back at her. It was shocking how much she was starting to look like a Fury. Like Ty, who had once seemed so exotic and beautiful. It wasn't that their features matched perfectly, or that their complexions were the exact same shade. It was in their abysslike eyes, in the curve of their lips. They looked like daughters of the same underworld.

As she shrank away instinctively from her own image, the glass became more translucent; the moon was coming out from behind a cloud and all of a sudden she could see into a beautiful backyard. Everything beyond the glass seemed to be giving off a mesmerizing red glow.

The garden. Like the one in her dream.

That's where the flowers were. That's where *her* flower was. Looking at them made her chest swell in anticipation. Her life was in that garden.

Bing-bing. The text message chime lurched her back to reality. Back into "Em" mode.

It was JD. *Where are you? Not at play? Need to see you. Now.*

Em looked down at her phone, then back up at the window. Now, when she looked outside, she saw nothing but a blank expanse of dirt, and gravel being tossed by the wind. The flowers were gone. *Shit.* Her palms began to sweat. What the hell . . . ? She'd *seen* the garden there, just a second ago. So close. Had she done something to make it appear? Or was she hallucinating?

Maybe she had to channel her Fury-self to get into that garden. Kind of like Crow had kept saying—he was going to *give in to the darkness*; he was going to channel the forces that had brought them. Something like self-hypnosis. Just a few minutes. Just long enough to see the garden, find the white flower, and end this once and for all. Maybe the garden was locked, somehow, protected against intruders by the Furies' power.

Eating the seeds would break the curse. Eating the seeds would make her human again. Whole again. She would be free. She took a shuddering breath. If she was free, was she casting this curse onto someone else?

And if so, did she care?

There was a sound in the distance, screeches of laughter that morphed at the last minute into a scream.

She was close now. And they were coming.

Placing her back against the wall, Em slid down to the floor. She shut off her phone. She put her head against her knees and prepared to enter the darkness one final time.

CHAPTER TWENTY-ONE

"Where am I?" Skylar's voice trembled on the dark, bare stage. Her face was lit in a purple glow. The audience was silent in its seats. "Fled is the kindly light; deep darkness blinds my eyes; and the sky, buried in gloom, is hidden away."

She covered her face in her hands and JD turned a knob on the light board, fading the purple glow into a deeper, reddish gleam. He was sitting in the auditorium booth, his left knee bobbing anxiously up and down, trying to focus on hitting his cues but hardly able to concentrate. They were halfway through Act Two, and JD was counting the minutes until he could escape, grab Melissa, and perform the ritual described in Mr. Feiffer's letter.

"You're more nervous than the actors," Ned whispered.

"Just got a lot on my mind," JD said back, sliding one of the dimmers up to the top of the lighting console. Skylar was bathed now in a rich, red spotlight. The madness was starting to overtake her character; her head was thrown back in despair, revealing a creamy, birdlike neck.

JD's ribs felt tight. He wished desperately that Em had come with her parents to the play. She needed to know what he was planning to do—and why. If she'd been here tonight, he would have taken the leap and told her everything. That he loved her. That he would do anything to save her. That he'd found a way to banish the Furies for good, while keeping everyone safe. He wouldn't be too late, like Mr. Feiffer had been.

He thought of the way it would feel to put his hand on Em's waist and pull her toward him. He imagined finally kissing her the way he'd wanted to for so long.

"Dude, blackout. Blackout!" Ned nudged JD's arm, and JD scrambled to hit the correct button, which plunged the stage to black. "Let's hope the audience thought that was a dramatic pause."

"Sorry," JD said. "I spaced." As he brought the lights back up for the curtain call, he pulled out his pocket watch to look at the time. Almost ten o'clock. He had to hurry.

Out in the lobby with his family and Em's parents, JD cracked his knuckles and absently dismissed any congratulations thrown his way. He had to think—fast—of a way to get Melissa out of there.

"Mel, want to get some late ice cream? The place up on Route Twenty-Two is still open."

She looked at him skeptically. "Why?"

"Because I have a craving for rocky road, that's why," he said.

"You buying?" Melissa asked. "You owe me."

"You have no idea," JD said drily. And then, to his parents: "Don't wait up. We're going to have sibling-bonding time."

"All right," JD's dad said. "Don't go too crazy. And be careful—the storm may have cleared but it's still slippery out there."

He practically dragged Mel through the parking lot to his car. The moon was high in the sky, so bright that it looked like a floodlight. The air was damp with the promise of more rain. He could see a mass of clouds gathering on the horizon, black and fleecy, like a herd overtaking the sky.

"What is up with you?" Mel shook off his hand as they speed-walked.

"We're not going for ice cream," JD said, unlocking the car doors and motioning for Melissa to get in. He waited until the car was moving to tell her the truth. "I need you to do something for me. It's going to sound crazy."

She looked over at him from the passenger side of the car and tucked a piece of hair behind her ear. The moonlight made her freckles dark against her pale skin. "This doesn't sound good," she said with a nervous laugh.

JD cleared his throat and clenched his hands around the smooth steering wheel. Outside, past the windshield, Ascension's fields and farmhouses sped by.

"Mel, there's something going on. Something you need to know about. And I need your help to stop it."

She scowled at him, trying to gauge whether this was the setup to one of his elaborate practical jokes. "If you're joking, I'm not in the mood," she warned.

"Neither am I." JD pulled onto Dillon's Road, a long, winding route that bisected the town and would take him over to Silver Way—and the entrance to the Haunted Woods. "Listen, Em is in trouble. She needs us."

"Em's in trouble?" Melissa's voice raised with concern.

He nodded. But before he could say anything more, his sister interjected. "Where are we going?" she asked sharply. They were almost there.

"We're going into the woods," he said. "The Haunted Woods."

She shook her head violently. "No. No. I won't go there," she said.

He knew the feeling. His mouth was dry. He felt desperate, and guilty, too. But Melissa had to help him. It was the only way. "Melissa, it's okay. It's the last time we'll go there. I promise."

"*No,*" she repeated. "Absolutely not."

"Melissa, we have to. It's not an option."

"Pull over," she said. "Pull over or I'm getting out of the car." When he looked over he saw that she was gripping the door handle.

"Calm down, Mel. I'm pulling over, okay?" He swerved onto the side of the road. His heart was beating against his ribs. They were surrounded by darkness and crickets and bullfrogs in the distance.

"I have to tell you something," she said, not looking at him. There was a pause. Then she spoke again, though her voice was so soft that he could barely hear her. "It was them. When I saw someone at my window, it was them."

"Who?" But he knew the answer.

The Furies.

"Ali," Melissa said shakily. "She scares me. So do the others."

"They scare me, too," JD admitted. He turned to her, and reached out for her hand. "They terrify me, actually. And you know what I'm going to do tonight? I'm going to get rid of them. Once and for all."

"What do you mean, *once and for all*?" Melissa asked, withdrawing her hand from his. "You can't make people just disappear."

JD sucked in a deep breath. "They're not people," he said.

"They're not *people*?" Melissa echoed. "What does that even mean?" While he tried to think of a response, she said: "You're freaking me out."

The wind was whipping hard enough to shake the whole car. Still, JD didn't know how to explain.

"They're after Em. I think that's why they were at our house that night."

"Like they're haunting Em?" she asked.

"Yes," JD said. "That's pretty much the only thing I'm sure of."

"Drive," she said, pointing down the road. "Just go. Before I change my mind."

In what felt like seconds, Silver Way approached on their left. As he made the turn, he heard Melissa take several shallow breaths.

"It's going to be okay," he told her. "You have to trust me. I swear I won't let anything happen to you."

And he wouldn't. He wasn't going to take his eyes off her. The second he thought she was in real danger, he would snatch her away from the flames. Hopefully the psuedosacrifice would still work, as it had for Drea's dad. A *willingness* to sacrifice an innocent . . . like that Bible story. Abraham.

The woods towered like a wall in front of them as JD parked the car. He got out and retrieved two backpacks and a can of gasoline from the trunk. Melissa eyed the supplies warily, hugging herself. The wind whipped her hair around her face. She looked so small.

"You have to trust me," JD pleaded. "If not for me, then do it for Em."

"Don't try to make me feel guilty," she said. "I've already agreed, haven't I?"

That's when he knew she was on board. He threw her the lighter of the two backpacks and clicked on his heavy-duty flashlight. "Follow me."

She nodded. "I'm right behind you."

They made their way quickly beneath stooped pines and the incandescent moon, moving at a pace that was somewhere between a walk and a run, even as the clouds continued to encroach on the sky and the wind tore shrilly through the trees. Branches tore at JD's sleeves and backpack but he didn't care. He had to keep moving. To stay still was to succumb to the evil that permeated these woods. As they walked, he gathered up pieces of kindling and small sticks to burn. Then there was a whistling behind him, in the trees.

"Is that you, Mel?" he asked sharply. It stopped.

"Is what me?" she replied. "I didn't do anything."

They knew. They were here.

By the time they stepped out into the gloomy clearing, both he and his sister were short of breath.

A few lights flickered inside the house, and the air was practically buzzing with energy from the oncoming storm—or maybe from the Furies' presence.

There was no way of knowing whether Ty and the other

girls were inside; JD just had to hope that the ritual would draw them in from wherever it was they existed. He felt sick to his stomach, nauseous with nerves and doubts. But he thought of the case inside the Furies' house, the one with Em's pen and Drea's pin, and it stoked the fire of anger inside him.

He indicated silently to Melissa that they should go around to the back of the house. To the garden. She nodded.

They went as quietly as possible, staying close to the walls. JD was practically afraid to breathe. He kept imagining the shadows transforming, taking shape, morphing into Ty's wide smile or Meg's staring eyes.

"The garden is so beautiful," Melissa whispered.

JD stopped and looked at her over his shoulder. "What are you talking about?"

"What we're walking through. It's pretty." She gestured all around them.

All JD saw was a charred patch of dirt, dotted with charred stumps and dead, strawlike stalks of grass. Errant stones, once part of a garden wall, lay scattered around the yard. Whatever Melissa's joke was, he didn't get it. "Whatever, Mel, let's just keep going."

"It's hard to believe something so beautiful could be so bad," she said, reaching up to make a picking motion with her fingers. Then she passed her hand toward him. While she was doing it, it looked like a miming exercise. But as soon as their fingers touched, JD felt a jolt run through him. He felt something

312

between his thumb and his pointer finger, something like a stem. He blinked.

The garden seemed to grow in front of him, with greenery shooting up from the ground and pushing forcefully over high stone walls that were miraculously erected out of the rubble in a matter of seconds. It was like watching a movie in fast-forward. The enormous garden of flowers crystallized in a flash of magic, framed by drooping willows that sprouted instantaneously from blackened stumps.

"Holy shit," he whispered.

This was the place. It was time.

"Stay here," he mouthed to Melissa as he started unpacking his backpack. With one of the sticks, he scratched a large protective circle in the ground. He motioned that she should sit in the middle of it. She did. Her eyes were big and scared. He kneeled down and took her shoulders. "Nothing will happen to you," he said, digging out both snake pins from his pockets and pinning them hastily to her shirt. He had to move fast now. The moon was almost directly overhead. He arranged the sticks in a circle around her, some of them pointing vertically toward the sky, others in clumps on the ground, following the line he'd drawn in the dirt. He piled orchid petals, ripped from their stems, around everything. Then he ran back over to the supplies, grabbed the can of gasoline, and squirted a bit of that over the sticks. They'd been wet with spring rain. He needed to be sure they caught fire.

Melissa whimpered. "What are you doing?" There was panic in her voice.

"No matter what happens, don't move," he said. His hands were shaking. Then he repeated his vow: "Nothing will happen to you. I promise. Just don't move."

With trembling hands, he pulled a matchbook from his pants pocket. Was he really going to do this?

You know as well as anyone that this is dead serious, Ali had said. And she was right. He'd already lost one friend and he was in danger of losing another. All his paths were blocked. All except this one.

"You ready?" he asked Melissa.

She nodded but couldn't contain another whimper.

With every ounce of false confidence he could muster, he smiled at her—the same smile he'd given her a hundred times, over board games or the dinner table or at their grandparents' house when Grandma Rose started telling the story of the pickle jar. It was a smile that said, *We're in this together. I'm feeling what you're feeling. I've got your back.*

When she tried, and failed, to smile back, his heart nearly broke.

Now.

He lit the match, crouched down, and held the tiny flame to a piece of kindling. It nearly singed his fingernails. A trail of sulfur hung in the air once he shook the match out. Then another, and another. The branches caught fire almost immediately, and the circle went *whoosh*, up in flames like a domino chain of red heat. Then, crackling and popping, the familiar sounds of a campfire. He walked backward, taking in the scene.

"JD!" Melissa yelled, scrabbling toward the center. "What the hell? Where are you going?"

"I'm not going anywhere. It's okay, Mel." JD tried to keep his voice calm. He yelled so she could hear him over the distance and noise of the fire. "It's like a spell. I promise I won't let it get out of control. You have to trust me."

Melissa nodded, but she was shaking, and he could tell she was trying not to cry. In the light of the flames, her cheeks were pink-orange; her blue shirt looked black. Her eyes glistened, like tears were on the brink of spilling.

"Shhhh," he said. "Just a few minutes. You're safe."

JD looked around, waiting for the Furies to appear. Praying that they would, yet dreading the moment they did. When they showed up—*if* they showed up—what would happen then? Mr. Feiffer's letter hadn't included a spell or a chant. . . . JD felt sweat beading on his brow. What if he'd missed something? What if this wasn't right?

There was crashing in the underbrush nearby. Someone was coming. He and Melissa locked eyes, and he braced himself for impact. He waited to see Ali or Ty or Meg emerge from the trees. He spun in a circle, searching the darkness, his eyes already bleary with smoke, trying to guess where they would come from.

Then, a scream. Melissa. The crashing hadn't come from below. It was from above. A branch, falling from the tall maple tree next to the fire circle. He ran toward her in horror, but he wasn't fast enough—the branch slammed against the top of Melissa's head, and she collapsed in a heap in the center of the flames.

Oh god oh god oh god. He edged close to the flames, trying to get past them, but they were as high as his waist and he couldn't get to her. "Melissa!" he cried out. But she didn't move.

The fire was licking up into the tree now, racing over its branches. He took a deep breath, steeling himself to charge through the flames. But just then another sound came from behind him. A racing footfall. *Thump-thump-thump.* He whirled around, expecting the Furies to be at his back.

But it wasn't them.

It was Crow.

"What are you *doing*?" Crow's face was wild; fire-shadows danced across his face and deepened the black craters under his eyes. "You're going to ruin everything!"

"What are *you* doing?" JD barked back. "Go away! Stay away! It's under control!"

Crow pushed past him, looking around frantically for something. Crow began to stomp on the fire with his boots.

"*Stop!*" JD bellowed, diving toward him. It wasn't time yet. He landed on the dirt, and a sharp spray of dust hit his eyes and his mouth. But he brought Crow down with him. JD spat pieces of grit from his tongue.

Crow's elbow went into JD's ribs, so deep it felt like cracking. They were inches from the fire. JD could feel the sweat all over him—on his forehead, his arms, the back of his neck.

"What are you *doing*," Crow said, shoving a calloused hand against JD's face and pushing him down toward the ground. JD strained against it, feeling his muscles stretch like elastic, so taut that they might snap. *No. Let go.* He had to trust Walt. Crow was on the wrong side.

"I know you're part of this," JD panted. He reared back and kneed Crow right in the stomach, feeling his kneecap make contact, hearing Crow's sharp intake of breath. JD had knocked the wind out of him, at least for a second.

He flipped Crow over, felt his weight shift, taking the advantage. He pinned Crow to the dirt. He looked down and tried to catch his breath. There was a smear of blood on his right hand. It was red-brown and ugly. "I saw you with them. You're with the Furies."

Crow turned his face to the side and spit blood onto the ground, trying to catch his breath. "I'm *not* working—with them. I was—trying to—strike a bargain."

"A bargain?" JD huffed. The air was getting smoky and his

lungs were tight from exertion. He was worried about Melissa. Maybe he should put out the fire after all.

"I offered myself," Crow was saying between frantic gasps. "Instead. I thought it would save her. I saw it in a vision."

"Instead of who?" JD increased the pressure on Crow's chest. The heat of the fire was starting to scorch his face. *A vision.*

"Her," Crow gasped. "They wanted her. Em."

JD didn't know what to think, what to believe.

"But it's too late now," Crow said. He didn't look angry anymore. He just looked sad. "I was wrong. My vision was wrong."

Sweat was dripping down JD's face. It was hot, too hot. The fire was raging out of control. Soon the whole garden would combust. The moon was high, like a spotlight.

Melissa still lay motionless in a small, bare patch of ground.

And JD realized what he had done.

They'd all die—Melissa would die—if he couldn't stop the fire, couldn't get her out of there.

He scrambled to his feet just as a scream tore through the air.

When he turned around he saw Em come running out of the Furies' house. She was sobbing. Babbling. "It's almost time," she was saying. "You saved me."

"Where are they? Where are the Furies?" He tried to take Em's shoulders but she pushed past him, moving into the garden, thick with smoke and flame. She was shoving aside the rippling tide of flowers, as though she'd lost something there.

"Em!" JD shouted.

Crow had climbed to his feet next to JD. "That's not—," he started to say.

"Shut up!" JD yelled. "I can't think." He needed to douse the flames—*now*. He lunged for the fire extinguisher he'd stolen from the auditorium, but Em blocked him off, a blissful smile on her face and a beautiful white flower in her hand. She grabbed his face on either side with surprising strength and a shock went through him as her lips touched his.

Adrenaline.

Fiery heat.

Desire.

"I love you," he whispered.

Another frenzied voice broke into the chaos.

"What are you *doing*?" a girl shrieked behind them.

He broke away from the kiss as a mess of dark brown hair whipped past him. The smell of Ivory soap and cocoa butter lingered in her wake. *Em.*

Stunned, confused, and utterly frozen, he watched as Emily Winters—another Emily Winters, the real Emily Winters?— plunged into the circle of flames.

CHAPTER TWENTY-TWO

Em flew out of her trance like a bullet, immediately confronted with the insane scene in front of her.

There was a circle of raging flames over there, to her right. She could just barely make out a person in the middle of the circle. She looked closer. It was Melissa.

Just next to the fire, two boys wrestled in the dirt. Em squinted. It was JD. JD and . . . Crow?

And then, right there, on her left, amid the greenery . . . Ty. Ty, holding a big, beautiful, white flower. So white it practically glowed. Ty was holding it aloft so that the bright, big moon shone down on it like a spotlight.

It was midnight. Maybe she even heard a bell tolling somewhere in the distance. She couldn't tell if it was real or in her imagination.

The flower.

It was midnight, and the albino flower had bloomed.

She wanted to reach for it. She wanted to so badly. To have it and rescue herself and stop the transformation. But there was no way she could get the flower and also get to Melissa in time. Em could see she was the only one to save Melissa. The boys were rolling around, too consumed in their own competition, and there was no one else. No one but her. All this for one mistake. One for which she had apologized. It wasn't right.

She wasn't going to let Melissa die. She wasn't going to let another person get hurt because of her. She scrambled to her feet and propelled herself forward with unnatural speed. If the Furies wanted to take her down, so be it—but she wasn't going to let anyone else die. She covered the ground in seconds and threw herself into the flames. She didn't see a fire, just the chance to save someone other than herself. For once.

It wasn't the searing pain she imagined. Instead it was pinpricks of heat dancing on her skin and an immense pressure, closing in on all sides, like the force of a freezing waterfall coming at her body from every angle—so cold that it feels hot. Except this was so hot, it felt cold. She came out on the other side, within the circle, and saw Melissa at her feet. Em fell to her knees beside her.

"I'm going to get you out of here," she whispered. Melissa's skin was slick with sweat, and her eyelids were fluttering. She hoisted Melissa's body into her arms.

She tried to plot her way out of the fiery maze. It was just darkness and smoke everywhere, like in Crow's vision. Flames were reaching up around her. The threads of blackness pulled at her heart: the same sticky, angry web she'd been walking through for months.

No more.

Through the wall of smoke and flames, she adjusted her grip on Mel, who was cradled in her arms like a baby. Like when they used to pick her up and throw her off the dock at Galvin Pond when they were all so much younger. She sheltered Melissa's body with her own, and attempted to move out of the circle of fire. She took one step backward, and then another. Meanwhile, the flames grew higher and hotter . . . higher and hotter . . .

She braced herself—cringing against the heightened sensation—and finally managed to twist her torso just enough to deposit Melissa's body safely across. She could feel the fire eating away at her skin, and smoke filling her lungs.

Smoke was all around her, trapping her, flames lit by JD— just as Crow had seen it.

But he'd misunderstood.

They had all misunderstood.

As she shoved Melissa's body just outside the flames, she stumbled. The heat ripped at her; now she could feel it everywhere, in her skin and teeth and hair. It was like a fist of pain gripped her from all sides.

Burning flowers. The smell was horrible, intense, searing her nose, making her feel as though her whole mind were on fire. Maybe it was.

And then, suddenly, the pain stopped. There was a high-pitched but very faint ringing in her ears, almost like a hum. Almost like a song. The darkness began to swallow her. But it was different from before. This sensation was strangely soothing, like rocking on a gentle wave. A rowboat swaying ever so slightly. In its embrace, Em felt peaceful. And in an instant, she understood.

I love you, JD, she thought. *It was you all along, but I didn't see it until too late.*

I love you, Gabby. I love you for forgiving me. For showing me what real justice and real forgiveness is.

And Crow . . . Thank you for teaching me what sacrifice means.

I love you, Mom and Dad, and Melissa, and Drea. God, Drea, I'm so sorry. We should have known all along—the Furies are evil, and to defeat them, we needed pure love. Not tricks and books and rituals.

You know why the Furies left last time?

Not because of a banishment. And not because of a flower.

Because Edie was willing to give up her own life for yours.

Love. It's why they kept me from JD.

Because love is the only thing that can kill them.

A scream. A piercing scream that ripped through time, thoughts, space, reality. A silvery scream.

A strong wind began to blow, sucking her out of this world and into another. Stronger and stronger, like a hurricane. A shrieking darkness spiraled around her. The cloudy vapors contained Meg's and Ali's leering faces. Their eyes were glass; their bones showed through their perfect skin. She couldn't look away—she was being sucked into their vortex. Time seemed to be collapsing in on her, heavy and charged.

The dark ocean around her turned to bright, bright white.

She heard voices.

You'll never be rid of us.

We tried to teach you a lesson.

The words were a patchwork of sinister sounds, a dissonant chord of desperation.

Em could practically hear them scraping against the dirt, trying to keep their footing.

She watched from outside herself—from nowhere, or everywhere—as Ty started screaming. Her precious white flower began to shrivel. In an instant, the petals withered to a papery brown. And Ty began to transform. Her eyes smoldered, dark red and black, like coals. She wavered, twisting in the breeze. Em saw it but also *felt* it, as intimately as if her own body were disintegrating into thin air.

"She didn't get what she wanted," she heard Crow say.

Then there was a huge burst of flame, rocketing them all off their feet. An explosion. The orchids. The Furies' faces. The silhouette of a tree—black against a charcoal sky. An icicle, melting rapidly into a pool of dirty water.

She kissed eternity.

And then, with a final howl, everything went silent.

CHAPTER TWENTY-THREE

There was the smell of fresh flowers. But not orchids. No, something lovely, and calming, and *right*.

A quiet beeping went on in the background . . . It was the sound of eternity, patiently waiting for her, waiting for her, waiting . . .

Em's eyes fluttered open.

The house was gone. There was no garden.

Ty, Meg, and Ali were gone too. A ripple of relief washed over her, tickling her toes. She didn't know whether to trust the feeling.

Groggily, she lifted her head and blinked several times.

She was in a hospital room. A bouquet of yellow roses, sprays of lavender, and big, bobbing gerbera daisies lay on a table by her head.

And then, seemingly from nowhere, JD was standing over

her, holding out a hand. "You're awake," he said with gruff relief. "You're okay."

"What—what happened?" Her throat was hoarse.

"They're gone," JD said.

"Are you sure? What about Crow? And Melissa?" Em said, struggling to sit up. She wanted them all to be okay.

"They're fine. You're at the hospital. Your parents are just downstairs getting coffee—you've been out for a while."

The words made Em's heart soar and her stomach drop simultaneously, leaving an airy, empty space in the middle of her body. "JD," she whispered. "Am I okay? Are you okay?"

He leaned down to wrap her in a bear hug, and her queries were muffled in his jacket.

"We're okay," he said. "All of us. Thanks to you."

Thank god. And then he let Em go, but not too far. Cupped her dirt-streaked face in his hands and then put two fingers against her throat, feeling for a pulse. Em felt it beating softly against the pads of his fingers.

"You're alive," he said.

He was so close.

A burning sob lodged in her throat. *Please, let it be true.*

"Is it . . . Is it really over?" The words floated out of her, as though spoken by someone else.

His face broke into an uncontrollable smile and his hands tightened around her. "Em," he said. "It's really over."

"How . . . ?" she asked.

"I'm honestly not sure," he admitted. "But you did it, somehow, when you saved Melissa."

"JD, all that stuff that happened this winter . . . I never meant. . ." She faltered. How would she ever be able to say how sorry she was?

"I know," he said, cutting her off by placing a finger on her lips. "You don't need to apologize anymore."

They stayed that way for a few seconds, centimeters apart.

And then he leaned in even closer and replaced his finger with his mouth, kissing her the way she'd always wanted him to. Slowly, carefully. She drank him in and kissed him back. *Can you feel this? How right this is?* She knew he could. She melted into him, reaching one hand around the back of his neck and hungrily pulling him closer.

He smelled like dew in the morning, like new growth.

As he pulled away, grinning stupidly, Em squeezed his hand and tugged him back. She put her mouth close to his ear—close enough for her lips to brush against the tiny hairs on his cheek.

"I love you, JD," she said. Finally. The words felt so natural, so easy to say.

"I love you too, Emily," he said.

And they kissed again—a kiss better, deeper, and sweeter than revenge.

EPILOGUE

The bell on Emily's windowsill issues a tiny *ding*. She looks up at it, smiling, and scribbles a note on a scrap of paper. Drops it into the basket on her end and pulls it over to JD's house. She watches him come to the window, pluck the paper from the basket, and read it.

"You're on, Winters!" he shouts from less than a hundred feet away. "I accept your challenge. What time?"

"After dinner! My mom is making pizza."

He holds up a finger and moves from the window. When he returns, he is holding a pen, with which he writes a response. The basket creaks its way back over to Em's side of the line. She feels like giggling the entire time.

Save room for popcorn, JD's note says. *It'll be your consolation prize after I beat you in Scrabble.*

"You wish!" she yells.

He flashes her a grin before disappearing; Em turns back to her laptop, where Crow's demo album is playing. He's moved to Boston, into an apartment with a few musicians he knows from Berklee. She and Crow text sometimes.

Em smiles with a trace of nostalgia.

He is doing well—not drinking, not smoking, and getting some gigs with his new band. One of the songs has even been getting some radio play around Boston. It's her favorite.

It's called "Emily."